I AM
HEATHCLIFF

STORIES INSPIRED
BY
WUTHERING HEIGHTS

CURATED BY
KATE MOSSE

THE BOROUGH PRESS

The Borough Press
An imprint of HarperCollins*Publishers* Ltd
1 London Bridge Street
London SE1 9GF
www.harpercollins.co.uk

This paperback edition 2019
1

First published in Great Britain by HarperCollins*Publishers* 2018

A catalogue record for this book is available from the British Library

ISBN: 978-0-00-825746-0

Typeset in Century Expanded LT Std by
Palimpsest Book Production Ltd, Falkirk, Stirlingshire

Printed and bound in Great Britain by
CPI Group (UK) Ltd, Croydon, CR0 4YY

Praise for *I Am Heathcliff*:

'Visceral writing that lays bare the savagery of Heathcliff'
Financial Times

'Inspired by *Wuthering Heights*, these tales of toxic relationships, an entirely disturbing episode of stalking and necrophilia, blighted lives and bleak landscapes reveal that contemporary responses to Emily Brontë's endlessly controversial classic can be equally stark, cruel and shocking'   *Daily Mail*

'Tales of toxic relationships, a hungry, howling, anorexic ghost, drug addled lovers and blighted lives and landscapes ... But there are surprises in store, too. Crime writer Sophie Hannah delivers a high school musical murder mystery while Louisa Young's *Heathcliffs I Have Known* is a furious, funny, riotous rant on the role of this supposedly romantic hero'
Sunday Express S Magazine

For EB, in whose
footsteps we walk

CONTENTS

FOREWORD BY
KATE MOSSE

'My love for Linton is like the foliage in the woods: time will change it, I'm well aware, as winter changes the trees. My love for Heathcliff resembles the eternal rocks beneath: a source of little visible delight, but necessary. Nelly, I am Heathcliff! He's always, always in my mind: not as a pleasure, any more than I am always a pleasure to myself, but as my own being.'

THERE IS A HANDFUL of books that exist beyond their time and space, beyond the circumstances of their invention: novels that are significant, novels that are beloved. Familiar friends. Their characters step off the pages of the novel and into the real world, into a public conscience to be used ever after as shorthand for a certain sort of person. Archetypes, I suppose. Stories that seem bigger than the books that contain them. *Wuthering Heights* is such a book. Cathy and Heathcliff are such characters.

Published in 1847, *Wuthering Heights* is a novel that changes its character and colour with every reading, yet remains uniquely and absolutely itself. It is variously a Gothic novel of obsession and revenge; a story of ghosts and bad dreams; a novel of opposites – light and shade, wild Nature versus taming civilisation, storm versus calm, violence versus tenderness, revenge versus forgiveness, the North versus the South; a novel of race and class, of the powerlessness of women's and children's lives; a novel about poverty, property, and wealth; a novel about how the sins of the fathers (and dead or powerless mothers) are visited on the next generation; a story of two houses – Wuthering Heights and Thrushcross Grange – on the Yorkshire Moors; a story of the shifting of time and how the land goes about its business indifferent to human emotions; a novel of order and disorder; of violence and the consequences of violence, of hate and the consequences of hate. Most of all, of course, it is held up as the most epic of love stories. But is it? It is a novel of obsession and all-devouring emotion, certainly, and about the nature and endurance of love, but romance it is not.

The telling of the story is complicated, and, though any reader picking up this collection will know the bare bones of it, it's worth spending a moment thinking about the architecture of the novel. *Wuthering Heights* starts at the end – in 1801 – when a southern gentleman, Lockwood, calls upon his landlord and 'solitary neighbour', Heathcliff. The old farmhouse, Wuthering Heights, sits isolated and exposed to all elements of wind and weather, in sharp contrast to the comfortable, well-appointed Thrushcross Grange where Lockwood has come to recover from an unsuccessful love affair. Confused by the household he finds at Wuthering Heights on his first visit, he is drawn back. Trapped by a snowstorm, and obliged to stay the night, he finds a sequence of names – Catherine Earnshaw, Catherine Heathcliff, Catherine Linton – scratched into the paint of the windowsill. When he falls into uneasy sleep, his dreams are haunted by the ghost of Cathy trying to get in at the window. In one of the most violent scenes in the novel, Lockwood drags her white wrist across the broken glass to force her to let him go. Heathcliff distraught and wild and desperate into the chamber.

This is the brilliant framing device that whets the reader's appetite and sets the narrative in motion.

When Lockwood returns to Thrushcross Grange the following morning, his head full of questions, he persuades the housekeeper, Ellen – Nelly – Dean, to tell him the story of Heathcliff and Catherine Earnshaw. Explain the connection between the two houses and families, going back a generation, Nelly speaks of the 'dirty, ragged, black-haired child' brought into the Earnshaw household and given the name Heathcliff; of the six-year-old Cathy and her jealous, bullying brother Hindley, of the growing affection between Cathy and Heathcliff, and of the very different household of Edgar Linton and his sister Isabella at Thrushcross Grange.

The fragment of dialogue from Chapter IX between Cathy and Nelly Dean quoted above – and which gives our collection its title – is at the heart of the novel. For *Wuthering Heights* is not a love story as we know it – or certainly as Victorian readers might have considered it – but rather a novel about the nature of love, of what happens when love is thwarted or distorted or traduced, of what happens when like and unalike come together. Cathy is thinking aloud, imagining herself married to either Edgar or to Heathcliff, in the same way she once scratched the three different names – the versions of herself – on the painted sill of her window at Wuthering Heights. Heathcliff overhears only the first part of her statement – that it would degrade her to marry him – and storms away devastated, so does not hear the second and most fundamental part of what Cathy believes.

He does not hear her say: 'Whatever our souls are made of, his and mine are the same.' He does not hear her say that she loves him.

Heathcliff is gone for years, and, when he returns a wealthy man, is governed by revenge rather than love. He has killed the best part of himself, the part of himself that is Cathy. Tenderness is gone, leaving only cold self-interest. He finds Cathy married to Edgar Linton, and, in spite, marries Isabella. The first part of *Wuthering Heights* ends with the death of Cathy, having given birth to a daughter, and Heathcliff's grief at losing her for ever.

The story of the second generation – the children of

Heathcliff and Cathy – is less well known (and, in adaptations, often ignored altogether), but it is what gives the novel its unity, its balance. Heathcliff mourns Cathy, yet plots against her daughter. It is not until he abandons hate and only love remains, that they can be reconciled. Finally, the line between the living and the dead is blurred, and all that remains is peace. It is left to Nelly Dean, when Lockwood returns to Yorkshire in 1802, to recount the story of Heathcliff's recent death, and bring the novel to a close. The final words are given – as are the first – to the outsider narrator, Lockwood, as he looks down upon the three headstones on the 'slope next the Moor': Cathy's is 'grey, and half buried in heath'; Edgar Linton's is 'only harmonised by the turf and moss creeping up its foot'; Heathcliff's is 'still bare'.

So, what makes *Wuthering Heights* – published the year before Emily Brontë's own death – the powerful, enduring, exceptional novel it is? Is it a matter of character and sense of place? Depth of emotion or the beauty of her language? Epic and Gothic? Yes, but also because it is ambitious and uncompromising. Like many others, I have gone back to it in each decade of my life and found it subtly different each time. In my teens, I was swept away by the promise of a love story, though the anger and the violence and the pain were troubling to me. In my twenties, it was the history and the snapshot of social expectations that interested me. In my thirties, when I was starting to write fiction myself, I was gripped by the architecture of the novel – two narrators, two distinct periods of history and storytelling, the complicated switching of voice. In my forties, it was the colour and the texture, the Gothic spirit of place, the characterisation of Nature itself as sentient, violent, to be feared. Now, in my fifties, as well as all this, it is also the understanding of how utterly EB changed the rules of what was acceptable for a woman to write, and how we are all in her debt. This is monumental work, not domestic. This is about the nature of life, love, and the universe, not the details of how women and men live their lives. And *Wuthering Heights* is exceptional amongst the novels of the period for the absence of any explicit condemnation of Heathcliff's conduct, or any suggestion that evil might bring its own punishment.

What of today? Will a new generation of teenagers, of readers, be introduced to Cathy and Heathcliff by teachers at school, or librarians, or be inspired to seek the novel out by collections like this? I think so. I think their reactions will be much as my own more than forty years ago, for, despite changes in our lives and expectations – the frantic pace of life, the banishment of boredom, and the lack of solitude – the confusion of first loves and deciding which of our selves we might be (as Cathy does when trying to decide between Heathcliff and Edgar Linton), these emotions are as commonplace now as then. Even if the language and style of the novel might seem to belong to another era, the conflict and story do not.

∞

The history behind the novel and its author is also well known, and has grown a little shabby with retelling. For the most part, over-attention on the biography of a writer is a way of diminishing the power or the uniqueness of her or his imagination. But, in the case of EB (and indeed Charlotte and Anne), there is some justification. Her sense of indifferent or careless Nature comes in part, surely, from the terrible losses they suffered: the early death of their mother and their two older sisters – Maria and Elizabeth – dying as a consequence of neglect and ill treatment at their school. The remaining four children, three girls and a boy, were then tutored at home and, taking refuge in writing and their imaginations, created a secret language and magical universes filled with stars and fantasy. Penning stories and poems on tiny fragments of paper. The freedom and claustrophobia of walking around and around the dining-room table in Haworth at night when the household had gone to bed, the sisters reading passages aloud to one another. The relentless ticking of the clock, the creaking of the wooden floorboards, the wind wuthering in the trees in the graveyard in front of the parsonage. The death of their aunt, and the increasingly dissolute behaviour of their brother Branwell, disappointed and drowning in drink and opiates, and debts. And then, in 1847, three novels published under the pen names of Currer, Ellis, and Acton Bell. Astonishing novels that spoke of the iniquities of the world, of the position of women without income, of violence and passion and of landscape.

Reactions to *Wuthering Heights* at the time were mixed. Dante Gabriel Rossetti described it as a 'fiend of a book – an incredible monster'; *Atlas* as a 'strange, inartistic story'; and *Grantham's Lady Magazine* as 'a compound of vulgar depravity and unnatural horrors.' *Douglas Jerrold's Weekly Newspaper* said: '*Wuthering Heights* is a strange sort of book – baffling all regular criticism; yet, it is impossible to begin and not finish it; and quite as impossible to lay it aside afterwards and say nothing about it.' However in the years after Emily Brontë's death, the novel's reputation took root: Lord David Cecil considered it the greatest of all Victorian novels, and Matthew Arnold said: 'For passion, vehemence, and grief she has had no equal since Byron.'

In modern times, critics – such as the great Elaine Showalter, Sandra Gilbert, and Susan Gubar – as well as novelists and poets, from Daphne du Maurier, Helen Oyeyemi, and Margaret Drabble to Sylvia Plath have all admired, considered, been inspired by Brontë's 'fiend of a book'. Playwrights and choreographers, artists and composers too, in print, in opera, and song, in ballet, and plays, on screens large and small.

Here, just a few examples: Genesis's 1976 album *Wind and Wuthering* and Kate Bush's chart-topping 'Wuthering Heights' released two years later, both of which use direct quotations from the novel itself; the all-female Japanese opera company Takarazuka Revue, and the Northern Ballet Company; Hotbuckle Productions Theatre Company, and The John Godber Company, in a version adapted and directed by Jane Thornton; the leading Asian touring company, Tamasha, with a piece set in the deserts of Rajasthan.

And, of course, film. The earliest known screen adaptation was filmed in England in 1920, though the most famous is the 1939 black-and-white starring Laurence Olivier and Merle Oberon (and David Niven as Edgar). It omitted the second generation's story, but was firmly situated on the Yorkshire Moors, as was Andrea Arnold's 2011 adaptation. Luis Buñuel's 1954 Spanish-language adaptation, *Abismos de Pasión*, was set in Catholic Mexico, and Yoshishige Yoshida's 1988 version was set in medieval Japan.

The sheer ingenuity and range of work inspired by *Wuthering Heights* is testament to the power of the ideas within the novel, the depth of characterisation, and the emotional intention of the story. As technologies change what can be achieved on screen and stage, there will be ever-new interpretations of the text, shaped and refashioned, keeping the passion for the story alive in new generations of audiences all over the world.

Now, here is this collection, published to celebrate the bicentenary of Emily Brontë's birth in 1818. I won't spoil the surprise of the stories that follow by summarising the work of the wonderful writers who have contributed, except to say that the pieces are wide-ranging and clever, moving and thought-provoking. Interestingly, a majority are set in modern times, rather than in the period of the novel or indeed EB's own time. Some are about what we would call – in modern terms – violent and toxic relationships; others about the collision of grief and identity; some are visceral and savage, and others infused with the emotion and beauty of *Wuthering Heights*. There is even the promise of a school musical! What the stories have in common is that, despite their shared moment of inspiration, they are themselves, and their quality stands testament both to our contemporary writers' skills, and the timelessness of *Wuthering Heights*. For, though mores and expectations and opportunities alter, wherever we live and whoever we are, the human heart does not change very much. We understand love and hate, jealousy and peace, grief and injustice, because we experience these things too – as writers, as readers, as our individual selves.

I'll end where we began, with Emily Brontë's words – and what is surely one of the most beautiful closing paragraphs in all of literature – as Lockwood looks down on the graves of Heathcliff, Linton, and Cathy. It's a magnificent full-stop of a sentence.

'I lingered round them, under the benign sky; watched the moths fluttering among the heath and the harebells, listened to the soft wind breathing through the grass, and wondered how any one could ever imagine unquiet slumbers for the sleepers in that quiet earth.'

TERMINUS

LOUISE DOUGHTY

T WO YOUNG WOMEN ARE standing in a hotel lobby, on either side of a polished-wood reception desk. They are staring at each other.

It is a Tuesday in February. Outside the hotel, lorries bump and thump along a dual carriageway. Beyond the dual carriageway, there is a wide esplanade, and beyond the esplanade a beach, where grey and brown waves chop against the pebbles, and a red warning flag furls and corrugates in the wind before straightening with a snap.

'Do you have any form of identification?' the young woman behind the desk asks politely, lightly enough, but the thick ticking of the clock on the wall behind her makes the query sound emphatic.

The hotel lobby is empty, apart from the two women. Victorian-era, once very grand, it has a vaulted ceiling and curving staircase, but the carpet is frayed now, the furniture worn. From the bar and restaurant on the other side of the

11

lobby comes the faint smell of disinfectant and cabbage, even though no one has cooked cabbage in this hotel for over fifty years.

The reception desk is shiny oak; the brass clock ticks loudly; the walls are painted a leaden green colour that hints at a sanatorium. At the end of the reception desk is a white plastic orchid in a brown plastic pot.

Who are you?

Good question.

The other young woman, the one in front of the desk, is called Maria. Maria has never been asked for identification at a hotel before, but then she has never shown up like this, walking in off the street with no luggage, a small backpack, and a stare in her eyes. A beanie hat is pulled low over her black curls, and there are shadows beneath that stare. The receptionist is slender, with a neat navy jacket, and fair hair in an immaculate ponytail. Her skin is very fine, the only make-up she wears is a slick of pale lipstick. Maria knows how she looks to this young woman. They are each other's inverse.

Maria reaches into the backpack and hands over a driving licence. The receptionist glances at it and hands it back. She doesn't write anything down. Maria scans the receptionist's face for signs of suspicion or hostility, but her expression is a calm, professional blank. Maria thinks how habituated she now is to interpretation, how experienced at watching a face.

In high season the room the receptionist offers – a deluxe

double with a sea view – would be over two hundred pounds a night, but it's a Tuesday in February, and Maria gets it for eighty-five. Breakfast is included.

'Would you like to pay now or at checkout?' the receptionist asks.

Maria has two credit cards that she has never used: when she applied for the mortgage on her flat three years ago, the broker told her it would be good for her credit rating to have a couple of cards, or even a small loan, as long as she made the repayments on time. The mortgage companies liked evidence of an ability to service debt. This amused Maria at the time, the idea of a company thinking that being in debt already made her a more attractive proposition. She never uses the cards, and, as she pulls one out of her purse, she takes a quick look to check that she has even bothered to sign on the back. She hands it over. That's how easy it is, she thinks. She can't use the joint account, but she has the credit cards. The bill won't arrive for a month.

Why didn't I think of this before?

The deluxe room is medium-sized and has mushroom-coloured walls. There is a huge sash window, almost floor to ceiling, that looks straight out over a narrow ornamental balcony with rusting ironwork, across the dual carriageway to the sea. Maria drops her backpack, sits on the bed, and stares at a distant oil rig, blurred against the horizon, the brown-and-grey water still chopping and falling, the red flag furling and snapping repeatedly. After a while, she closes her eyes, begins to breathe deeply, and falls into a short but intense sleep.

When she wakes it is still daylight: just. She rises from the bed, switches the kettle on, makes a cup of tea, and returns to the bed, sitting upright and sipping the tea while she stares at the flag, the oil rig, the rearing waves. She thinks to herself, quite distinctly, *So this is what it feels like, a breakdown.* She thinks, *To get the full benefit, I must not attempt any decisions, not even small ones.*

She sips her tea. She watches the flag.

After a while, she needs the loo. The small bathroom also has a huge sash window looking out to sea, with a net curtain. She thinks, *I can watch the sea while I pee*, and feels a disproportionate amount of pleasure at this unexpected bonus. She thinks, *In the short time I have been in this room, I have become obsessed with watching the water. I never want to take my eyes off it.*

She lowers her jeans and sits. The bruise on the front of her right upper thigh has spread and altered: it's now the size of a side plate, the centre of it still purple but fading to red, almost lacy, at the edges. By tomorrow, she knows, it will be tinged with yellow and green. She finishes on the loo, pulls up her jeans with haste, returns to the bed without washing her hands. She sits there, then, staring at the sea until the light fades and the beach darkens and the flag and oil rig become invisible and there are only the sounds in her head: the blur and blare of traffic beneath the window; the crashing of the waves that peaks above the cars and lorries intermittently; the occasional tinkle of something blowing against a nearby balcony – just the sounds, the lift and fall of them in the dark, that's all there is. She cannot move.

Eventually, with a certain effort of will, she goes back to the bathroom, pees again, and brushes her teeth. She removes her shoes and her socks and her jeans – folding and placing them neatly on the chair in the corner for easy access – and gets into bed, pulling the thick duvet with its slightly shiny cover up over her shoulder, tucking it beneath her chin. *Decide nothing, think of nothing.* She's hungry, but she can't order room service, doesn't even know if they do room service, as she can't get up to look at the hotel information folder. Just before she falls asleep, she reaches out to the bedside table and checks that her phone is still turned off, as she has done several times an hour since she left her flat that morning. She falls asleep to the crashing of the waves.

In the morning, she wakes gently. She lies still for a while, eyes closed. The sounds are still there, they colour the room like tea leaves steeping in water, and as they do, she is filled with a sensation she realises she hasn't felt for a long time: calm. She is lying on her side in a foetal position. Very, very slowly, she unfurls.

She makes an instant coffee, pulls back the curtains, watches the sea in the morning light: it, too, is calmer. *The sea is me. Or I am the sea.*

Eventually, hunger gets the better of metaphor.

Over breakfast in the deserted dining room, which also overlooks the sea, she does some calculations. In the grey light of day, rested, she feels amazed that she has spent eighty-five pounds on a good night's sleep. View or no view, she thinks, you could get two pairs of shoes for that. Decent shoes. Paying that much long term is out of the question. She can put it on credit for the time being, but sooner or later that bill will roll in, and she has eight hundred and thirty-three pounds of savings. That won't do ten nights, let alone the rest of her life.

The rest of her life is too large a thought to grasp. She tries, momentarily. She sips her pleasingly hot coffee, which has come in her own little silver pot, pursing her top lip over the white china cup and taking it in in tiny amounts, inhaling it almost. She tries again: but when she looks beyond the next few days, the weeks and months to come, the enormity of what is to be accomplished, it is as if her imagination shudders and baulks like a nervous horse approaching a high fence.

Six hundred and seventy pounds of her savings came from her Uncle Malcolm – her father's cousin, who lived alone in a council house in Loughborough and always used to say to her, 'When I've gone, all I've got is yours.' Her father had taken the precaution of warning her not to get excited – Uncle Malcolm was a car park attendant for Tesco, and scarcely had a bean. All the same, when he died of lung cancer at the age of seventy-two, Maria felt guiltily excited to inherit a few hundred quid – poor old Uncle Malcolm. It was the first time she had ever inherited or won anything, the first time anything had come her way that wasn't earned. She was so excited she had put it in a building society account and done nothing with it because she didn't want it to be gone. 'That's right, duck,' her father said. 'Save it for a rainy day.'

Maria and her father both believed in rain. Maria's mother had died of leukaemia when she was fourteen, and her father had heart disease and hadn't worked for years. Maria had grown used to the idea that orphanhood was looming, had grown into it, and in due course her father died when she was twenty-two, leaving her just enough for the deposit on a one-bedroom flat in a new development on the edge of the Recreation Ground, where, on Sundays, she was woken by the malice-free shouting and swearing of the local five-a-siders and the occasional bump of a football against the boundary fence.

That was one of Matthew's observations of her, very early on. On their second date, they walked along the canal towpath after dark, and in a tunnel he stopped and pushed her against the wall. They kissed for a long time in the cold and dank. He pressed on her, his weight, the rough cloth of his jacket with its folds of pockets and buttons and zips, and murmured into her hair, 'Maria, Maria, you're an orphan, you're all alone . . .' She cried, then, a little drunk from the wine at dinner, and he held her for a long time, until her feet began to go numb inside her thin suede ankle boots. After a while, he pushed the dark, crinkled locks of hair away from her damp face and looked at her, and she closed her eyes then, knowing he was watching her. He bent his head, to kiss the butterfly-fragile skin of her closed lids, one after the other, then her salty face, and said, 'You'll never be alone again, now,' and something inside her melted and let go.

And even now, sitting sipping coffee in this crumbling wedding cake of a hotel, she can feel that warmth, inside, if she thinks about it, how good it felt, the release of it, to give it all up after all those years of being brave.

After breakfast – a fat sausage, surprisingly good and herby, bacon a little flaccid, a glistening fried egg, and congealed beans – she goes back to reception. A pale young man is on duty, tall and thin, body like a long drink of water. She wonders if this hotel only employs pale people with fine skin. She hesitates, waiting for him to look up and wondering if she can remember how to be charming. The young man carries on tap-tapping at the keyboard behind the desk with his thin fingers, and looks up one microsecond before it would be obvious he was deliberately ignoring her.

'I'm Room 212,' she says. 'I'm thinking of staying a few more nights. Would you do me a deal if I did?'

Without speaking, he keys her room number into his computer and then wobbles his head from side to side in a small movement, pressing his lips together. 'Can't do anything on a sea view room, sorry,' he says. 'They're in such high demand.'

Pointedly, she glances around the foyer, where the only other people in sight are a bulky white-haired man in a motorised wheelchair, and a tiny Asian woman she guesses to be his wife, who finishes tucking a tartan rug over his knees before turning and bustling to the Ladies.

'Really?' she says, turning back, fixing the young man with her gaze and thinking, *Have you any idea how much I need a break, you skinny git?*

He shakes his fine head. His fringe flops. She has the feeling that, if he thought he could get away with it, he might examine his nails.

She rests her arms on the shiny wood of the reception desk and leans forward, hoping her posture is indicative of a woman who is not likely to move away before she has been accommodated.

He gives a sigh that contains only the merest hint of melodrama. 'Let me see what I can do . . .' He taps away. 'I could give you a reduced rate on a compact double. No view.'

The compact double has just enough room to walk around the bed, and when she looks out of the window, it is into the brick blank of a building she could touch with the flat of her hand if she lifted the sash and leaned out. But she can afford it for another three nights.

She walks a lot. She walks around the shops, the brash, loud chain stores in the Churchill Shopping Centre, where she passes clothes she isn't looking at along the rails. In the pretty little Lanes, she pauses and stares into boutique windows, looking at the cashmere wraps in skin colours and shoes displayed at angles and chunky necklaces that look so cheap they must be really, really expensive. Occasionally, looking in those windows, she wonders about going inside, just to warm up, but the women behind the counters look back at her in a welcoming manner. She doesn't want anyone to speak to her; she doesn't want anyone to be friendly.

At least once each day, she goes down to the beach and stomps along it for a while, tipping forward as she forges against the wind, clenched and braced, enjoying the crunch and sink of the stones beneath her feet, until she is pleasantly exhausted and takes refuge in a café where she sips hot tea from a polystyrene cup and does some more staring. *Staring is my job now,* she thinks. *I'm getting really good at it. This will work,* she thinks. *Walk all day. Watch telly in my compact cube in the evenings. Go to bed early.*

Just before she goes to sleep each night, she picks up her phone from the bedside table and looks at it without turning it on, feeling the shape of it in her hand, the weight of all the messages accumulating inside. She puts it inside the drawer, next to the Gideon Bible, and closes the drawer very gently, as if the phone is a small, sleeping animal and she doesn't want to risk disturbing it.

On the third morning, as she is crossing the foyer on her way to the breakfast room, the pale young man calls her over, 'Miss Crossley,' he says.

She greets him with a smile. They are almost old friends now. She struck up a proper conversation with him the day before, after she lost her key card on one of the beach walks. He ended up confiding in her that his wife is expecting twins, that she is from Romania, and they met over karaoke, that he is excited but nervous about becoming a father. She has worked out that his supercilious air is borne out of a touching if misplaced belief that the hotel he works for is quite posh. 'Morning,' she says, cheerily.

He hands over a hotel envelope. 'Your brother left this for you.'

She takes it with an automatic hand and turns away, scarcely registering the young man's brief look of disappointment that she doesn't say thank you, when they got on so well the day before. She grips the letter in her hand as she crosses the foyer, and her knees are weak as she stands waiting for a table at the entrance to the breakfast room. Later, she will query her actions at that point, how swiftly she defaulted to automatic pilot, how normal that felt.

She doesn't speak to the young woman who leads her to her table, hardly hears her as she puts the menu in front of her and reminds her to help herself to the continental buffet if she'd like fruit or cereal before her cooked option. She opens the envelope with shaking fingers and sees that inside it is a hotel compliment slip, folded in two. She unfolds it as the young woman pours her coffee, and doesn't even acknowledge her with a look.

The compliment slip has four words on it, in blue biro.

I am you, remember?

Maria thinks, then, of how when her train arrived in Brighton three days ago, she felt such pleasure at the fact that the station was a terminus – she had come to the end of the line, the edge of the country, and from now on it was the open sea. And it is with a solid and unsurprised kind of feeling, a cold feeling, quite devoid of emotion or panic, that she looks out of the breakfast-room window and sees, standing on the steps of the hotel and looking right at her, a compact young man in a dark-grey coat, staring at her with a smile. He isn't her brother.

The world closes down, as if a lid is being brought down on a coffin. She can almost hear the thump of the nails being hammered in. In the tiny, box-like room, with the view of the brick wall, Matthew guides her by her elbow to the bed and sits her down. She has the irrational thought that this would not be happening if she was still in the room with the view – as if, somehow, that would have enabled her to fly out to sea. He sits next to her and strokes the side of her face with the backs of his fingers while she looks straight ahead. He talks to her very gently, explains how disappointed he is, how sad he was when he came home to her note, how his first thought was to go down to the canal and sit by the side of it and slash his wrists and throw himself into the water with stones in his pockets to weigh him down. Was that what she wanted?

Was it? He has missed her so much. He has been crazy with worry.

Afterwards, they lie together under the shiny eiderdown. He has pulled her close, and his skin feels clammy against hers – the room is stuffy. 'The thing is,' he says. 'I am you. And you are me. We can never be separated Maria, because we are the same person. Don't you remember? I told you. You were only half a person when we met. And then we met, and we joined, and we became a whole thing, and that's the way it will always be. We can't exist without each other.'

She lies next to him, breathing steadily. It has not been too bad so far. There will be more to come later, in two weeks or six weeks or six months. It will come, then. This is only postponement.

She props her head up on one elbow and turns to him, managing a smile. 'How did you find me?' she says, still smiling, as if it has all been an enormous game, and that is when his hand comes at her from nowhere, to grab the underside of her chin and force her head back against the headboard with a bang.

The pale young man who works behind reception is still on duty when Matthew comes to check Maria out of her room. Maria and Matthew have come down from the room together, but Maria sits and waits in the armchair on the far side of the lobby, her beanie hat pulled down low.

Matthew stands at the reception desk tapping the edge

of his credit card on it while the pale young man looks at his computer.

'No, it's all paid for,' the pale young man says, 'your sister paid in advance when she checked in, didn't she mention that?' He glances past Matthew's shoulder, across the lobby to where Maria sits, looking at the door.

'Oh,' says Matthew, giving a final brisk tap and slipping the card back into a pocket, 'No, she didn't, she must have forgotten.' He slides the key card across the table. 'We're all done then.'

'Was everything OK for your sister?' the pale young man asks, looking down at Matthew and tipping his head very slightly to one side.

Matthew stretches a smile without parting his lips. 'Lovely,' he says, 'she's had a lovely break.'

Matthew crosses the lobby and takes Maria by her arm and guides her out of the main entrance, holding her backpack in the other hand. His car is parked in the small car park right in front of the entrance to the hotel.

As they reach the car, he stops and turns her to him, then moves his hand up to the back of her head. He laces his fingers in her hair and pulls her face towards his and kisses her with all the passion of a drowning man. Maria hears a passer-by, an elderly voice say, fondly, as Matthew's teeth clash against hers, 'Oh, look . . .'

After the kiss, Matthew releases her and turns to unlock the car door, and at that moment, Maria looks around and sees the young woman from reception in her navy jacket, standing in the hotel entrance, behind the glass-panelled door, looking out at them both. Maria is close enough to see her own reflection layered against the young woman's face and to know that the young woman is, in that moment, seeing her for who she is. It would take no more than a couple of steps.

Matthew turns, puts his hand on her arm again and pushes her gently into the car. By the time Maria has put her seatbelt on and looked back at the hotel entrance, the young woman has gone – or maybe she is still there, and it is simply that Maria herself has moved away and is no longer reflected in the glass panel of the door. Perhaps it is just that the light is different.

Maria thinks, *She will have forgotten me before she has crossed the hotel lobby, lifted the wooden hatch on the reception desk, and gone to join the pale young man who will talk about his twins.*

On the long drive back up to the Midlands, Matthew chats away about what he has been doing, about how the cat threw up on the bedspread yesterday, but he was in such a panic about finding her, he left it. It's going to be her job when they get back, sorry, but she can hardly blame him.

Maria sits with her head resting against the side window, staring at the flash and rush of the passing countryside as they speed up the motorway, and when she doesn't respond, he makes a snort of disgust – she knows he will bring her surliness up later – and turns on the radio. He turns it up so loud that the signal is distorted and the music wavers and blares. He sings along, loudly, tapping the steering wheel with his fingers and accelerating as he changes lanes in a way he knows makes her nauseous.

Maria says nothing. She thinks about the sea. She thinks about the red flag that flew in the wind on the pebble beach, and the shush and crash of the waves, and how the sounds seemed to magnify on that first evening in the hotel, as darkness fell, as if they were all that there was, out there in the calm of night. She thinks of how the rise and fall of the waves felt like the rise and fall of her own heart, how she could see her body rising and falling in that water, arms splayed as she floated on her back, hair pooling around her head. She thinks about her reflection in the hotel-lobby door that morning, twinned with that of the young woman.

The young woman is called Anya; her pale male colleague is Neill. When Anya returns to the reception desk, she says, 'Have you done the printouts yet?' and Neill replies, 'No I was going to go on my break now, I can do them later if you want.'

Anya shrugs, thinking that it's so quiet, these winter mornings, they go by so slowly, she would rather be busy any day. 'No it's all right,' she says, 'go on your break, I'll do them.'

Neither Anya or Neill will think again about the sallow young woman with dark curly hair and the brother who came to pick her up, not even when they hear on the news the next day about the accident that afternoon, the two fatalities on the M23. The inquest into the deaths, some months later, will blame the driver of the car, Matthew Burton, for changing lanes too quickly, but it will get little publicity and there will be no reason for either Anya or Neill to make the connection.

Neill's wife will have given birth to their twins by then, a boy and a girl. Anya will never tell him that she has loved him since the first week they met on their training course two years ago, the same course where he met his wife, loved him distantly and without hope, as you might love a pair of shoes or a cashmere wrap you can't afford to buy.

February passes slowly in Brighton. On the pebbled beach, the waves continue to lift and crash, the red warning flag flies for the rest of the month, and to Anya it seems as though winter is never-ending, just keeps rolling around and around, and that summer and the busy season is both a far memory and will never come.

ANIMA

GRACE McCLEEN

T HE MEN ARRIVED IN the afternoon with horns and with dogs. Rain came in swathes; mist was cold on my skin. I slipped out after lunch. There was only packing to be done, and I didn't want to stand and watch. 'You'll like it,' they told me, 'you'll see. Just give it time. You'll learn to be a lady,' they said. 'Oh miss, such airs and graces, you'll have – you won't know yourself!'

It was this that concerned me. 'But can I come back?' I asked them.

'Of course,' they said. 'But you won't want to. You'll be so busy with your new life there. It's time you grew up, anyway. You've been left to your own ways too long. You can't stay here for ever. It's time you went into the real world.'

I was sure I would be content to stay here, amongst these fields and woods, this hill, for the rest of my life; I did not care if I never discovered the 'real' world, but I said nothing. I could always run away, I thought; if the new place was as

29

bad as I imagined, I could run away and come back here. But then I couldn't stay; they would send me back. Could I live in the wild? I wondered, as I watched them label vests and socks; What would I need to survive there?

It wasn't sadness I felt that day, but disbelief that this could be happening. I had never lived anywhere but here. I didn't know if I could. It seemed inconceivable. I wasn't sure how my body would function. So there was no sadness, only shock, only amazement that such a thing was taking place. Stupor, I suppose.

I couldn't stand around and wait for the car to come any longer, so I crept away that afternoon, despite the weather, and, hidden by the bare blackberry canes, stole down to the fence at the bottom of the garden. Nothing seemed real, though I strove to experience each and every thing as I never had before. I passed the place where I fell and scarred both knees when I was four, the tree where John the gardener had built the lookout for my seventh birthday, the orchard where every September we harvested apples, the place where I laid out supper for the hedgehogs. I touched lichen, caught the sharp stink of badger, noticed the colour, even now, of the dead leaves on the ground, stepped on mushrooms and heard the curious slippery squeak their flesh made as it sundered – and I saw, smelt, heard, and felt nothing. I couldn't yet feel the rain, which was heavier now. Each drop left only a numbness behind it that might be cold or might be hot, a small presence then absence, a coming and going too slight and too numerous to keep count.

I reached the fence and looked over the land. There was not much to see, I realised; nothing remarkable to another; but each bush, each stream, each thicket, was essential to me. I wondered suddenly if it would remain when I had gone, and then wondered, because I could feel nothing, if I had already left it.

I stood, thoroughly wet now, knowing I would be in for it when I got back. And that was when I saw you: a low brown shape slipping by the hedge, your gait dishevelled, paws black, your tail a little too long. A few minutes later I heard the hunt.

I saw them in the distance, saw the horses, dogs in troops, tails a forest of spears, caught the whining and shouting, squelching and screams, shouts; 'Get over!' 'Get up!' Whipping and hupping: 'Hup! Hep! Hup! Hep!' You ran right by me, and my heart beat once, so hard that for a moment I couldn't breathe. And there and then I came to life.

Horns blared. You answered in sharp breaths and a patter of feet. You were still trotting – why didn't you run? Perhaps you were already tired. I didn't know how far you had come. But as I watched you disappear, it was my legs that turned to water, my skin that stung, my chest that was suddenly tight. I had forgotten I had to get back. In a second I had climbed the fence, snaring my skirt, and dropped down the other side. Then I was up and running after you, through the empty field, rain blinding me. I entered the wood after

31

you. There was screaming in the air. I wasn't sure if it came from within or without. And in the grey midst of winter the whole world caught light.

I lost you, and when they came crashing behind me, I fell back and waited. I knew you would outwit them – you always outwitted them, dozens of times. You would double back and leave them panting, and then you would disappear, and later, when it was safe, I would find you. I ran through the thicket. I hacked brambles apart. I knew where your den was; I would meet you there and see that no harm came to you. I said the words in my head and I know you heard me. I would get there before them. But even the ground could not hold you. Even earth vomited you out. Like some prophet of old, there was no place for you, or for me that day; we were driven out, dispossessed, disinherited, and I knelt, or rather my knees did, when I saw they had found you before me; I watched as they hit the ground with pipes and with spades; as at one end of your home dogs began to bark. The dogs wagged their tails – they were such stupid creatures! They yapped and they whined; foolish noises for such large animals to make. If you made a noise it would mean something, I knew; it would make sense. I had heard you at night and you sounded like a demon. There was thunder now and rain like tarpaulin, banging in sheets, or maybe the banging was in my head, and I watched as they clamoured for you, unashamed in their lust. I should have shouted. I should have screamed and run at them. Could a child have done that? A girl of twelve? Perhaps. Why didn't I, then? Why didn't I stand up and save – I see now – both you and myself?

The first time I saw you, you were trotting along the top of the cornfield. The sun was rising, and when it caught your fur you looked as though you were cloaked in blood. I had never seen anything so beautiful and at once so familiar; I had the strangest feeling that I had, for the first time, seen me. After that I always looked out for you. I knew there was only one. You were the one the grown-ups spoke of. And they too spoke as if you were one, not many; not really animal and not really human. Not spirit either. What, then? An exile, a devil, the whipping boy of centuries. An ancient carrier of wrongs. You were the massacre, I learned. You were the terrorist. You were the alien. You and me both. And though they hated and killed you, they wrote stories about you and sang songs. You were a trophy. They eviscerated you and stuffed you, over and over, as if to reassure themselves there was no way you could come back to life. They put you in glass cases above fireplaces, or painted you on signs above doors where you swung in the breeze at the end of chains – as your brothers and sisters swung at the end of ropes, and, now, unable to move, I realised you would too this day, before they were done.

You were a legend and didn't even know it. You were immortal. And that afternoon I understood: they must kill you for you to live on.

∞

So they dug down. They sank steel rods into the ground and pushed you out. A difficult birth; you did not want to be born. Who would into such a world? They sent in forceps: a mastiff. He came out dragging you, but before he could kill you they took you away and let you hang, and I began to see that my worst fears were not dark enough: these men had a plan, but death was only a fraction of it; time made up one half and pleasure the other. They took you down and gave you to the jaws of the dog. He received their offering ungraciously, tugging clumsily in his hunger. Your skin was pulled back from your skull. You looked absurd, surprised, as if you were smiling. Absurd was the first thing you would look. There would be others.

The dog was excited, then confused. He could not pull any harder, but they made sure that he did: one pulled you, another his hind legs. Short sharp pulls. Your head came away bloody, dishevelled, fur in your eyes. You looked concussed, stunned. Stunned was the second thing you became. There would be more.

Your eyes were so bright at that moment. They were enormous. I was not sure if I was kneeling or standing or lying down; my own body seemed to have evaporated. We were both merely eyes, mine weeping, yours steely; looking on at the world's fun; playthings both; whirligigs; spinning, elevated, enthralled; borne high on a rhapsody of pain. They held you by the fur so that your mouth panted, showed small teeth. You looked like you were grinning. You looked mad now. Mad was the third thing you became.

'Look at this creature!' they said. And you certainly were a spectacle. They laughed and spat now, having removed their king and vanquished their leader – for you are their leader: you led them, not the other way around. The hounds bayed and jostled, in frantic anticipation. Their saliva descended in strings. The men held you aloft by the scruff, and you hung like a dead thing. You knew you must use only awkward effort each moment called for. You knew already, as I did not quite yet, that it was too late, yet still you played the game; you were a magnificent player – the best; you played your part so beautifully, down to the puny snap at the pole with which they touched the side of your jaw; down to the way your mouth clapped shut as they dropped you – careful to keep their hands out of harm's way – into a sack. And there you hung for an instant; a man on his way to the gallows. Though there would be no more trial now, that chapter was over; or if there were to be one, I sensed even now, it had barely begun.

The company were overly loud as they rode back through the wood. They were washing their hands with their laughter; without laughter they would honour you even as you were destroyed. I followed, breath rasping, stumbling over bare furrows, blinded by rain and by tears. I, your witness, your watcher, your other. Betrayer. Self.

Did you know me? Even now, in this hour I disowned you? When I stood silent by? I knew you. It was I who watched you from the beginning. You are the one who came out of the woods at the end of the day. You came out of the woods where the thorn trees grew thickly, out of the woods and into my life. They said not to encourage you, but I couldn't help it. A person can't look truth in the face and go back again. And you were truer than anything I had ever seen and more alive. So I watched and I courted you. At night when you played with your children, or fought, or made love. Early in the morning and late in the dusk, I saw you saunter leisurely with a bird or rabbit slack-necked in your mouth. Left you scraps from the table when their backs were turned, though I also knew that you slaughtered far more than you could carry away; hens, ducks, geese; night after night. I smelt your stink, heard your rustle, found the hole in the ground where you came and went that looked like an empty socket in a head. I thought you saw me too, because once or twice you stopped and looked back or looked up, and our eyes met, and when they did it was as if we had spoken, though not in any language I knew of. Once we stopped feet apart, surprising each other in the lane. Your expression changed but a whisker. You barely lifted your head, simply slipped sideways into the hedge. Afterwards I thought there must be some residue, evidence, but I came away empty-handed as if waking from a dream, and, as if bereaved, found I could not remember your face.

So here we are. At the end of all things, it seems. They have taken you to the long field, and when I reach it I fall to the ground winded, and though it lurches beneath me like a wave, strangely, I am almost at peace now, in the midst of utter loss; because the loss is utter, because I am in the midst of it. Perhaps I would not be if I were further from the centre, if the loss were one degree less.

They whirl you once in the air and then let you go. And even now, for a moment, my heart leaps in hope and I think they are setting you free, it is over, they were simply teaching you a lesson! It was just a trick, a nightmare – they have caught you and now they will throw you back! I clamber to my knees then stagger forwards, weeping, cheering, ridiculous, as I watch you scarper. But a sound makes me turn. Dogs, pouring over the field after you. There is no reprieve. It is simply round two. They have not forgiven you at all, they hate you more than I knew. And I stand as if halved, split asunder, and watch you. A small thing, moving slowly.

In dreams I have seen you since that time, wearing a diadem of thorns. I have seen you at the foot of a tree, a wolf with a red hide, a man in sheep's clothing, with a snout and hairs on the backs of his hands, a creature who bids me speak. I, your cowardly apostle, your doubting disciple, your false friend, was silent when it mattered; was with you and was not; went with you to the end of the earth, was there when the field came alive and leaped like a wave. I was there when you ran your last race.

The rain was too heavy to see. I saw. The wind blew sound this way and that. I heard. You were running all out now.

I told you, you should. I told you that earlier, but you wouldn't listen, you would only trot. I am sorry to say you were not a great runner; the dogs were. I didn't see when they overtook you. I looked away. I understood heart attacks now.

I couldn't see what the dogs were doing, there were too many. They swarmed, climbed over and under. I guessed you were at the centre. For minutes blackness wiped me out. When I looked again you had escaped. You were so much cleverer – and still had strength left, even now. But numbers prevail; someone spots you. You are recaptured. And finally, they deign to murder you. Piece by little piece.

I learned that day what a slow business it is to die; how tenacious life is even when the creature who possesses it doesn't want the gift any more. My heart was everywhere now, in my fingers and eyes, in the balls of my feet, beneath the soil, running through streams, through veins of leaves and of trees. My heart took up the skies. A man came with a terrier on a rope. The group broke for a second, and I saw you, huddled, still standing.

Imagine being eaten alive.

The intimacy. Do you form a bond with your consumer? I thought you would be dead many times over, but the dogs took tiny bites. It was as if they were humans; we could eat things just as well as they. They took tiny bites, but there were hundreds. I couldn't imagine all of those mouths. The hatred in them. The desire.

At some point I fell down, went out like a light. When I

came to they were hoisting you up and a dog came too; thrashing and mad-eyed. You were limp now. No more than a piece of rag. I saw then the secret: you were attached to a rope; whenever you were close to quitting they lifted you up. Now they were swinging you by your tail, and the dogs jumped after you clumsily, threshing mid-air. You flew, suspended above that sea of saliva, breath, rain, and teeth. I thought you were dead. But you were not. The man knew you could not last. You jerked to life – still had such power! You had been playing, an excellent sportsman; you didn't flinch, even in agony. The dogs became delirious. You were let down amongst them.

When I look back on that afternoon now it was too homely, too unpretentious a death to be violent. They were merely scrubbing a board, raking a lawn; it was housework, nothing more, and you were a figure of fun; there was nothing tragic about those tugs at the line. You had crossed the border of pity a long time ago, horror wasn't far behind, and after that was the ridiculous – because now you were nothing; an object, ludicrous, staggering slightly; something to make men either laugh or throw up their lunch.

They pulled you back and forth, teasing the dogs, helping them out; it was only right, was how it was done, these final gestures, this inching away of life; jerked you from side to side for variety; set you right side out like a jumper, then once again turned your insides out.

In the last moments, what was a living creature became

39

a blank space, an observer looking down upon itself. You, too, only astonished now at what they had done to you. Your eyes were wide with the thought of it and would never close. It was this that killed you, this miracle.

Once more – as if fondly – as if for old time's sake – the man lifted you, and a dog came up too, the others mad with envy because he was close to you. Though it wasn't you any more, I could see that now; just a piece of something; a mat; road kill; a ludicrous tatter with goggle eyes.

Because I was silent, now I speak. And what can I say? That I loved you. That the spectacle swallowed me whole. That I went inside it. Horror sucks you inside. That I would murder now too, if I could. That I have dreamed many times since then of what I could do.

When they had gone I buried what was left of you in the open field with my hands, and for three days and nights after, in the new room, in that unfamiliar place miles from here, where I remain but can never return to, I lay with you in the belly of the earth and imagined we both had never been born.

Now, though I am older, and each day the universe is a mighty stranger, I occasionally glimpse you sometimes at the borders of vision. You appear for a moment then evaporate.*

*Cathy's words: '. . . if all else remained, and he were annihilated, the universe would turn to a mighty stranger'.

I first saw you trotting along at the top of the cornfield as the sun rose. I could not speak because you were beautiful, and afterwards I went and walked. I thought there must be some sign you had been, some proof of your presence. But there was none.

You left no trace and nor did you wait. You went on ahead and I followed as best I could, grasping a knowledge available for a certain time only.

You went into the woods where the thorn trees grew thickly. Into the woods and out of my sight.

A BIRD, HALF-EATEN

———

NIKESH SHUKLA

I LOOP THE WRAP over my thumb and across the back of my hand. It goes over my hand three times, tight, and then around my wrist, three times, tight. There's a ritual to this. I bring the wrap up from my wrist in between my little and ring finger and then back down to my wrist. Up again, between ring and middle, and back down. Up again, between middle and index, and then back down. Each time, the wrap forms an X across the back of my hand. I loop it between thumb and index and then across the palm of my hand, to lock it in. I wrap the remainder of the cloth around my wrist and then Velcro it closed. I flex my hand, open and closed. It feels tight, taut, tethered.

I repeat the ritual with my weaker hand. This one always feels looser. I love watching people perform this ritual quietly, meditatively, with ease, in changing rooms and on YouTube videos. I look at my own fingers, shuddering slightly under the wrap, and clench my fist.

When I have wrapped both my hands, I pick up my gloves and take three shallow sips of water, heading to the thin sweaty alcove of heavy bags. I'm the only one in here. I come when it's quiet so I can concentrate.

When the bell rings, I hold my fists up over my face and I drop my chin. I am hunched, and standing with my feet a shoulder apart.

The bell ring is a short sharp electronic burst, like when you're called forward at the bank. I always choose the bag in the middle. It's milk-chocolate brown with a silver strip of gaffer tape that acts as a waistband around its middle. It's the heaviest bag here.

For the first three minutes, I punch quickly and lightly, jab-cross, repeatedly. First at your nose. Then at your stomach. Jab-cross nose, jab-cross stomach, jab-cross nose, jab-cross stomach. I try to maintain a consistent speed so that I'm working my arms, ensuring that the muscle memory is kicking in. I don't want to fling my arms out at you uncontrolled. I want my body to be seasoned to swivel from the hips, the turn of the foot, so that the power is coming from my entire body, and my arms are giving me the necessary distance from you, and my fists can carry the full force of my core.

The first time I got punched, I was intervening in a theft. Some guy was pulling on my friend Rachna's bag, which she had slung over her shoulder, while I was oblivious, trying to hail a cab. I heard her shouting, 'You can't do that, you can't do that,' and turned around. The guy was pulling the bag so forcefully that their heads were nearly colliding. It was over her shoulder, securely, so she'd need to take it off for him. He wrenched her so close as she was shouting, I saw her accidentally bite his nose. I ran towards her and pulled on the bag myself. The bag-snatcher let go, and for a pregnant second, I saw something in his eyes that wasn't aggression or frustration or anything – it was powerlessness.

He punched me on my nose. And he ran off.

I don't bruise very easily, but I felt the imprint of his knuckles on my face for days.

It was the first time I'd been punched.

I'd been in scraps before, but the thing about scraps in the boys' school I went to, they were all about grabbing each other by the shirt on the shoulders and pulling, like a strange undressing wrestle.

When the bell rings, I take off my left glove. The knuckles on this hand always throb after each round. I practise the swivel in my hips. One of the trainers has told me I'm too stiff, I need to relax into my shots. Keep my knuckles on top. Every movement is still alien to me. You watch the way fights are choreographed in films, and each punch is syncopated to a stirring score, each movement, every duck and weave, is a seamless piece of a dance. Here in this gym, the walls drip with the splatter of several people's sweat. Here in this gym, the old hi-fi that still has cassette decks spits out Ed Sheeran or whoever is big on Radio 1 at that time. Here in this gym, the most balletic of boxers are the ones under eighteen. Here in this gym, you see interlopers like me. We who need this bag to represent something to us. Each sound is like tapping a sofa – flat, undramatic, clunky. Usually, the bag is a manifestation of ourselves. The implication, when we shadow-box, is that we look at ourselves in the mirror, because the first person you have to defeat in the ring is yourself. You box yourself in the mirror. You visualise your face on the bag.

Most people are here because they never defeated that person in the full-length mirror. You can tell, we're the ones whose eyes never leave our reflections as we move around the gym.

The bag, you are never allowed to let drop, not if you want to be quick.

I put my glove back on.

When the bell rings, I launch at the bag with power this time. I jab, jab firmly, then follow it up with a powerful cross, a pow to the centre of your face. Immediately I duck and arch my entire body in a semicircular movement to the left. As I rise, I meet the side of the bag with a left hook. My left hooks are telegraphed from miles away. It's as if I need the duck and weave, and the big powering up of the arm to act as my inner force. I need those movements to make my hook an effective one.

When we eventually fight though, you'll see it coming

from miles away and step out of it, and I'll drop my guard and you can strike everywhere.

You and I train at different times. I've chosen my hours to coincide with when I think you'll be at work. My lifestyle allows me to be here at unsociable hours, when the club first opens. All the while, you're at work.

I wonder if you think about me as much as I think about you.

I vary the combo this time and follow the left hook up with a right hook. The bag is swinging about on the chain wildly.

I saw you in the city centre last week. It was the first time I'd seen you in your normal clothes, not your boxing gear, and it shook me. Not that you looked like a regular person. More that you being a regular person made it harder for me to visualise your face on this bag. You wore a white shirt. Polyester. I could see through to the outline of a vest. You wore grey trousers, and worn black shoes. You had one hand in your pocket, and the other held your phone to your ear. You were listening intently and looking up at the sky as you paced. You didn't see me. I stopped and waited for you to notice me. But you didn't. When I saw you had breezed on past me, I turned and followed you. I wanted to see where you went when you weren't at the gym. Who you were in your real life. I got twenty steps before I realised I was exhibiting problematic behaviour. And I only realised I was exhibiting problematic behaviour because I walked into the path of a bike as I crossed the road behind you. The cyclist swore at me – unnecessarily probably – but it was enough to shake me.

What did I observe in those twenty steps?

That you walked with confidence.

That you had to look upwards in order to concentrate.

That your entire body seemed relaxed. You looked like you belonged in that body, you owned that skin, no one had ever given you a reason to doubt yourself.

It made me angry. That you were seemingly at one with yourself.

I told the cyclist to go fuck himself, and turned around, returning to my office, to my desk. I stared at a half-drunk mug of coffee and picked it up. The cold of the handle against my fingertips as I gripped it tightly was a comfort. My colleague Chloe passed my desk and looked at me quizzically. I put the mug down and smiled at her, banging at the space bar on my laptop to wake it up.

'You OK?' she asked.

I shook my head. 'No,' I replied, quietly, and with enough finality to show her that she was not to enquire any further.

The second time I was punched, I was on a train coming home from London. It was late and I was drunk. I played a film on my laptop and pointed myself at it while I ate chicken strips, dipping each one deep into a small carton of barbecue sauce. I was too drunk to concentrate on the film, but it was action-packed enough to catch my attention occasionally. When I finished my McDonalds, I shoved all the detritus into the paper bag and shoved it under my seat in an effort to pretend the entire shameful transaction never happened.

The barbecue sauce must have slipped out of the bag because I felt a shuffle in the seat behind me turn into a shouting man.

'There's shit on my shoe,' he bellowed to the empty carriage.

I looked up at him. He was greying, wearing a blue raincoat of the kind that only businessmen with no imagination seem to purchase, and clutching a can of Fosters.

I looked down at his shoe. He wore black dress shoes. I could see a speck of burgundy on the right one. Presumably some of my barbecue sauce.

'Sorry boss,' I muttered and offered him a napkin.

He launched himself at me with his fists. He punched me twice in the face before I could react. In launching himself at me, he lost his balance and fell on me. I was so shocked. I sat there flinching and cowering, waiting till he regained his balance and stood up.

I cried.

I could feel his knuckles embedded in my cheek. I could feel the slime of his neck sweat by my mouth. I turned back to the laptop and carried on watching my film. As if nothing had happened. He straightened himself up and apologised, before picking up his bag and disappearing down the train.

I sat there, rooted to the spot till my station arrived. I ran off the train, down the steps, and up the other side to the exit. I ran out of the barriers and I ran to the taxi rank.

I jumped into a car. As the car pulled away from the station, I saw him emerge, eating a chocolate bar and staring at his phone as if he had not a care in the world.

I didn't tell my wife I'd been assaulted. I don't bruise, and so apart from my cheek being tender to touch, there was no sign of the impact of his fists on me. I got off the train in fear. I hurried to the ticket barriers. I prayed for a short queue for taxis. I couldn't rationalise the casualness of the assault. I couldn't bring myself to comprehend the escalation from a dab of barbecue sauce to a full-blown attack. All I knew was that I was attacked, and ultimately that it was my fault for being careless with my rubbish and for not reporting the unnecessary reaction sooner.

The day I signed up to the boxing gym, my wife asked me what had brought on the sudden interest in the sport.

'I just want to protect myself,' I said.

'Then take up self-defence,' she replied. 'I'd love to do that too.'

I couldn't explain to her that boxing would help me take up room. Boxing would give me space to occupy unapologetically, and no one would think twice about hitting me. I would have the confidence to dodge, to take a punch, and if required, hit back.

My first class, a technique one, was when it started.

I felt out of place the entire time. People had brought their own equipment. I was lost. I couldn't skip. I took some gloves from a bin next to the toilets. The communal gloves stank of the sweat of many people. I was dripping with sweat myself, from ten minutes of skipping uselessly and shadow-boxing self-consciously. I put the gloves on without wraps and flexed my fingers. It stank.

You were my partner. The first thing you told me was that you're a Southpaw. I didn't know what that meant until I was unexpectedly hit repeatedly. You leaned in, and, due to your height and reach, you were able to deliver shots I couldn't block with my elbows. Also, you were happy to use force. We'd been instructed only to tap each other while we were learning the techniques. That didn't deter you from hitting, hard. And asking me to hit you back hard.

'It's OK, harder,' you kept telling me.

The sensation of being hit when it's part of the game, the sport, it was confusing. It hurt. It also niggled at something else in me. Why was I not learning self-defence? Maybe my wife was right. Instead, I'm learning to hit but also be hit.

I observed you everywhere around the gym. You took up space. From the way you left your wraps in a heap on the floor after a session, through to hogging the middle of the gym when you skipped, through to the way you winked at everyone.

And after a while I wanted to take that space away from you.

The moment came at the end of our second technique class. I'd tried to avoid partnering up with you, but you sought me out.

'I like to train with the new guys,' you told me between

rounds. 'See whether you're tough enough to stay or you'll just stop coming cos you like box-fit but not boxing. Which are you?'

Why does it matter so much? I said, in my head. 'Dunno,' I mumbled aloud.

The instructor shouted out another combination before I could muster up the courage to say it out loud.

Before I could drop my chin and put my fists up, you jabbed twice, pushing me back, and gave me a left hook that caught me on the ear.

It caught me by such surprise that I dropped to the floor.

The instructor rushed over.

'You OK?' he asked. He looked up at the room. 'You better defend those shots or you'll be dropping as well,' he bellowed to the rest of the class.

You took your glove off and gripped me under my arm, pulling me up.

'Hit me,' you said. 'Hit me.'

So I hit you. As hard as I could. You were that space on the heavy bag we aimed for, pretending it was a nose. You were ready, and used your left glove to bat my shot away as hard as you could.

'Hit me,' you repeated.

I repeated my movement. You did the same parry, this time harder.

'Hit . . . me,' you said, slower, quieter.

This time, I was slower, and I tried a shot, but you ducked and pushed me back.

'I said hit me,' you said, laughing.

I unVelcroed a glove and put it in my armpit. I undid the other. I looked at you and shook my head.

'Box-fit's on Tuesdays,' you said. 'See you then. Fly away bird, fly away. Before I eat you. There are lions here, and we're hungry.'

I cycled home, raging, turning over and over in my head the perfect argument with you, the perfect shots, the perfect retaliation. At home, my wife asked me how the class was, and I shrugged. 'It was OK,' I said. I didn't want her to know I felt humiliated because she was right. I didn't have the stomach to fight. Only the desire for self-preservation.

What was it about you that made me obsess over your words? There was something, a gauntlet, a challenge.

As I worked the bags by myself on Tuesday and Thursday afternoons, I noticed you in the sparring club. Here the more amateur-level boxers gathered, to spar with the one or two pros training for matches. I worked the bags, quietly in the corner. I wondered if you noticed me. You waited your turn like everyone else, but were never chosen to spar.

Different strands of different pecking orders, I wondered. You were nobody here, so you were somebody there.

One day you saw me, and I flinched. I was between rounds, peeking out of the corridor of heavy bags at you. You smiled and flapped your arms like a bird, giggling to yourself. People turned to see who you were gesturing at, and all they saw was me, the chubby person, trying to get in shape. Someone shook their head at you, which made you drop your grin.

You kept looking at me, and gestured to the ring.

The day we spar, I leave work early for a meeting that doesn't exist. I go for a run around the harbourside, and then a jog to the gym. Outside, I wrap myself.

I loop the wrap over my thumb and then immediately across the back of my hand. It goes over my hand three times, tight, and then around my wrist, three times, tight. There's a ritual to this. I bring the wrap up from my wrist in between my little and ring finger, and then back down to my wrist. Up again, between ring and middle, and back down. Up again, between middle and index, and then back down. Each time, the wrap forms an X across the back of my hand. I loop it between thumb and index and then across the palm of my hand, to lock it in. I wrap the remainder of the cloth around my wrist, and then Velcro it shut. I flex my hand, open and closed.

You're in the changing room when I enter. You're talking on the phone, to a colleague about something to do with your work. I look you directly in the eye, the entire time I'm in the changing room. You barely notice me till I walk into the gym.

I face you in the room, both in our corners. Everyone has left except people coming in for a class. We're nobodies in the ecosystem of this gym.

I stare into your eyes. I've obsessed about every second of this fight. I know how to dodge your arms. I know how to move backwards quickly. I have worked out every scenario in my head.

You made me do this. Maybe this was your plan all along. You flap wings at me. The bell rings. I drop my chin, hold up my fists, and breathe.

THICKER THAN BLOOD

ERIN KELLY

August

'IS THAT THE BRAND-NEW iPad?' Heath was up to his shoulders in the hot tub, one dry arm resting on the side, finger on a screen that was tiled with images of Cat. He had his back to Izzy, but could tell by her tone that she would be twisting the hem of whatever ridiculous garment she was wearing. 'It's just, if you drop it in the water, that's the third one this year.'

'I paid for it,' he said through a rigid jaw, 'and if I do drop it, which I won't, I'll pay for a new one.'

'It's just, it's the waste?'

Heath reached for another bottle, the eye tattoo winking with the flex of his bicep, and uncapped it with his teeth. Four beers down and it was still too early to tell whether drinking would make him relax around Izzy or stoke his irritation with her. Either way, he was too busy to be interrupted: on the Instagram phase of his nightly cycle through Cat's social media accounts. He'd already done Twitter and Facebook, and after Instagram, would have to work his way through what he thought of as the associated accounts, the people she called her friends, and the 'man' she called her husband. The associated accounts were in some ways more revealing than Cat's own, as a friend might catch her dropping her guard, exposing the misery behind her heavily filtered life. When it happened, he could go to her. She could only pretend for so long, even to herself, to be totally jazzed about this life Ed had given her, this life of farmers' markets, group holidays in Provençal *gîtes*, charity fundraisers, and strawberries and cream at Centre Court, and fucking *golfing* holidays.

It was a low-activity evening: Cat had liked a couple of things but hadn't posted herself. If he was lucky he'd only have to go through the cycle once and he'd be done in under two hours.

'Oh, why d'you have to—' began Izzy, but the tablet pinged with a notification, and this time Heath snatched it away from her outstretched hand. A new post, a touching attempt at an arty selfie. She was in the garden, aureole around silhouette on the back wall of the Grange, the tumbling violet moor an invitation, an unmade bed laid out behind her. Heath felt the usual sick stirring deep under his belly. He shifted position, hiding himself under the bubbles in case Izzy thought it was for her, then returned to his study of Cat. Why had she kept her face in shadow? Had she been crying? Tears made most women ugly, but when Cat cried her face bloomed pink and white.

Izzy stopped mouth-breathing on the back of Heath's neck and appeared in front of him. Christ, she was all done up for seduction. Her hair described the barrel of a curling tong, and she was dressed in an awful chiffon kimono thing she called cruise wear. It was supposed to be floaty and seductive, but it was covered in sequins and getting close to her felt like pressing up against a rose bush.

Another ping. Ed had just made his annual Instagram post. Heath was on it in seconds. It seemed that Ed was doing a life-drawing class in the Scottish borders as part of a stag weekend. The charcoal sketch was crap and the woman they were drawing wasn't even attractive.

It meant, though, that Cat was on her own at the Grange for the first time in ages. He could be there in forty minutes. Pulse hammering, he got out of the tub just as Izzy sank into the bubbles.

'You can have it to yerself,' he said, heaving himself over the edge. He dried himself roughly on a towel, pulled on a tracksuit, took a bottle of Laurent Perrier from the drinks fridge, wrapped it in a towel, and threw it into his sports bag.

'Where are you going? It's nearly nine o'clock.'

'Gym,' he said. Izzy looked at the green bottles lined up

on the edge of the hot tub, but she had learned, at last, not to challenge him.

His feet found their path in the divots and tufts they'd walked for as long as he could remember. He could've run the route from the Heights to the Grange in ten minutes, but he didn't want the champagne to fizz, and anyway, he needed to clear his head and think about how he would say it. Below and to the west was the first estate he'd ever built, shoebox houses whose tiny gardens were mocked by the moor. In front of him, the dipping midsummer sun made a thin gold thread on the horizon. A single dazzling bead shone through a hole in the rocky crag that marked the midpoint between her house and his. He'd kissed her for the first time at the foot of those rocks, when they were both fourteen, kissed her, and that was as far as it had gone, the wanting getting worse over the years, and the conversation grinding in ever-decreasing circles. It had taken him years to realise they were all excuses.

'Foster siblings still count,' she'd said at first.

'Don't be daft. There's no law against it.'

'In the eyes of society, though.' Since when did she care about society? Though they'd been raised under the same roof, she was not his sister; he was her possessor, not her protector, and they both knew it. Whatever they had, it was something thicker than blood.

Then, as they got older: 'It would destroy our friendship, Heath, can't you see that?'

'Let it!' he'd roared. 'Let it . . . smash this misshapen thing and put it back together a new way, the right way.'

Her head had gone into her hands. 'Will you listen to yourself? Smashing, misshapen. You're so bloody *intense*. It was all right when we were kids, but you can't want to carry on like this for ever.'

It was all he did want. He couldn't remember a time he hadn't wanted it, from the inseparability of their childhood to the present physical ache for her that was so constant he wore it like an extra body part.

'I mean, come on,' she'd laughed. 'Can you honestly see us pushing a trolley around Waitrose together, going to parents' evening?'

'*Waitrose?*' This was coming out of nowhere.

'I suppose not. The rate you're going, we'll be lucky to afford Morrisons.'

He'd been horrified. 'This is about *money*?' She knew he was struggling, but he'd never thought it mattered to her. To his shame, tears pricked his eyes and made a stone in his throat. He turned his face away.

'No. Or – not only. It's about – a kind of life I want.'

'A life you *think* you want.'

She'd rolled her eyes. 'This is exactly what I'm talking about! You don't know me as well as you think you do.'

'I know you better than you know yourself.'

But it had niggled at him for months afterwards, and because she seemed to believe that she meant it, he'd gone off to prove himself, starting as a labourer and going in with a mate, flipping properties from Salford to Harrogate. He'd worked on himself, too: got strong and lean. And while he was watching the money stack up, picturing her face the day he walked back into Cat's life, Ed had stepped in, all breeding and family money and red chinos – and she'd fallen for it. The image of them together, of Ed's hands on Cat's skin, was a film Heath couldn't stop watching even when he closed his eyes. The sick knot of desire inside him, deep and low, tightened like the balling of a fist.

Heath approached the Grange from the back, took their old path along the side of the house, stopping at the window where he and Cat had spied on Ed and Izzy a lifetime ago, taken the piss out of their wooden toys and their side partings. How had they gone from that to this? He leaned against the stone lintel and closed his eyes, not against the memory, but the present. His longing was so powerful that he could almost smell her.

He opened his eyes to see Cat on the other side of the glass, looking past him, out onto the moor. He took a beat to savour how she looked when she didn't know she was being watched. Her hair was a mess of waves, she wasn't wearing any make-up, and she looked closer to her girlhood self than Heath had seen in years. She'd lost weight for her wedding and never put it back on, fallen in with that crowd of skeletal ladies who didn't lunch, all blow-dries and nails. But there was a blown-rose blowsiness to her tonight, and some meat on her bones again, and her name slipped out before he could announce himself.

'*Cat*,' he breathed. She screamed and leaped away from the window. 'It's only me. I'm sorry, I thought it'd be a *good* surprise.'

He'd expected her to push up the sash and put her arms around him, but instead she glanced over her shoulder, held a hand up in conciliation to someone behind her.

'It's all right, Ed,' she said, throwing up the sash window. Heath felt winded. What about Scotland?

'It's him, isn't it?' said Ed. Even in his fury, Heath had room for a pulse of satisfaction that he'd been Ed's first guess. He liked the idea of being at the forefront of Ed's mind, wandering around in there with mud on his boots.

'For God's sake, Heath.' Ed was still in the same outfit from the Instagram photo, and Heath had the feeling he'd somehow been tricked into visiting the Grange. 'What *is* it with you and windows?' There was something in Ed's tone Heath hadn't heard before. Usually he at least managed to feign civility for Cat's benefit, but now a trembling dimple in one cheek suggested he was trying not to laugh at him.

His fingertips tingled. Something was very wrong.

'What're you *doing* here, Heath?' said Cat.

The truth – that he had come here to claim her – sounded ridiculous now, even in its diluted version: 'I had to see you, that's all.'

She looked – was that *pity*?

'All right!' said Ed. 'I've put up with your Jeremy Kyle crap out of politeness, but enough's enough. You can't just keep turning up here. I won't have you upsetting Cat in her condition.'

In her condition. Cat's glow: Ed's newfound confidence. Heath went very cold, then very hot. She had the grace to drop her eyes, at least. 'Due in February,' she said. 'Don't look like that. I want you to be happy for me.'

But he had dropped his sports bag in the shrubbery. He was back at the Heights in nine minutes, a personal best. Izzy was still awake, after making her own raid on the drinks fridge, so he took her to bed for the first time in months. It was simple mechanics, drainage and release: it had to go somewhere, and Izzy was so grateful she cried.

February

Heath spent Valentine's eve closing a deal for his next development with a new contractor. They'd be building in Hertfordshire on the edge of a nothingy plain they thought was real countryside. It would be his biggest project yet, and it got him away from women. It was bad enough seeing Cat's body changing on a screen, without her parading the real thing in front of him. The men celebrated their signatures with dinner in the hotel restaurant. During the meal he'd left his phone charging behind the bar, on silent. After they'd shaken hands and parted, he retrieved his phone, and, in the second it took to register the twenty missed calls from Izzy, her number flashed up again over Cat's picture.

'I don't know how to tell you this,' she started, and he knew. He staggered into a wall as though he'd been shoved. 'I'm with Ed now,' sputtered Izzy. 'Detached placenta. The doctors did what they could, but it was too late. The baby was a little girl. They're calling her—' He threw the phone at the far wall. The screen shattered Cat's face into shards, then went black.

He bypassed denial and went straight to guilt. He should never have left her. He should be with her, holding her hand, catching her soul before it slipped away for ever. The impulse propelled him to his feet, but the vertigo lurch told him he wouldn't get a mile up the motorway before he lost his licence or worse.

Anyway, he couldn't trust himself to be in the same county as the child.

'Triple whisky,' he said to the barmaid, after she'd picked up the mess of silicone and glass. She bit her lip.

'I'm not supposed to serve . . .'

Heath slid a fiver her way. 'Charge the drink to the room, and that's for you.'

She was a good listener, Lenka or Lilja, or whatever her name was, keeping the drinks coming, and nodding in all the right places when he talked about Cat.

'I mean, what kind of hospital lets a woman die like that in 2017? More to the point, what kind of man allows that to happen to his wife? Put another double in there, that's a good girl.'

He woke himself up the next morning by calling her name. The twist of his mouth opened up a deep scratch from the night before. There was vomit on the floor, and a single artificial fingernail snapped on the bedside table. Everything after Izzy's phone call was a blur. He remembered the bar, note after note after note changing hands, and then his own slurred apology, I'm sorry I'm sorry I'm sorry, and a soft accented voice; I don't want anything to do with this, you're seriously messed up, you need help.

March

Ed sent a 'polite request' that Heath stay away from the funeral. It's immediate family only, he'd said. I'm sure you'll understand. A pathetic attempt to have the last word. Immediate family. What else was Heath if not that? They *were* each other, so where did that leave him now?

She was buried where she'd got married, the pretty, if weather-beaten, little church on the hill. The sky was a glowering pewter that matched the lead on the roof. Heath parked his old site van at an angle on a grass verge, and slung his tool bag on a random overgrown grave. It announced his intentions before he understood them himself.

Wind made murmurs in the heather on the hills. He had the moor to himself except for a couple of ramblers, zipped to the chin in purple Gore-Tex, walking expectantly towards the church. They waved at Heath from a distance, but up close something in his eyes must have warned them off, because they changed tack and went the long way around, on the other side of the dry-stone wall. Good. They could go somewhere else for their brass rubbings.

In the churchyard, the same family names repeated on the headstones, more proof that Cat should've chosen him, an injection of fresh blood, over these inbred bastards. Heath ran his tongue over his gold tooth, the only treasure he'd take to his own grave.

Cat was in the wrong place, in Ed's family plot. Tasteful white lilies banked knee-high, half-obscuring her name in marble. Catherine Linton, beloved wife and mother, and then the days of her, the childhood that had been his, and the short adulthood Ed had stolen from him. If he could have, he would have carved his name next to hers, but he had brought the wrong tools for that.

Heath kicked the lilies into the undergrowth. In the settling dust cloud of yellow pollen, he placed the single red rose he'd bought that morning. The florist had offered to take the thorns off it, but he wasn't having that. He took one last picture of Cat, bringing the total of her images on his camera roll to 1,259.

He didn't decide to dig so much as find his foot on the shovel, turning the loose earth. Knowing that he would be her last as well as her first kept him going even while the graveyard around him began to frost. Sweat loosened the spade in his hands, but it didn't slow his pace. When dusk drew in, he drove over the graves, let his engine idle and used the dipped headlights as torches. When the earth was at shoulder height, he tore the skin off a knuckle jemmying open the lid, but euphoria hid the pain because then they were together again, even if his was the only breath misting the night. She was cold: she wouldn't look at him. One hand teased out the soft length of her hair, while the other worked at his zipper, heedless of the blue light strobing on his back, deaf to the car door's slam and the footsteps, the police officer's shadow on his back, and only half-hearing the voice that said, 'Jesus Christ, I thought we'd find him nicking lead off the roof. I thought I'd seen it all, but *this* . . .'

But he was down deeper than they could reach him, and by the time backup came he was spent. He'd undone Ed, he had beaten even death and laid the final claim to her. Nobody could take that away from him.

The back of the police car had tinted windows. The moon was bright, and the moor was silver, the way it used to look when they were kids.

September

The hospital was hundreds of miles from home. Fenland, not fells, beyond the perimeter wall: reeds and water instead of heather and gorse. His room had a toilet, a sink, and a tiny window. Other patients had the night terrors, but Heath lived for the small hours, and the scratching at the fortified glass, and the little white hand that reached for him and told him she still wanted him, that she had always wanted him, that he had known her better than she knew herself.

ONE LETTER
DIFFERENT

JOANNA CANNON

'Yorkshire isn't what it used to be.'

Ellis's mother addressed the kitchen window of the holiday cottage, as if the entire county had spread itself out before her, waiting for an evaluation. They'd only been there half an hour, but her mother had already found herself a dishcloth to run over the draining board.

'It's the same as it always was, Carole. Still sandwiched between Lancashire and the North Sea.' Ellis's father didn't address the kitchen window, but carried on opening and closing the drawers and the cupboards, because when you walk into a holiday room, the first thing you do is look at all the empty space and wonder how you might go about filling it.

'There's no view. The brochure promised a view.' Her mother rinsed the cloth under the tap, and gave herself something else to wipe. 'Brochures aren't what they used to be either.'

There was a view, it just wasn't the one her mother had

expected to see. It was a view of another, identical holiday cottage, a recycling bin in the back yard of a pub called The Cow and the Canary (a ridiculous name, said her father), and a single, wooden bench decorated in graffiti, because there are certain things in life that are so important, they need to be written down somewhere to make sure they are always remembered.

'There's a view from my window. You can see the edge of the moors if you stand on tiptoe.'

Ellis looked at each of them in turn, but her parents didn't answer.

She turned and headed back to her room, listened to the sound of her feet on an unfamiliar staircase and the echo of herself in another house. Unlike the carpeted world they usually inhabited, the cottage had floorboards and flagstones. It made every noise more important than you intended it to be.

'Ellis, you sound like a herd of elephants,' shouted her mother. 'Do try to be more graceful.'

It took seven trips for her father to unload the car. Ellis watched from the bedroom, using her rucksack as a step and breathing silence into the glass. People go on holiday to escape their lives, yet her mother seemed to have packed as much of their life as she could into the back of the Ford Focus and brought it along with them.

'I'm fairly sure they have frying pans in Yorkshire,' her father had said that morning.

On the seventh trip, her father just carried one thing. The photograph. Ellis wasn't surprised to see it, because it accompanied her mother everywhere in its tired gilt frame, but she was surprised to see it carried in all by itself. Perhaps her father was worried about dropping it, or losing it somewhere between their car and the front door of the cottage, or perhaps it was just that the photograph weighed far, far more than you might think.

At home, the photograph lived on top of the television. Ellis found that her eyes always seemed to move upwards and she would catch herself staring into the past, no matter what TV programme she had wanted to watch. However, in the holiday cottage, after several false starts, her mother decided the photograph should be placed on the kitchen windowsill.

'There,' her mother said. 'That's better. Now it feels like home.'

So her mother had her view after all. Even if it wasn't a view she had ever expected to see.

They all ate fish and chips that night, and stretched out their motorway legs on a walk around the village, but it still took Ellis a long time to find her sleep. The bed was decidedly difficult. It was wooden and panelled, and Ellis thought it seemed more like a coffin, but she could never say that to her parents, because any reference to illness or dying had been hoovered out of their conversations. They lived in a sterile world now, where no one got sick or passed away, for fear of opening a door none of them would ever be able to close. As well as the bed issue, there was a lot of noise, too. Mainly from the bar at The Cow and The Canary. But there was something else. The house creaked and complained each night, as it settled itself into sleep, in a way their own house never did. Any sound Ellis made was nurtured, grown somehow by the floorboards and the leaded-glass windows, until even the sound of her own breathing seemed to be carried away down the landing, and passed around from room to room.

Ellis had reached an age when her parents didn't know whether to cut her free or tie the knot a little tighter. *Before*, they had examined every inch of her existence, but now, *after*, it felt as though she had finally been allowed her freedom, but she only ever cashed it in in order to drift around the outskirts of her parents' lives, waiting to be questioned. Everything in Ellis's life fell into either before or after. She was divided into two people, and no matter how hard Ellis tried, she never seemed to be able to glue the bits of herself back together.

'I'm going for a walk,' she said from a doorway, on the morning of the second day. 'To the moors, probably.'

'Right.' Her mother was rearranging the cushions on the sofa. Diamonds or squares. Crouched in corners or pulled out into a line.

'Enjoy yourself.' Her father returned another paperback to the little shelf next to the fireplace.

'I'll be back later.' Ellis pulled a cagoule over her head. 'Hopefully. I mean, it can get quite wild up there, can't it? So who knows when it might be.'

She waited for as long as she could, to see if someone would fit words into the silence, but no one did, and so she lifted the latch on the front door.

'Ellis,' her mother shouted.

Ellis smiled before she turned.

'Why don't you tie your hair back from time to time, love? It would really suit you.'

There was a path between the two holiday cottages. It didn't really look like a path until you were close up, but Ellis found she always noticed the things most people seemed to miss. The path was overgrown with grass and weeds, and the grass and weeds were just wet enough to change the colour of her trainers and bathe her ankles in yesterday's rain. Either side of her journey was the litter of other people's holidays. People who had managed to spot the path as well, and who had left small pieces of themselves, like clues, along the way. She studied the clues as she walked. A receipt from the off-licence. A child's glove. A plastic football, abandoned, perhaps, by a disinterested dog. After a few minutes, she reached a fork in the path and studied the alternatives to see which looked the less travelled.

'It's the one on the left for the moors.'

The boy leaned against a gate. His skin was bleached like the wood, and his eyes were the grey of a battlefield sky.

The landscape seemed to have borrowed back all of his colours.

Ellis looked up at the path. It was steeper than she had expected.

'It's not as bad as it seems,' said the boy. 'Come on, I'll show you.'

He began climbing. Ellis frowned at the boy, but she followed him anyway, because she couldn't think of any reason not to.

'You're staying in the other holiday cottage,' he shouted as he walked, the distance growing between them.

It wasn't a question. Ellis said 'yes' anyway.

'What's your name?'

'Ellis.'

He turned and looked at her. 'Isn't that a boy's name?'

'It's either. It's Irish shorthand for Elizabeth.'

'You don't sound Irish. Are you Irish?'

'No, I'm not, but my mother says you can always borrow, can't you?'

Ellis waited for the discussion. There was always a discussion.

'Cool,' said the boy, and he carried on walking.

She smiled. When she looked up again, he had moved further away, and Ellis tried to be heard and catch up all at the same time. 'What's yours then?'

'I'm Leo,' he shouted back, and then, 'no, I'm not, but you can always borrow, can't you?'

∞

As they walked, there must have been a point where grass turned to moorland. Ellis hadn't noticed where exactly that point was, but now, all around her, everywhere was held at the moment when purple becomes brown, when walkers become trespassers. The point when you had to let go of the need for a path.

'It's not that far,' said Leo. 'It just looks that way.'

They were there before she knew it. When Ellis lifted her head, it seemed as if the whole world had unfolded itself when she wasn't looking, and she stared across blankets of heather, towards the sea. It looked like one shade at first. A single layer of dark pigment, painted on the landscape. It was only when you studied it, when you really creased your eyes, you realised there were so many colours, it was impossible to discover them all with a single stare.

'From the car, it looked as if it was all brown,' she said.

Leo stopped walking and sat. There wasn't a seat, but it didn't seem to bother him. 'You need to stop sometimes, to see things properly,' he said.

Ellis sat next to him, because when something didn't bother other people, it didn't bother her either.

'I never knew there was so much space left,' she said.

'Five hundred and fifty-four square miles.'

Ellis turned to look at him.

'I'm an only child. I read a lot.' He spoke without returning her gaze. 'Are you?'

'Am I what?' Ellis knew what he meant, but she needed time.

'An only child?'

She hesitated. Some questions were more difficult than others. 'I'm a twin,' she said eventually.

'Cool,' he said. 'Identical?'

'I guess so. I'm flat-footed though, and I wear my hair different. Sometimes, my voice is louder.'

'I can't imagine anything more brilliant than being a twin.'

'Actually, it's the least brilliant thing there is.' Ellis drew her knees to her chest. 'In fact, there's just one thing less brilliant than being a twin, and that's being a twin when you're the only one left.'

It was a lot easier to let the words go when you were on the moors. There was so much more space for them all to fall into.

They sat on the same bank of grass. So close, their arms almost touched, but he still didn't look at her. 'That's really shit,' he said.

It was the best description Ellis had heard so far. 'Yes,' she said. 'It is really shit.'

'What was her name, your sister?'

'Eleanor. Ellie,' she said. 'Ellis and Ellie. One letter different.'

'One letter, but a whole person.'

'People forget that,' said Ellis. 'They only look for the bits they miss seeing.'

'Come on.' Leo brushed at the heather on his coat sleeves. 'Let's walk on, and then we can stop and talk some more.'

Before she stood, Ellis glanced at Leo's legs, where the

78

material of his trousers had ridden up. The bruises were purple, like the heather. He saw her looking and turned away.

The next morning, he was waiting for her on the wooden bench. She spotted him from the kitchen window, as she was rinsing her cup and trying to avoid looking at the photograph.

'I'm off out again,' Ellis shouted.

Her mother had discovered a vacuum cleaner in a small cupboard under the stairs, and she was admiring all its attachments. 'There's no need to shout, Ellis. Why does everything have to be at full volume?'

Ellis closed the front door as quietly as she could.

'Hey.' She walked over to the bench and looked over Leo's shoulder.

'All these people.' He ran his hand over the graffiti on the bench, tracing the carved names with his fingertips. 'Why do they do it?'

'To stay remembered?' Ellis said.

It was a question, but Leo didn't answer.

'It's why we write things down, isn't it?' she said. 'So we don't forget them? I guess it's the same with people.'

'Is your sister's name here?'

'No,' Ellis said.

Leo took a key from his pocket. He found a space near to where the boards of the seat curved into a leg, and she watched him scratch an E into the wood.

79

'Come on,' she said. 'Let's go back to the moors. But don't walk too fast, I'm tired.'

'Tired?'

Ellis told him about the noise. Not the noise from the bar at The Cow and The Canary, but the other noise. The noise she couldn't quite put her finger on.

'It's like a tapping. It sounds like someone's trying to get into the house,' she said.

'Or out.'

'Out?' They were on the overgrown path now, and Ellis stopped next to the child's glove. Time had begun to steal it away, and blades of grass curled around its fingers.

'Doors and windows,' said Leo. 'They keep people in, as well as keeping people out.'

She waited for him to elaborate, but he just carried on walking.

Now, they always met by the bench. And Ellis would watch, each day, as Leo carved another letter into the wood.

He twisted the tip of the key into the dot of an i. 'It'll be time to go home soon,' he said.

Each morning they'd returned to the moors, and every so often, Ellis made sure she stopped and creased her eyes, to be certain of seeing all of colours. They always walked in silence, and only spoke when they found somewhere to sit. Ellis didn't ask about Leo's bruises, and Leo didn't ask about Ellis's sister, but Ellis talked about her anyway, because all the space seemed to pull the words out of her.

The words her parents were never still enough to hear. Ellis talked about the noise, and how she could still hear it each night, about what it might be.

'A bird?' she said. 'Or a mouse? Perhaps something's trapped in the chimney breast?'

'I've told you what it is,' Leo said.

It was the last night before Ellis found out the truth. She did what everyone does in really bad horror films, she did what she promised herself she'd never do. She left the coffin bed, and tiptoed out on to the landing. When she peered over the bannister, she realised exactly where the noise had been coming from.

It was her mother.

'She was walking around the house,' Ellis told Leo on the last morning, as they watched their separate lives returned to the back of each car. 'The shuffling and creaking. It was her slippers on the floorboards. Up and down. Backwards and forwards. Room to room. She never stops.'

Leo pushed his key into the wooden seat.

'She must do it at home as well,' Ellis said. 'Only I can't hear because of the carpet.'

'I was right all along, then.' Leo brushed at the wood. 'It's someone trying to get out.'

She didn't answer, and after a moment she heard Leo sigh.

'She's trying to get away from it, Ellis. The grief. She

thinks if she keeps moving, she'll manage to leave it behind. All that misery. Everyone does it.' He returned the key to his pocket. 'There,' he said. 'Finished.'

Ellis looked across.

'The "s" was really hard,' he said. 'It's difficult to draw a curve in the wood.'

She was going to say something, but the words disappeared, and all she managed to do was frown and say 'Why?'

'Because,' he said. 'Because what would you do if you're worried you'll forget something?'

Ellis stared at the letters and looked back at Leo. 'You'd write it down,' she said.

It wasn't a question, but Leo answered anyway.

'Exactly, Ellis,' he said. 'Exactly.'

Half an hour later, Ellis watched from the back of the car. She hadn't studied Leo's father until now. He was wiry and loud, and he pointed and shouted instructions at Leo and Leo's mother. He looked like a man who had made a lot of anger for himself, but hadn't yet decided where to put it.

'You spent a lot of time with your friend this week,' her mother said from the front seat.

'I did.'

'Where is he from?' Her mother pulled some knitting out of a bag for the journey, because if her legs weren't allowed to move, at least her hands could try to make up for it.

'I don't know,' said Ellis.

'What does his father do for a living?'

'I'm not sure.' She watched Leo climb into the car. 'He didn't say.'

'Whatever did you talk about then?' said her mother.

Ellis was going to wave, but Leo didn't look back. His father's car turned slowly on the gravel, and Ellis watched as it crossed the bridge by the pub and was swallowed up by a line of cars heading towards the main road and back into a pool of ordinary lives.

'We talked about all the other things,' she said.

Their own car climbed out of the village, her father pressing hard on the accelerator to make up for the weight of all their things in the boot.

'The sun's really caught you, Ellis,' her father said.

'The wind's done your hair no favours, though,' her mother said. 'Are you sure you don't want to put it in a ponytail? I've probably got an elastic band in my bag somewhere.'

Ellis said no, no her hair was fine just as it was, and she listened to the knit-and-purl click of her mother's needles, and leaned her face against the glass.

'I don't get the attraction of it.' Her father nodded at the heather through the car windscreen. 'Far too bleak for my taste.'

Ellis watched the moors roll by, and thought how much she would miss it. The space. The being still. She felt as though she had left all of her thinking up here, but Leo had said that was fine, because she could always go back another time and collect it again.

'So bland,' said her mother. 'So brown.'

'Stop the car!' Ellis shouted from the back seat. 'Stop the car right now!'

Her father pulled straight into a space at the side of the road, and both her parents stared at her through the gap between the front seats.

'Are you not feeling well?' said her mother.

'Turn off the engine!' Ellis was still shouting, and for once her mother didn't criticise the volume. 'We need complete silence. We need to be still so we can see properly.'

Her father cut the ignition. The only movement was a gentle rocking of their car, as other vehicles whipped past them on their way to somewhere else.

All three stared through the windows.

'What are we supposed to be seeing?' Her mother peered up at the sky and down at the tarmac, although she seemed to take in very little between the two. 'I don't know what you want me to look at.'

'Wind down your windows,' said Ellis. 'Wind them right down, until there's no window left, and stare properly.'

They did.

'Now do you see all the different colours?' Ellis pointed. 'Do you see them all? Can't you tell that everything isn't just brown?'

Ellis's mother put down her knitting and began to crease her eyes.

They lingered for a while in that lay-by, under the grey of a battlefield sky. They watched the moths flutter amongst the heather, and listened to the whisper of a breeze through the grass, before her father turned the key of the engine once more, and they started on the long journey home.

THE HOWLING GIRL

LAURIE PENNY

I N THE END, IT was the edge of panic in Jamie's voice that decided her.

'Hey, it's good to talk to you. Really good. I've missed you, G.' The number was unlisted, so for Grace the greeting was an ungloved fist, right up under the ribs, no warning. How many years had it been since he'd said her name like that? Her initial in his lovely long-ago-and-far-away mouth like that?

He had a problem, he said, something he was working through, and it would be wonderful if she could help out – but it would be better face-to-face. Would she come up?

Somewhere inside her a barricade started to dismantle. A white flag waved after months and years of siege. We're starving in here. Let us come to terms.

Jamie laid it on thick. Unusually thick. The new place was so lovely, even in winter, so healing – the perfect place to write, or – was she still writing? Anyway, it was a nice place for a break, and they could talk in private. Could she make it?

Grace made a noise that gave what she hoped was a convincing impression of looking at her calendar and thinking it over. Jamie would absolutely pay the train fare, least he could do at short notice, he'd book it now, no problem at all – but could she come soon? Next weekend?

She could.

The cottage was a two-mile ride from the deserted station. She asked the taxi driver polite questions about his life, and didn't really listen as he told her how old his kids were, how many years he'd been in the country, and what the weather would be like this time of year wherever it was that he was from. He asked her the same sort of questions about London, and she stared out at the rushing darkness, and contemplated lying about having a husband, having a child, or at least plans for one or the other. In the end she simply said that she was working too hard to think about those things. Concentrating on her career right now. Maybe some day.

'London,' said the driver, making a sympathetic clucking sound. 'You young women can have a very bad time there.'

She didn't know what to say, so she said nothing, and eventually he turned on the radio.

She was going to see Jamie again, and he needed her. She couldn't resist that. Not even after ten years, and he probably knew that well enough, she acknowledged to herself, as the taxi took knuckle-whitening turns through the blood-black tunnels of grasping trees that all country roads turn into at night.

The thing was, he really had sounded glad to hear her voice.

Later on, she would remember that, and wonder.

Jamie was waiting on the threshold. His hair doing that thing. His face doing that thing. Casual trousers low on his hips, and a cup of tea in one hand as he took her coat and gave her 'the tour'.

'The tour' took quite a while. The house was old, old enough for a lot of people to have lived and died in it, refurbished with that soft, warm lighting everywhere, calm and quiet, like an upscale restaurant before the punters come in.

'The tour' was an excuse for Jamie to show off, which he did graciously, and also for them to talk, for the first time in a long time, about a lot of things that didn't matter, like how it made sense that you weren't allowed to just knock out a wall of a four-century-old cottage, no matter how much you wanted a kitchen island, or how much it cost to have original hardwood floors stripped, re-sanded, and painted – a lot, but you should have seen the carpets. The previous owners had been vandals, truly, people who put paisley on floors ought to be shot, and he was only ninety-nine per cent joking, he'd do it himself, he was ethical like that.

The cottage was warm – almost stuffy, all the windows were shut and locked, and Grace supposed it made sense.

The wind stampeded over the moors outside, bitter, and the windows were all single-glazed, old-style, just thin glass between you and the terrible dark. Still, she remembered how much Jamie used to long for fresh air, when they'd lived together.

In the terrible one-room studio in Turnpike Lane – you couldn't call it a bedsit these days, but that's what it was, no turning-around room between the end of the bed and the oven – he used to creep up onto the windowsill, perch among the ashtrays, and sip down the dirty traffic-stinking air from the crack in the skylight. Sometimes he'd do it in the middle of the night, after they had fucked, before they fucked again, the streetlight making his skin luminous and alien, his flat white bum and the signature-line of his spine, as he turned to look at her like a drowning kid looks at a life raft.

She really had loved him.

It was important, Jamie was explaining now, to have simplicity, comfort, minimalism, if you were doing real creative work. Grace was waiting, just waiting, for him to use that Danish word that had been in all the lifestyle magazines, but of course he would never be that obvious. He simply led her into the living room, with its low, squashy sofa covered with sheepskins, its low-burning fire, the delicious rich scent of pine and cinnamon from some hidden, noiseless diffuser.

'It's gorgeous,' she said, meaning it. 'It feels so—'

'—so safe, doesn't it?' Jamie liked to finish people's sentences.

It was only after you really knew him that you discovered

how special this ability really was: Jamie could finish your sentences without listening to a word you'd been saying. He had a natural ear for the rhythms of speech – it was part of what made him so good at what he did – he could predict people's words. Most people are tragically predictable, she remembered him saying, more than once, wafting a spliff between slim fingers, conducting the conversation.

Jamie had what songwriters called a lean and hungry look – a boy who wanted so much from life. You wanted him, and more than that, you wanted to be the thing he wanted, even as he stared over your shoulder at the curve of his own future strutting by.

In the downstairs toilet, which Jamie referred to bizarrely as the half-bath – as if she were intending to buy the house – Grace checked herself in the mirror and decided she would do. People told her, approvingly, that she looked young for her age, and she worked out to videos, and she kept herself just a little bit hungry all the time, not being silly about it, not like she used to, but still, the regular empty noises inside were a growl of approval: tomorrow you will take up no more space than you do today.

And if sometimes she woke up in the middle of the night, groggy and half-animal with hunger, groping for carbs, that could be solved by stripping the kitchen of danger foods and keeping something around empty enough to stuff down until her stomach was soothed back to sleep, like one of those orphan animals on the manipulative reality shows, curled on a blanket that smelled almost like mother.

'You look good,' said James, when she came through to dinner, changed out of her travel clothes.

They talked about what they had both been 'up to', as if adulthood were a minor crime. She talked about her copy-writing jobs, and he talked about his third novel and the TV deal, in a way that allowed them both to pretend that they were discussing similar lives, that she didn't already know all of it. Mostly from her mother, for whom 'successful writer' far outweighed 'soul-sucking mindfucker'.

Mind you, there was a lot that her mother didn't know.

Jamie sliced the woody stems off fat, stiff spears of aspar-agus, blackened them in butter until they wilted; cracked two huge, translucent duck eggs over the cast-iron pan, and fried them so that the edges frilled into doilies. There were slabs of thick dark rye bread slathered with some sort of delicious savoury stuff – wild mushroom spread, he explained, bought that morning from the farmers' market. It was dank, musky, fantastic, like licking the armpit of Christ.

Grace ate the whole thing as neatly as possible. She could see Jamie watching her, deliberately saying nothing. He had always got on at her about her table manners. She ate like a pig, he used to say, not like a girl.

'I just thought it would be great to reconnect. Talk about how stuff's going. I know that – well, I know you weren't happy with how things ended between us, and that made me unhappy.'

Grace heard the word *sorry* thundering in the negative space of the conversation.

He asked her how she was, repeatedly, in all sorts of ways. He asked how work was – fine – how her sister was – fine – whether she was still in touch with so-and-so, and how they were.

'I'm really glad,' he said, and again, he seemed to mean it, like a man who has just been told that the lump is nothing to worry about.

She put her fork down.

'OK, what's this actually about?' she said, annoyed enough to forget that he had never liked that sort of question. 'Are you in some sort of anonymous thing?'

'Pardon?'

'My mum's ex-boyfriend was in some sort of junkies-anonymous cult. He had to call everyone he'd messed around and apologise. Then if they didn't forgive him, he yelled at them. Seemed a bit dodgy. I wondered if this was one of those things.'

'Ah. No. No, not really.'

'It's OK if it is.'

'You know, I actually know a lot of people who've been helped by that programme. But no. This isn't that. Why?'

'You seemed to be circling around some sort of apology. Maybe. I don't know.'

Jamie's eyes narrowed – they really did, that was the weird thing, he was the only person she'd ever met who actually narrowed his eyes when he was angry, like he'd read it in a book and practised.

'Apologise for what?'

'I'm sorry,' she said. 'Forget it. Never mind.'

She remembered that she was alone in a remote place with a man who liked to choke people during sex and hated having to ask because it killed the mood.

She blinded her second egg with the edge of her fork.

'It's good,' she said, letting the cold yolk clam over her tongue.

He laughed, low and sudden.

'I suppose I did want to apologise. In a way.'

She raised both eyebrows, her mouth full of egg.

'I don't know what for, specifically. For being young and dumb, I suppose.'

'We were both young,' she said, wiping her mouth. 'And we both could have behaved better.'

'Yes, yes, that's true,' he nodded. 'We both could. I suppose we both have things to apologise for.'

'Well, then,' she swallowed, 'I apologise.'

He went to the toilet – the half-bath. While he was out of the room she wrapped the buttered toast in paper napkins to throw away later, somewhere Jamie wouldn't notice.

The sheets in the spare room were cool and clean on Grace's arms and legs, rough impersonal comfort, like she imagined the best sort of hospital bed would be, where you're ill enough to need care that comes at the click of a button, but in no pain you can't bear.

She woke up hungry. If she was honest, it happened more nights than it didn't, always a couple of hours into a forget-table first dream.

A raw emptiness shook her awake with the branch of a dead tree battering on the thin window. A wordless wanting to cram herself with something thick, bread or cake or cock or love, all of it dangerous, nothing safe to hand.

The knocking continued, rapping the sleep from her, focusing the hunger. Maybe if she drank cold water, that might fill her, but it was never enough at night. It had to be sweet, or heavy, or both.

She sat up.

There were no trees on that side of the house. Something else was knocking.

Grace turned her head very carefully, and saw a dead girl outside the window.

Her hand was very thin and very white, cheap fabric stretched over sinew, and there was something about her face that seemed horribly familiar, even though it kept flickering in and out of focus. Dreaming, Grace was obviously still dreaming, and so there was no reason to be afraid. It didn't feel at all real, and when things didn't feel real, they felt safer.

The dead girl looked so cold out there.

There was something wrong about the way the light hit her: she looked overexposed, permanently caught in someone else's snapshot with the flash on too high and the strange glowing rabbit-eyes. Could she even see?

She opened her mouth, and that was wrong, too, it opened much too slowly, a paper flap, and it was all black inside, and a terrible noise came out, something like an obsolete machine screaming.

That was enough.

Grace dragged the thin curtain across the window and lay back down, deciding she wasn't hungry any more, because she was dreaming, and in a minute she'd be in another dream, the sort where you could eat as much as you wanted, chocolate cake and school-dinner food, chips and beans and bacon, all the dirty stodge you really wanted, and when you woke up you felt so guilty, so out of control, until you remembered it was OK, you'd dreamed it. Compared to that, dead girls in the garden weren't so scary.

Grace used to think about death far more. Not in a frightening way – at least, it wasn't frightening to Grace, although she learned not to talk about it too much.

But she would mention it, sometimes, often, to boys after they fucked her, because she found it excited them. The thought of her cold.

They would hold her close and stroke her face and look sad.

She didn't actually want to die. There were some days when she felt it might be a lot less hassle just to conveniently and without much of a fuss suddenly be dead, but the truth was that she just wanted to be allowed to hold life lightly. That would have taken too much explaining, though, and poetic, intellectual boys were always far more interested in dead girls, or the idea of them, an idea of girls who went cold quietly and cleanly, without shitting the bed or screaming, because they were hollow inside to begin with.

The next day they went for a hike, even though she didn't have the right shoes. She had brought big, worn-in biker boots, but you needed extra ankle support for hiking.

'What's the difference between walking and hiking?' she asked, halfway up a hill, her breath serrated, her cheeks grated raw by the wind.

'Hiking has more intent to it,' said Jamie. 'It's more mindful.' He stopped to let her catch up. 'Also steeper,' he conceded.

He had taken it up, he said, last year, to take his mind off the publicity.

Last year, Jamie had been shortlisted for three major literary prizes, and although he hadn't won any of them, it was generally acknowledged that sooner or later it would be his 'turn'. This time the gongs had gone to, respectively, a very young white woman who wrote a searing novel about sexual violence, a middle-aged black man who wrote a searing novel about the impact of the Dutch slave trade on eight generations of a fictional family that was nonetheless interpreted as autobiography by every critic, and a transgender Asian lesbian whose novel, a magical realist retelling of an Icelandic saga set in modern London where all the main characters were foxes and pigeons, was also universally described as 'searing'.

Jamie, the underdog, was noted for his grace in defeat in

every interview. There were lots of interviews. Critics suggested implicitly that his book might have swept the board of trophies if it weren't for the general mood of political correctness lingering around like a ripe fart in a gentlemen's club.

Photos of Jamie gallantly kissing the hand of the very young female author as she went to collect her award made the rounds, and if Grace recognised the look of confusion in her face, frozen in the moment of interruption on the way to her spotlight, she was probably being ungenerous.

But Jamie's book was stunning, all the same.

It was about a young man who retreats to one bare room in despair at the state of the world, and who gradually transforms into a wild animal. Various lovers arrive and attempt to save him, and all of them end up mauled or eaten, until at last an enigmatic Russian waitress works out how to tame the creature. There was bestiality and body-horror and a dash of pop philosophy. The whole thing was disgusting and delicious, a book made by fermenting rotten things until they tasted intentional.

Grace savoured every page, cried at the end, and hated herself for it. She recognised the room in the book, the room where the creature was trapped. It was awfully like the room they'd had in Turnpike Lane all those years ago, when they'd been hungrier and younger, and had nothing to do but hurt each other. The dusting of mould on the walls. The stink of roll-ups soaking into everything. The books on every surface. The bloodstains.

She could understand why it hadn't won the prizes – the other books had had more range, more human interest, and fewer gratuitous scenes of wolf-men having deep thoughts about Zizek while eating their own shit. But it was damn good, all the same. That was the annoying part. The problem wasn't just that Jamie acted like he was a special boy with a special talent.

The problem was that he was right.

He was the sort of boy you followed up mountains in the wrong shoes.

She picked at a blister later in front of the fire.

'Don't you get lonely?'

'Oh, I'm in London half the time – and usually when I'm here my assistant comes out. Or Julia. Honestly, I wish I could be here all the time.'

It was only the second time he'd mentioned his wife.

'Does Julia like it out here?'

'She loves it,' said Jamie, his back turned, fixing something in the kitchen. 'She was the one who encouraged me to get it. Did all the painting herself – she loves that sort of thing. Decorating. Fixing things up. She's thinking of retraining as an interior stylist. Are you hungry?'

Jamie made dinner.

He fed her a rich, brutal stew of devilled kidneys – so old-fashioned, deeply savoury, simmered in some sort of dark wine. There were crushed potatoes oozing with butter, and more wine to go with them, and winter vegetables simmered until they sighed and gave up their juices.

Then, some sort of decadent chocolate treachery made in tiny fancy individual pots. Normally she wouldn't dare, but he'd been to some trouble. She couldn't refuse, it would be rude, even though she was imagining every teaspoonful on her hips the next day.

'You need to try this,' said Jamie. 'I made it for you. Go on. You don't eat enough. I'm going to feed you up, girl.'

He dug a spoon into the smooth surface of the dessert and lifted it to her lips. It tasted of everything she'd ever wanted to get away with.

He tucked a finger of hair behind her ear, and again, Jamie was the only person she knew who could make such a cliched move feel thrilling. His fingertips brushed the down on her cheek so lightly, summoning something in between loss and wanting.

After that, things escalated rather quickly. All she had to do was let it happen. In fact, it was better if she let it happen.

He tugged his shirt over his head and showed the full miracle of what five years of clean living could do to a previously etiolated human body.

It was all she could do to remember to hold back, to be shy, to let him lift her hands to his chest, and then lower, to look down, to stay still, to let him lead.

'It's all right,' he said, 'everything's all right.' And it was, she supposed. It was perfectly all right.

From somewhere outside her body, Grace watched Jamie fuck her, and wondered how she'd been hung up on this for so long. Really, he'd never been all that good, had he? He did the things that girls were supposed to like in a perfunctory way. Then he got down to it, filling her up thoroughly and hurriedly, as if she were a non-disclosure form.

He came quickly, whimpering and falling forward onto her.

Grace got up to take a piss, because no amount of post-coital cuddling is worth a bladder infection once you've had one. She padded into the dark kitchen for water, not a snack, she wasn't going to eat, she was full, had been filled, she was going to ignore the leftovers on the side and the thick fresh bread, and just be in the moment, the stone tiles leaving cold kisses on her feet, the hiss of the tap and the dead girl standing right outside the kitchen window.

The glass dropped out of her hands. It didn't break. She saw it rolling away over the stone with a drowning sound.

When she looked up, the dead girl was still there, and of course, this time Grace recognised her, and of course. Of course.

The dead girl was mouthing something, saying something without sound.

Let me in.

Fuck, she looked so cold and hungry out there.

Grace looked down and noticed that her hand was already halfway to the lock on the window.

She screamed then, really screamed, and Jamie came running.

If she had had time to think, she might have expected

the dead girl to vanish, to have to explain what she'd seen, why she had screamed, over and over, sounding like a crazy person while Jamie did his concerned nodding thing – you've always been mental, can you stop it with the attention-seeking for just a few days, you're an embarrassment, this is why I can never tell my friends about you.

But when Jamie skidded to a halt, she was still there, glaring silently at the two of them.

'What the fuck!' said Grace. 'What the fuck, Jamie, what the fuck is that?' And then she was just saying fuck over and over, under her breath, like some sort of nightmare porno.

'Can you please stop overreacting?' he said, his face a twist of panic, not looking at the window, where the dead girl's face, that horrible, familiar face, was pressed in longing.

There was no breath to mist the glass.

'Fuck that, it's me,' she said.

Because that's who the dead girl was.

'When you called me, the first time,' she said. 'You thought I might be dead.'

'Yes,' he said simply.

'But I'm not dead,' she said.

'I think we've established that by now,' said Jamie, drawing her close, tender, shivering. She smacked his hands away.

'Unfinished business,' said Jamie, 'isn't that it?'

'Right. So you thought – what? If you were kind to me, if you fucked me – it – would go away?'

She was still staring at the dead girl, the twisted version of the kid she'd been ten years ago, and for the smallest fraction of a second she could have sworn they shared a look of understanding. *I know, right?*

'You do know your dick doesn't have magic powers, don't you?' she said.

Jamie shook his head. 'There's no need to get dramatic about this.'

'There's every fucking reason to get dramatic,' she said, half shouting.

'Calm down. It's all right. Come here.' Jamie put his arms around her, but she wriggled away, staring over his shoulder to where the dead girl, dead Grace girl, was raising a pair of oozing wrists in accusation.

There was so much she had made herself forget.

She had wanted more, once, hadn't she, until it got too much, and it was better to crush all the wanting away. To waste away. All that wasted time.

She shoved Jamie away, and went to sleep on the sofa.

In the morning, Grace went for a walk by herself.

She was positive the dead girl, the Grace-girl, wouldn't be there in the daytime, if only because in her mind there seemed to exist some sort of vague code of conduct for creatures who come from wherever it is this one did. Just in case, Grace didn't look to right or left of her as she headed down the track to the village. Fixed her eyes on a random point in the middle distance, a tree, a signpost, switching the focus whenever the object got too close, like her father had taught her to do whenever she would get carsick on long journeys. Grace couldn't remember if it had helped, but it had kept her quiet.

Grace went through the village, stopped at the single shop to pick up a few important things, and to post a letter that, given the circumstances, absolutely couldn't wait. She walked for an hour until she reached the outer limits of her own boredom. Grace had really never seen the point of just walking. Whatever it was that other people find inspiring about nature just didn't seem to do it for her. Grace smoked two cigarettes outside the closed-up pub, sucking down the dirty smoke and longing for the city.

Then she went back to the cottage to warm up.

Jamie was still sleeping it off. Grace opened the windows to let a breeze in, then went from room to room turning up every radiator. The place was beautiful, Jamie was right – cosy and tasteful without being too pretentious. It felt safe here. Bright and dry and safe.

She had bought fish fingers and chicken nuggets from the corner shop – the sort of meat so processed it forgets it's dead. Grace shoved the whole lot in the enormous oven, which still smelled vaguely of yesterday's feast.

She had also bought cheap ketchup, and milk that was not organic, and real bargain-bin tea, full of tannin dust, the ancient price sticker peeling off the packet. The proper stuff, she thought, mentally supplying the punchline: proper tea is theft.

She made herself a cup of strong tea with two sugars. She made herself go out to the front garden and sip it while it was still sweet and scalding. And she made a plan.

Her stomach yawned, and she decided to feed herself. She went through Jamie's cupboards and found some crackers and jam, ate them over the bin, not even bothering with a plate.

Then she went through every room in the house, lighting the scented candles, dimming the main lights, fluffing the throws and pillows just so. She put on music – the gentle pop of fifteen years ago that she had never had the cash to go out and dance to, the sort of music people with more comfortable lives listened to on rooftops in the cleaner parts of town, surrounded by hothouse plants, with well-cut clothes, and cold drinks in their hands. Kissing. Appreciating each other. Stupid, simple things to want.

She turned the music up. It woke Jamie, who came padding in on long, bare feet. He narrowed his eyes in that studied way, seemed to consider commenting on the music, and then groaned and threw himself across one of the sofas. A man hogging a life-raft.

'My head. Jesus. That was a lot, last night. Sorry for sleeping so long.'

'Seemed like you needed it.'

'Yeah.' Jamie winced. 'Yeah. Hadn't been getting a lot of sleep, what with—' he waved vaguely at the window.

She put a cup of black coffee in his hands, just brewed,

and took one for herself. She wanted to tell him it was fine, but it wasn't fine.

'It's been going on for weeks. Every night. Banging on the windows. Wanting to be let in. I can't write. Can't sleep. Can't think of anything else.'

'So what, you thought you'd call me up and see if fucking me and telling me I was pretty would make the – the whatever it is – make it go away?'

'I'm sorry,' he said. 'I'm really sorry.'

'For what? The sex, or the dead girl with my face, or – whatever you were trying to do, inviting me here?'

'I don't know. Everything. I'm sorry for everything. I'm a shitty, shitty person. I've always been a shitty person.'

'You're not a shitty person, Jamie, you just do some shitty things, and you ought to stop saying you're a shitty person and just try not to do so many shitty things.'

He looked at her. 'Well, that was eloquent. You should write a self-help book.'

'Fuck you.'

'I'm—'

'What are you going to tell Julia?'

His hands tightened around the coffee cup. 'She's got nothing to do with this.'

'Maybe she should get to decide that.'

Anger flashed across his face, and he almost stood up, then, and Grace took a step back, and then Jamie's body had a kernel panic at the sudden movement, and he seemed to deflate.

'Telling her any of this would only hurt her. I can't believe you'd want to do that. To another woman.'

Grace said nothing. Best to keep him wondering. He might not play along otherwise.

'Get up now, Jamie. I've thought of a way to fix your problem.'

'Now? It's getting dark.'

She told Jamie to go and stand out under the eaves by the back door.

Then she went from room to room, getting everything in order, took the food out of the oven, and set it on the table in clean white dishes.

Chips and beans and bacon. Mayonnaise and chicken nuggets. Chocolate cake, with the thick cheap icing that always tasted of birthdays in the school holidays. A fat jug of livid orange juice, pure livid liquid sugar. Candles, napkins.

'Is that for me?' Jamie called in through the door.

'No,' she said.

'What's going on? It's getting cold out here!'

She threw him an extra jacket and scarf.

Then she took the keys from the cupboard, and opened every window in the house.

'What the fuck are you doing?' Jamie hissed. 'She'll come. She always does. She'll get inside.'

'That's the idea. I thought – I don't know, if she wants to come in so badly, why not just let her in?'

'This is stupid and reckless and I don't endorse it.' Jamie shivered.

107

'Fine. We'll go back inside and shut all the windows and have a nice quiet evening. I'll call Julia up and tell her how nice it's been.'

'Bitch,' he said quietly. 'Selfish bitch.'

Grace smiled to herself, and waited. The night crawled up the skin of the sky like a bruise.

It didn't take long.

The smell of butter and sugar and salt and filthy yummy fried things was hugging the house by the time the dead girl arrived. They spotted her through the hall, outside the kitchen window, in the old paddock.

She stood at the open window, shivering in and out of focus, the light inside soft and buttery and inviting.

She seemed to look about her, as if there had been some mistake. Grace was reminded of those videos of the rescue animals, the foxes and badgers that kind people took care of and then set free in the woods, opening up the carry cage, and how they'd hesitate and take scared little steps, wondering if it was too good to be true, before pelting away to freedom.

The dead girl started crawling in through the window. Her cold hands smacking wetly on the countertop, her hair hanging in hanks over her pupil-less eyes. The thin white meat of her marbled with rotten black thread-veins.

She went straight to the table and started eating, and eating, and eating.

When the feast was finished, the dead girl, her face now flushed and warm, went to the giant fridge. She tore the door off its hinges, unhooked her jaw like a snake, and started slowly, methodically pushing things inside her mouth.

'Hey!' yelled Jamie, and the girl's head snapped around. Jamie clapped a hand over his mouth.

The Grace-girl seemed fuller now, her edges more defined, as she tiptoed into the front room and started to take off her wet clothes.

She peeled them off systematically, piece by piece, dropping them one by one along the corridor. She was quite naked by the time she got to the front room, thin as a bad-faith argument, her white belly extended only a little above the dark triangle of her pubis. Not fashion-thin, or sexy-thin – she just looked ill, the familiar old scars red-raw and shiny-new, slicing into layers of memory. Grace elbowed Jamie.

'Stop staring,' she hissed.

'Seriously?'

'It's rude.'

Padding up to the low, dry heat of the fireplace, the dead girl tilted her head in time to the music, considering the couch, a little nervous – a stray animal that hasn't been given permission, thought Grace, and then the dead girl smiled, really smiled, for the first time, and wrapped her arms around herself, and curled up on the sofa, tucking up inside the thick sheepskins.

The fire purred.

The dead girl closed her eyes and smiled.

'What the hell is happening?' whispered Jamie.

'I don't know, really,' said Grace. 'But whatever it is, I think it lives here now. I'm going back in.' Grace realised as she said it that that was what she was about to do. 'It's cold out here.'

'Are you mad? You can't go in there.'

'I think I can. There's plenty of room on that sofa.'

'I'm not going in.'

'No, I think that'd probably be best. She might still be hungry.' Grace patted his arm. 'Call your wife. She'll come to get you from the station.'

Jamie swore at her.

Grace grinned, and went inside to get warm.

FIVE SITES, FIVE STAGES

LISA McINERNEY

Market stall

'ARE YOU SURE NOW?' Cass's brother asked. 'Is that the lot, like? Is that the lot?'

'Yes, that's the lot,' Heidi said down the phone. 'To my knowledge.' She did not want it assumed that she had control over Cass, or that she might know exactly what Cass was doing and when, given a specific time or scenario, given a mood or a string of evocative words. The street was throbbing, but she looked at her fingernails, the middle one now bald of the lemonade-coloured gel they'd chosen together – Heidi had been picking at it; they were, the pair of them, fiddlers and fidgeters – she brought her fist closer to her face as if needing to examine some new defect. 'The second you know, let me know how she's doing,' she said to Cass's brother, but he'd hung up. She wasn't sure whether he had heard her begin to speak.

Around her there was much going on. There was a market at one end of the street, stalls selling crêpes or flat caps or posh cheese, people jammed up together, parting with their money in one way or another. There was a busker not far from her, forcing a folk version of a nightclub song. There were teenagers chirruping. It was an average day, and Heidi was chastised by it. Nothing catastrophic happened on days like this. Catastrophe would have the day bend for it, catastrophe would be insistently perceptible. The manner of catastrophe was this: it would not be trivialised by the paths walked by others or the air breathed by the oblivious. Those oblivious people would have looked to her like fiends or mutants, or at least the lines of their bodies would have shivered and warped. All objects would have seemed darker, even given that the sky was dark for July, heavy and close. Her knees would have buckled, she would have involuntarily howled.

As it was, she walked down to the market.

'What do we have here?' she murmured. She picked up a clunky pendant on a leather cord and was set upon by the stall-keeper.

'It's lovely, isn't it?' the stall-keeper said. 'That one.'

'Aren't they all?' she replied – dulled derision and down-cast eyes.

She was not searching for a get-well gift here. Here, there was just tat and lavish tuck, neither of which Cass appreciated, having a neat mind and a modest appetite. But she appreciated derision, especially of the subtle kind – their own language of little ironies and aversions. 'How tacky,' Heidi would say of people holding hands. 'I'm in *love* with love.' 'It's morbid,' Heidi would say of a bright print or a carousel. 'We're clawing away from the grave as if we think that's achievable.' 'Excruciating,' Heidi would say of sushi and pomegranate and salted caramel. 'Well isn't that fucking droll,' Heidi would say of students collecting signatures for petitions. 'I really hope you die before me,' Heidi would say to Cass. 'I honestly don't think you could cope with the separation if it was the other way around.'

Cass would appreciate Heidi bringing her a scornful report as much as a piece of jewellery or a knitted shrug or a second-hand book. She began to prepare her report. She moved slowly through the throng and paid close attention to expressions and exclamations. To her right was a stall selling home-made fudge.

Sugar's what we really crave, Heidi thought. *Sugar to keep us sweet.* There was something funny in this that she could develop. An axiom along the lines of, but at the same time taking the piss out of, Marx's opiate-for-the-masses. She thought she might like some fudge, and, more importantly, she thought Cass might get a kick out of her bringing her some, if she presented it in the correct way: a bag of pistachio-and-peanut-butter fudge and a new mocking proverb. 'OK,' Heidi said to this stall-keeper. 'I'll bite.'

He raised his eyebrows. He was young and wispily bearded. He pushed his hair back over his head. He was doing his damnedest to look handsome.

113

'This is atrociously bad for you, isn't it?' Heidi asked.

'It's all natural,' he said. 'Butter, sugar, and milk.'

'Yeah, but naturally bad for you. Like it wouldn't be good for, say, convalescents.'

'Everything in moderation,' he said, and coughed out shoddy laughter. 'But I dunno. Probably not.'

'Good,' she said. 'My girl's in hospital. And she'll get such a kick out of this because it'll drive her brother up the wall.'

The stall-keeper filled a bag as she pointed around the display. 'Sorry to hear your lady's sick,' he said.

'Oh, she'll be mostly hanging out in the waiting room,' Heidi said. 'Reading gushy magazines and listening to her brother *admonishing*. They won't keep her in.'

Lane off Bridge Street

She threw the fudge against the side of the Spar on Bridge Street. 'Fuck your fudge!' she screamed. 'Fuck it! Though' – in sudden, hissing contemplation – 'it might have fucking choked you, it was more like toffee . . . a fool and her money . . . Why the fuck is this happening now?' Less hissing. Sickly mewling: 'Like you didn't fucking time this, Cass.'

A young fella in a branded polo shirt came out of the shop and stared at her. She was thunderous again. 'What?' she roared at him. 'What the fuck do you want?'

'Calm down,' he said.

'Or what?'

He hovered, shook his head.

'Go and fuck off for yourself,' she told him. 'Clean up on aisle fucking two.'

The young fella clucked and went back inside.

'What my girl Cass badly wants,' she raved after him, first at his back, then at the stickered glass of the door that slid closed behind him, 'is a kick up the hole. Such a profound one. Like one where she could taste my fucking toecaps. Like one where I knock out her teeth from the inside. Fudge! Fudge, what would she say to that anyway? *You're a sap, Heidi. D'you love me that much, Heidi? How wretched you are, Heidi.* Or, *I'm not allowed fudge, Heidi. Are you trying to give me a heart attack? This is why my brother hates you, Heidi.*' She kicked out at the air, and the automatic doors came open.

Inside the shop she saw two dears, two skinny dears in Capri pants and Hush Puppies sandals, two skinny, non-smoking, cappuccino mid-morning, book-club dears in Capri pants and Hush Puppies sandals, staring at her as if they had never been her, or never experienced youth like hers, which was to her a light-headed inconsistency, a shape that stretched in all directions.

'Report me!' she cried. 'Go on, get your mobiles, call the police, tell them there's an angry girl, tell them she's offensive.'

She made for the lane at the side of the shop. It connected Bridge Street with the wide square around which were the pubs and clubs and restaurants. The square was often the subject of letters to the editor by the kinds of people who had never seen it after ten o'clock at night – the rigid and scared and judgemental. Heidi thought she needed a drink. She was beginning to feel dizzy and nauseous. What she had thought, this morning, to have been a lack of the hangover due to her seemed now to have been nothing but residual drunkenness, and so she was feeling it – the late, late night with Cass, the tasting of the top shelf, the pills and powders, and the mad conversation. Wherever it was, in the dark, that Cass pushed against her and held her – Heidi's face pressed to the wall, her temple to the brick – and didn't even reach under her clothes. Just held her there, under her weight. In her long thin arms.

'Bottle Rocket,' Cass said. 'Just stop. For a second. Just . . .'

The bitch. The weak and drunk and fearful fool.

Heidi was a third of the way down the lane. Behind her came a woman's voice.

'Can I help?'

It was one of the skinny dears. She held a set of car keys in one hand and with the other balanced a paper bag against her chest. She returned Heidi's stare. She didn't repeat her question, though Heidi waited for it.

'Is that what you think this is?' Heidi said. 'A cry for help? Like I'm not really angry? I'm just driven mad by the heat? I just need a cup of tea and a hug?'

The woman was an inch or so taller than Heidi, but so slight, so open and normal, that Heidi's coming for her caught her off-guard. She stood dumb as Heidi stopped toe-to-toe with her; when she stepped back it was awkwardly; she seemed at that moment a halfwit, and that was reason again for Heidi, whose spittle hit the woman's cheek. 'You don't understand,' Heidi said. 'I could stand here till Christmas trying to make you, but you'd never understand.'

River wall

The first time she met Cass's brother was in Cass's living room, from which Cass had hurriedly excised the parapher-nalia of their new and heady collision: philosophical texts with cigarette-paper bookmarks, wine bottles, paint pots. 'So, how long has this been going on?' Cass's brother had asked, and Heidi had replied, 'For ever, it feels like.'

The first time she had a run-in with Cass's brother was twenty minutes later, in Cass's kitchen. Heidi had been filling a glass from the tap when he'd come up behind her. He was light on his feet, like Cass, though he must have been three stone heavier, strong and broad and severe. 'Where did you come from anyway?' he had said. It wasn't a friendly question. 'She doesn't look good,' he had said. 'She doesn't look like she's sleeping. She's being short with me. She's dodging my questions.'

'I don't know what kind of relationship you two have,' Heidi had said, sipping. She was lying. She did know. She and Cass knew each other wholly, even at this point.

They had stared at each other for a while, Heidi and Cass's brother.

'I just want you to go away,' Cass's brother had said, steadily.

'That's unimaginable,' Heidi had said, also steadily.

Now Heidi, drained after her encounter with the skinny dear, dismayed that she had so furiously pelted away Cass's fudge, crouched against the stone-clad wall of an office that backed onto the river. She took out her phone. She pulled her sleeve down over her wrist and rubbed at its screen. She went on to open app after app, reading no new headlines, or social updates, chancing no new moves in her games. She thought she should stay put a while, in case the police were called. She wouldn't have bothered, if she had been the one wronged. But experience told her that there was something in her general air that made heavy implications, and in this way – in the set of her jaw or the roll of her eyes, in the evident chemical burstings in her brain – she was assumed to be a berserker. It might have been supposed that she'd do more damage further up the road. That she was in the midst of some episode.

If they just leave me the hell alone, she thought, *I can self-correct.*

She had taken her phone out because she needed to do something with her hands, and also because she thought she might call Cass's brother, and tell him that she would make her way over, permission or no permission.

If you let me see Cass, she thought, *I will tell you anything you want to know.*

Cass's brother. She could see the shape of the pain in

him. She didn't know what that kind of pain felt like, but the fear of it was such that she could imagine it. She felt great empathy for him, though she hated him too; she hated how he interfered, and she hated that he had made progress in demonstrating to Cass that she was better off without Heidi, and Heidi without her. Cass's brother fabricated empathy and wielded it well. He didn't understand Heidi, and she felt sympathy too, sorry that his world was so small and that he needed to confine Cass, that he couldn't just trust Cass and let her be. But mostly her empathy came from understanding his love for Cass. She felt connected to Cass's brother in a different way. An unrequited, sad compassion. The way one might feel for the recipients of overseas charity, a kinship based on knowledge of different kinds of suffering.

If you don't stop me seeing her, she thought, *I will try to help you understand her.*

She opened her Recent Calls list and looked at Cass's brother's phone number.

If I could make you see that Cass and I are one soul, ripped, she thought. *If I could show you that it's not only futile to try to keep us apart, but a great cosmic error that would bring you nothing but the shittiest of karmic payback. If I could find a way for you to understand, will you bless us? Will you let her shrug off your petty concerns about biology and morality and how life should be lived? Will you finally give her permission to be fucking well?*

On the river wall opposite, someone had painted the words

119

Global Warming Is Your Fault. The water was speckled with insects. It was brown. Not the brown of its mud bed reflected, but the brown of rust and industry and discarded things.

Heidi stood. She flung her arm back, so as to throw her phone at the far river wall.

She held her arm like that until the potential went. She bowed her neck. She put her phone back in her pocket and rubbed her forehead.

She would fix things as best she could. She would put their living space in order, she would give routine a chance, she would extol its virtues to Cass, she would get her out of bed in the mornings, she would placate the brother, she would keep a job, she would take painkillers only on prescription, she would make green juices, she would be diligent about recycling, she would write to the county council, she would campaign and lobby, she would be unflappable and intimidating, she would stop global warming.

Junction

There were red lights at the crossing, and she considered walking on anyway, into the traffic, taking her chances when her chances weren't good.

At this point nothing looked real.

There were various degrees of unreality as witnessed by Heidi and Cass, there were positive renditions and negative renditions. There were times when the streets were lit by hidden sources and everything took on a golden, under-skin glow. And there were times when it felt like their skins were so thin they were see-through, and their seams were likely to split and their insides were in danger of spilling onto the paths. There were times when Heidi thought of Cass as her evil twin, that she had been split from her in early childhood, and that, knowing this and feeling the distance keenly, the separation had damaged her. There were times when she'd wept for gratitude that they'd found each other. People looked on, in fast-food queues and ghost estates and patchy country raves, as she wept and clung to Cass. She didn't care. The corners of these spaces warped and peeled inwards. Space was a construct. Their bodies were unreliable. Nothing was real.

She had run away once. This was before Cass. She was a teenager then, and prone to such carry-on. The running away was not successful, and its duration measured hours rather than days. Just before she had run away she had thought of nothing but ferries, forging signatures, and honing wiles, and then she got only as far as the bus station in the very early morning. It was startlingly cold and hunkered on the only bench was a cockeyed man, who grinned at her. She had circled the station, gone to a friend's house, sat for hours in McDonald's, and returned home. But the planning of that unsuccessful escape had been sufficiently liberating. The mere act of considering flight had lasted her months. There was hope in it. To come to a point of despair but see beyond that another horizon . . . to run away from, but towards something . . . She understood it now. 'Cass,' she had said some months back. 'I was stupid, before you. But I was also brave.'

'Cass,' she had said. 'The problem with you is that with you I don't need to be brave.'

Running away was no longer a possibility because running away meant there was hope of better things, and what use was hope? If Cass was taken from her now – and if it didn't happen in the hospital it would happen through her vicious, hateful, fucker brother – what would she do? Cass had made it so that Heidi had forgotten how to be brave.

So she could run instead into traffic.

She did not believe in an afterlife as a rule, but rather, life in forms as yet incomprehensible to her. Life in terms of matter neither being created nor destroyed. Ongoing existence on a molecular level. Ongoing existence in vapours or spirit. Non-corporeal practical-nothingness, where maybe she and Cass would be each other, if they couldn't be with each other. And so on that basis—

—if Cass were to go—

—Heidi would have to go.

This thought, on this normal day, this thought was the one that buckled her.

If truth is a place, it is barely habitable

'Cass,' she had said. 'Listen to this.'

'Love is patient, love is kind,' she had read. 'It does not envy, it does not boast.'

'Imagine that,' she had said. 'What kind of love is that?'

'How sanitised,' she had said. 'And sexless. How pure and lifeless.'

Love, as experienced by Heidi and Cass, as discovered or excavated or eventually understood, was brutish and unpredictable, was as much from the viscera as the soul, was a physical pushing and pulling, was a state that caused insomnia and encouraged tantrums, was integral but occasionally unbearable, was defined by strife because mind and body craved and rejected it in cycles, was all of these fucking things, was raised voices, was sore knuckles, was pungent, was withdrawal, was music, was, at the sharpest point of it, hate.

Heidi sat on the low wall of the car park just outside the town centre and took out her phone again. Her fingers slipped on the plastic case. There was a feeling of mass in her throat. The roof of her mouth was parched and hot. She swallowed, and swallowed again.

There were things that perhaps now couldn't be fixed, but she needed to admit to having broken them. This pulled at her in the familiar way. The way Cass always did.

She phoned Cass's brother.

'There's more,' she said.

'Tell me,' he said.

'We bought a couple of grams of cocaine,' she said. 'I didn't have much, so if you didn't find it today, then she had the guts of that. She was taking Valium to sleep sometimes. She had a stock of it at her place, in the drawer of the bedside table. She'd only just gotten some, two days ago. So I don't know if that's still there, but if it's not it means she took that too.'

'I'll have to go and look,' Cass's brother said. 'I could have looked hours ago.'

'I know,' Heidi said. 'I'm sorry—'

'You're a coward,' Cass's brother said. 'I'd tell you to pray that she wakes up, for your sake, but you won't understand why, will you? Because you're not all there, Heidi.'

Heidi said, 'I know that,' or she said, 'Isn't that, after all, the problem?' She made some affirmation of understanding and acquiescence, some verbal agreement that she offered to the brother, some parity of the truth. Thus informed, Cass's brother navigated their monstrous love and went looking for what kernel of sickness he could crush, so he could bring Cass back to her, or lead Cass away from her. Heidi waited. In that moment the sky flashed, and she thought of new futures, and even the best of them frightened her.

KIT

JUNO DAWSON

I DESERVE NO LESS, but before you judge me harshly, I need you to know I'm not that girl. I'm really not. I'm not the cartoon-silhouette girl on the chick-lit novel with the kitten heels and shopping bags. I don't girlishly trip and stumble into whimsical new love affairs every time I leave the flat. I don't wait by the phone. I don't imagine what I would sound like with a different last name.

But he was different.

With him I became someone else. And so fast I shocked even myself.

The first meeting – mere weeks ago, although it feels like years – has taken on sweeping cinematography. They were refurbishing Pret A Manger, and I don't care for the battery-acid aftertaste of Café Nero, so I went, with a certain smugness, into our local independent, Roaster. It's all exposed copper pipes, Edison bulbs, and upturned tea chests as tables. I was raging at how a coffee shop could have possibly sold out of almond croissants before nine in the morning when first I laid eyes on him.

He emerged from behind the coffee machine, a vortex of steam hissing and swirling around him. Under his apron – thumpingly masculine with its coarse fabric and rusty fasteners – he wore a Breton shirt, rolled almost to the shoulder. Both forearms were a jotter pad of tiny tattoo doodles. Across his knuckles, from right to left, were the words CRUEL ABYSS. A tidal wave of raven-black hair, with flecks and stripes of silver, tumbled over his forehead and over his right eye. His beard was long, but not unkempt.

But it was the eyes. Isn't it always? Framed by a flat, dissatisfied brow were the bluest blue eyes I'd ever seen. Not wishy-washy grey-blue. Blue, like the sky.

He slammed the metal milk jugs around as though he was mad at them. I suppose no one particularly delights in making coffee for strangers on a Monday morning.

'Can I help you?' the girl asked, and I suspect she was repeating herself.

'Oh. Yes.' She rolled her eyes. She must have caught me staring at her colleague. 'A skinny latte and a porridge please.'

'Plain, cinnamon, or jam?'

'Cinnamon.'

He never once looked my way.

As soon as I got to the office, I exploded all over Nell. 'Oh my God! Have you seen that guy who works at Roaster?'

She smiled and put down her granola pot. 'Oh you must mean Dane.'

'Dane?'

'Great Dane. Irish? Blue eyes? Very . . . brooding?'

'That's him. Holy fuck, he's lovely.'

'Yeah, bit of a miserable fucker though.' She returned to her yoghurt, prodding it with a plastic spoon. I wished she wouldn't get plastic spoons when we have perfectly reusable, steel ones in the kitchen. 'Is granola good for you?'

'No,' I told her flatly, not done talking about Dane. 'When he looks like that, who cares?' I sat in my seat and switched my computer on. The familiar, stomach-deep dread at opening my inbox awoke along with the monitor. 'Although he is only a barista.' I stopped, knowing it sounded both snobbish and a little unhinged to be mentally planning our future. Why did it even matter what he did?

'Actually he's not,' Nelly said.

'Not what?'

'Not just a barista. He's a pretty well-known photographer too. His brother owns the Roaster chain – he just helps out I think.'

Well that changed everything. A photographer, an artist. That explained his bad mood. He'd rather be off, I thought, taking pictures of despondent Londoners, not being one. When I was at school I was briefly interested in photography, but my friend Bella told me I was being a hipster try-hard so I soon gave up the hobby. 'Oh, OK. Interesting. Do you know how old he is? Does he have a girlfriend? Is he straight?'

Nelly laughed. 'Oh Jesus. Stalker much? I dunno, babes. Erm, definitely straight. I think. No idea about the rest.'

There was only one thing for it. I counted down turgid minutes all through a hugely tedious brand meeting with a client before heading back to Roaster for lunch. Nelly reliably informed me they did delicious organic superfood salad boxes.

As I tried to decide between kale or quinoa, I saw an opportunity and took it. He was clearing the table just next to the chiller cabinet. 'Which do you think?' I asked. 'Kale or quinoa?'

At first, I thought he was either ignoring me or had simply zoned out. After a terrible silence where I feared he might just walk away, he realised I was waiting for a reply. 'Oh. Erm . . . personally I'd get the bacon-and-egg roll.' He offered a half-smile, a curl in the right edge of his lip.

I returned the smile. 'Kale it is.'

'Don't say you weren't warned. Rabbit food.'

I carried the little box of salad to the counter. It was almost two. I guessed the lunchtime rush was over. Sure enough, the waitress was sitting having her lunch, a Tupperware box filled with last night's chow mein, at the corner table. 'I'll have that and a skinny chai latte please,' I said.

He put it through the till before going to make my coffee. 'I'll bring it over,' he said.

'It's OK,' I replied, keen to start a conversation. 'You're Dane right?'

For the first time, he looked up at me, no doubt questioning whether we'd met before. I wondered, out of nowhere, if he had a lot of one-night stands. Did he think we'd fucked? That, at some point, he'd left my place, unshowered, in last night's shirt? Did he think he'd slipped his fingers inside me in the corner of a club or bar while we kissed wet, drunken kisses. Just the idea of his prowess turned me on. 'Yeah,' was all he said.

'I'm Catherine . . .' I said, but it didn't feel right, and neither did Cathy. 'Everyone calls me Kitty.' No, that wasn't quite cool enough for 'Dane' either. Kitty sounds like a little girl, or a woman who actively wants to be infantilised. 'Well, Kit.' There, that was better. Kit.

'Have we met?'

'No. I'm just a fan of your photography.' Wow, that sounded a lot less *Misery* in my head. It's true though. I'd spent half an hour in preparation that morning scrolling through the gallery on his website.

Dane bottles London's very essence in his work. Gang members trying to look inconspicuous in very conspicuous hoodies; rugby-playing apes in chinos on Clapham High Street; Romanian men changing into their Yoda fancy dress at the crack of dawn on the South Bank; Putney girls collapsing under the weight of too much Prosecco and too many teeth. Dane captures real London, not postcard London.

'Thanks,' he said, pouring the milk into my latte. I noted earlier he used blue milk instead of red. I didn't correct his error.

'I mean it. They really feel like London. There's no big fake smile. There's nothing polite about them.'

He looked at me again, and it was magnetic. I felt something tug on my innards. Tug them towards him. 'London isn't polite. If you catch its eye, it asks you what the fuck you're looking at.'

'Well . . . I love them. You shouldn't be working in a coffee shop.'

I wondered if I shouldn't have said that, but a wry smile crossed his lips. 'I'm just helping my brother out.' He handed me the latte. 'I don't know why; he's a real dick. Two seventy-five for a fucking thimble of coffee in what used to be a slum.'

'Yeah.' I don't mention that our high-end creative agency used to be a brothel. 'Gentrification, right?'

And with that, I sensed our time was up. A yummy mummy behind me waited impatiently for a floppy-haired little Hugo to decide what cake he wanted. 'Well thanks.' I smiled, not letting his eyes unlock out of mine. 'I'll see you around.'

He nodded.

That night, I touched myself in the bath and thought about him. I made lazy circles in the soapy water. A candle burned, the air was treacly with amber and oud.

I imagined myself going back to the coffee shop just as he's closing up, stacking the stools on the tables. He sees me, and, saying nothing, walks past me to lock the door. Taking hold of my arms, he pushes my back against the counter, already unbuckling his belt. 'You want me in you,' he growls in my ear, already kissing my neck, exposed like prey.

'Yes,' I whisper.

His hand ploughs my thighs, pushing the hem of my dress, and sliding my knickers aside. I'm already wet, in a way I get when I pleasure myself but rarely with a man. With his other hand he steers a fat pink cock – and it's in my head, so of course he has a porn cock – expertly into me. There's that familiar stab, the urge to reject it, push it out before it becomes all warmth and tingle and I melt into it.

The bathwater sploshed and bubbled as I thrummed myself faster, harder. Oh God. I wanted him in me. Closer, if possible.

There was nothing stopping me taking my work laptop to Roaster. Sometimes he wasn't there, and I'd get my cappuccino to go. If he was, I joined a strange, pathetic *Game of Thrones* regarding who got to sit at the hallowed tables next to the power sockets.

I want to stress once more that I wouldn't normally do this. In fact, if I weren't me, I'd judge my behaviour most severely.

I told a little white lie. 'The air conditioning is broken in the office,' I told him when he guessed my order without needing to ask. 'Skylights. It's like an oven in there.'

'Cool,' he replied.

Painting by numbers, I was soon able to form an impression of Dane Kelly:

1. He had a lot of friends who looked like him. They all had beards and sailor tattoos. They dressed in skinny jeans and band T-shirts. The ones who were thinning on top wore flat caps.

2. He really hated working in a coffee shop. He often muttered 'cunt' or 'wanker' under his breath as he breezed past. I wondered if he was confiding in me as he did so.

3. He frequently crept around the corner into the alleyway to smoke Marlboros and play on his phone.

I also learned he had a type. I'm sure to him, he believed he was one of those rare heterosexual men who have as many female friends as male ones, but I knew better. A steady stream of girls, all candy-pastel hair and nose-rings, all panda eyes and torn jeans, came to visit. They had no interest in being mere friends. All squealy and huggy, they threw their arms around his neck to haul him over the counter for a kiss.

I couldn't help but resent them. I wondered, again, how many of them he'd fucked, and each time his imagined mastery stirred me up. I believed he'd probably woken up tangled in most of their bedsheets, only to assure them in the vanilla morning light that the events of the night wouldn't soil their friendship. Each of the girls would smile gratefully, inwardly devastated, before heading off to their jobs at Beyond Retro or Rockit.

He seemed to favour one girl over the others, a painfully

thin model-type with toothpick arms, hollow cheeks, and full lips like some sort of Tim Burton fantasy. Peroxide lobotomy fringe. For her, he came out from behind the counter, joining her when he took his breaks. Interestingly, this girl seemed entirely disinterested in him. They shared a certain weariness, as if simply being alive were a terrible inconvenience.

I was doing some work one afternoon when I became aware of a shadow over my MacBook. I looked up and saw Dane standing over me. 'Hey,' he said. 'What are you doing tonight?'

I was stunned. Surely he wasn't asking me out?

'I have a gallery opening in Hackney tonight. You should come.'

'Oh, I . . . sure.' I actually had plans to go to the cinema, but I reckoned I could convince Eleanor to reschedule.

'Cool.' He handed me a flyer and returned to the counter.

I immediately fired off a message to Eleanor. *The insanely hot coffee-shop guy invited us to a gallery opening tonight. WE HAVE TO GO.*

What the fuck are you supposed to wear to a gallery launch of someone you desperately want to have sex with? I laboured over whether I should even change, or go in the office clothes I'd been wearing that afternoon. In the end, I went to an early spinning class and headed home to shower.

Having watched the type of girls who flocked to him, I decided that looking like a prefab wife in a short skirt and high heels wasn't going to impress him. I clawed through my wardrobe, hating everything. Why did I own so many floral dresses? Did I want to resemble walking pot pourri? I had a Guns N' Roses T-shirt from Topshop, but I don't look like I own a Guns N' Roses album (which I do not) so I wasn't sure if I could pull it off. In the end, I chose a simple white shirt with some spray-on skinny jeans. I picked out some heeled boots, but I couldn't shake the notion that I was more Kate Middleton than I was Kate Moss.

I met Eleanor outside Hackney Central. 'This better be worth it,' she said, puffing on a vape. I don't get vaping. If you're going to smoke, just bloody smoke. I don't know which is worse, cigarette smoke or smelling like a box of Milk Tray.

'I promise we'll see the film next week. Or at the weekend.'

'I'm going to hold you to that. And you're getting the popcorn.'

'Deal. I think the gallery's just down the street . . .'

'You look nice, by the way. A red lip suits you.'

'Thank you.' Everyone suits a red lip.

We didn't need a map to know the poky little pop-up gallery with people spilling onto the street was Dane's launch. Dozens of adults dressed as teenagers littered the pavement, cradling glasses of wine. 'This must be it,' I said. It was a balmy night, sticky and airless. I soon wished I'd worn a skirt.

We fought our way through the crowd, and I saw Dane

in the middle of it all, wholly different away from the coffee shop. He was laughing at something a friend was saying, head thrown back. White teeth, sharkishly sexy. Quite unconsciously, I pursed my lips, puckering up.

'Do you wanna go up and say hi?' Eleanor asked.

'No. No, we can't just go barging up. Let's wait for a good moment.'

We busied ourselves looking at his photography. In the small space we could only shuffle from image to image, following the herd. The pictures were quite wonderful, but by far too bleak and stark for my little flatshare. This new collection was mostly taken at the coast . . . possibly Camber Sands or Margate, I'm not sure. They seemed to be about the juxtaposition of natural and artificial. The black-and-white pictures captured disused power sub-stations, downed power lines, burned-out cars, washed-up shipwrecks.

One caught my eye in particular. A rare portrait of the girl with the peroxide fringe eating chip-shop-chips out of a paper cone. She was seated awkwardly, staring into her food. She looked upset, her brow furrowed, eyes down. I wondered if she was happy with him taking her picture. I imagined her asking him not to take it. Yet there she was.

I scanned the room and found her lurking in the corner like a fashion Gollum. I watched as Dane sidled up to her, slipping an arm around her shoulder. She wriggled out from under the embrace like that cat in Pepé Le Pew cartoons. I seethed, wondering if she knew how much I wished he'd wrap his arm around me. I would be so proud to be at his side, supporting this, his big moment.

Dane leaned in and whispered something in her ear, and she did manage a watered-down smile. At the same time, she – unconsciously or not – pushed him back, creating more personal space between them. My mind filled the gap with all sorts of scenarios. Did she have a boyfriend? A girlfriend? Is she an ex? Is she with his brother? I was almost sure there was a story, a history there. What I didn't question was that Dane was besotted with her.

Unless I could somehow get him to see me the way he saw her.

I waited for my moment. I saw him duck out for a cigarette, and I pounced. I followed him outside. He said farewell to some people who were leaving, and then I swooped in for the kill. 'Can I bum one of those?' I asked, hoping people still said 'bum'.

'Hey,' he said. 'You made it.'

'Yeah. Just thought we'd pop in on the way to the cinema.'

'Oh cool. Didn't realise you smoked.'

'Only with a glass of wine.' Not strictly true, but I'm not a total dork, I had smoked before. 'They're great, you know. Your pictures.'

'I don't know,' he said, eyes down. I could tell he wasn't just being humble.

'No they are. So different in tone from your older stuff.'

He shrugged. 'I wanted to try something new. Not sure it works. I wasn't inspired by London any more, so I left for a while. I just wanted to come back and take pictures of London.'

'Well sometimes,' I decided to go there, 'you have to go away to realise that you already had what you wanted the whole time.'

He laughed a little – a tiny snort really – but I was pleased I'd done it. 'Yeah. I hear that.'

I was brave again. 'That blonde girl?'

'God is it that obvious?'

I smiled. If I could win him over as a confidante, I was surely halfway there. 'Maybe a little.'

'I royally fucked that one up. I missed my chance by a mile. Timing is everything, everything is in the timing.'

Well isn't that a shame, I thought. 'Plenty more fish in the sea.'

'Maybe.' He finished his cigarette. 'My mam used to say there are as good fish in the sea as ever came out of it. Everyone thinks that's Shakespeare, but it's not. We don't know who first said it.'

'And it isn't even true. Overfishing. Look at poor cod.' With hindsight, do I know why I mentioned cod? No. Either way he laughed, more loudly this time. Worth it.

'I better get back in there. What with it being my party and all. I have to do a speech in a sec. You gonna stick around?'

'Sure.'

'Sorry, what's your name again?'

'Kit.'

'Oh yeah, that's it.' He vanished back inside, and I felt as if I were glowing all over.

Obviously I wasn't going to copy Miss Peroxide, but I did need to make Dane see me in that way. It started with the hair. I went to speak to my hairdresser, and said I wanted a radical change, something a bit rock chick, but nothing needy. He bleached just the ends of my hair before adding a bubblegum-pink tinge.

I went shopping for new clothes. Again, I couldn't wear the exact same stuff as her because I'm not a size eight, but I bought some simple black T-shirts and dresses from All Saints. I subtly changed my make-up, gradually adding more black kohl to the rim of each eye. It wasn't so much a makeover as a seasonal shift into autumn. No one in the office even noticed, really.

The day after my hair turned to candyfloss, I took my laptop down to the coffee shop to show it off. You can only imagine my disappointment when I found Dane wasn't working, nor did he drop by for free coffee as he sometimes did if he didn't have a shift.

And you can continue to imagine the disappointment when he wasn't there the next day either. As the days turned to weeks, gradual panic rose in my gut as the pink hair faded. In the end, I decided to be bold and ask Gaby, the nice lesbian with the nose-ring who works at Roaster. 'Hey, where's Dane these days? Is he on holiday?'

'No,' Gaby said with relish. 'Didn't you hear? He and his

brother had a huge fight about something. I don't know, he wouldn't say. Anyway, Dane quit and said he hopes Rich chokes on his own dick.'

'Oh wow.' Graphic.

Gaby shrugged, gesturing at the coffee shop. 'Dane didn't really need this anyway. He's earning like proper money for his photography now. He's doing something for *ID Magazine*.'

I nodded, but felt winded. I took my chai latte to a corner table and waited for my pulse to stop raving. How . . . how could he just leave and not say anything? I felt so . . . so cheated. How can someone just go? If TV has taught us anything, it's that feelings this strong deserve a rain-soaked farewell, some sort of crescendo.

He'd just gone. And I thought for a moment that maybe I'd imagined him.

There was only one thing left to do. I'm as good a social media detective as the next girl. No longer worrying it might look keen, I followed him on Instagram, and his 'Stories' told me he was still in East London at various bars and parties. He was looking after someone's French bulldog, so lots of walks in Victoria Park.

He only used his Twitter to promote art shows and stuff, and his Facebook was frustratingly locked-down. My finger hovered over the friend request button, but in the end, I decided against it. I wouldn't be able to bear the wait for his acceptance. What if he never accepted?

He did however follow me back on Instagram, which I

(giddily) took to be a good sign. I quickly raked back through a couple of years of pictures, deleting any in which I looked fat or basic. Taylor Swift gig in Hyde Park? Erased. Fourteen separate pictures of avocado on toast? Gone.

I quickly altered my username to Kit instead of Catherine. It's funny, isn't it, how our social media is really just a collage of the fictional version of us we want people to see. Online, I could be Kit so much more easily than in real life.

I don't know why I hadn't thought of it sooner. This way I could show Dane I was someone he could fall in love with. Better still, his Instagram was a menu of the things, the bands, the food he loves most. All I had to do was mirror him.

Dane loves 'doggos'. I started stopping poor dog owners on the street to grab a selfie with their pooches. Dane favours 'real' dogs over little floofy ones, so I – cautiously – threw my arms around every staffie and mongrel in East London. Sure enough, Dane double-tapped my 'doggos'.

I shouldn't have been surprised, but was a little disappointed to see Dane was also partial to a gym selfie. He was always self-deprecating: 'man, @trainersaffiq KILLED ME today #personaltrainer #goals #actuallydead', but I couldn't help but notice he looked suitably shirtless, sweaty, and poised in front of the changing-room mirrors.

I started echoing his routine. I made use of a gym membership I rarely troubled with. A couple of spinning classes in the week, and yoga on Sunday mornings. I didn't post as many selfies though. If girls post too many selfies, they're conceited.

I bet – in fact, I know – Miss Peroxide doesn't work out, so that was something we had in common that they did not. I found her in his follower list. She's called Sanne Vanderburg, and she's Dutch. Well, of course she fucking is. She barely posted, and when she did they were deliberately melancholic beach huts, dropped teddy bears, animal bones, and cool graffiti she'd discovered. I bet she's never posted a single picture of her dinner, the fucking witch.

I will never be as tall, thin, and striking as Sanne, but I supposed the good thing about getting my arse into the gym was that I could tone up a little. After a few weeks of my new regime, my friends, if not Dane, noticed. *You look amazing babes! SMOKING HOT!* and also *Are we calling u Kit now???* Naturally, the number of creeper pervert men sliding into your Requests inbox is directly proportionate to the number of selfies on your account, so they increased. Instagram also started trying to sell me liquid meal replacements and 'tummy teas', whatever they are.

But from Dane, only the occasional like.

On the day Beyoncé Instagrammed a caption saying MAKE IT HAPPEN, I decided to do just that. It had been a couple of months since he last worked at Roaster, and I wasn't brazenly going to ask him out, but I needed to get us into a situation where he could ask me on a date.

He'd sent a single tweet promoting his friend's band. Lockwood were playing that night at the Troxy. I wasn't planning on going out, but I saw from the chain that followed his tweet that he was going too.

A rational part of my brain told me this behaviour was getting ridiculous, bordering on stalking. But the fact I had never before felt compelled to act in such a manner made me all the more certain this was something worth exploring. If I hadn't sensed a seed of something between us, I don't think I would have felt so drawn to him.

It would go like this: I'd run into him in the crowd and be surprised to see him. I'd ask to buy him a drink because I think guys secretly quite like it when we take some of the ambiguity out of these things. We'd skulk off to some quiet corner, and I'd ask him what he'd been up to these last few months. Tipsy, we'd kiss, and miss the band's whole set.

I tinted my hair and shaved my legs and bikini line (just in case). I couldn't convince anyone to see the band, so headed to the Troxy alone. If anyone asked, I decided I was going to say I knew the bass player.

For a little-known act, the venue was humming, full of guys who looked like extras from *Peaky Blinders*, and girls who looked like Sanne. Strangely, now, so did I. The pink hair; the skinny jeans on a skinnier ass; some Converse; black eyes. I blended in. As I entered the venue and paid, I sensed some of the guys checking me out, and felt that strange cocktail of pride and discomfort.

The warm-up act was already on, and the queue was five-deep at the bar. People mostly seemed to be drinking pints of Fosters in plastic cups. I was nervous, and I needed something to take the edge off. I ordered a double vodka and soda.

Drink in hand, I wove through the crowd, politely stopping to watch the support act for a few moments. The lead singer looked scarcely out of puberty, and I wondered when I'd become an adult.

I was watching him mutter – an affectation – into the microphone, when Dane walked right past me. He's so tall he almost seemed to fly overhead before I could even register it was him. He was carrying two pints, spilling foam as he went.

This was it. My heart thundered. I followed him. I didn't want to lose him.

He slipped out of the fire exit into the smoking area. As I stepped into the night air, I felt the first nip of winter at my arms. I hadn't brought a coat. I embraced myself, cold.

Dane lit a cigarette, balancing his drinks on the ledge. I suddenly felt very exposed, almost naked. I couldn't go through with it. I went to turn back, when he looked up from his phone and saw me. Too late.

'Hi,' I said, forcing a bright smile.

'Hey,' he said, but there was a flicker in his eye. A flinch. Oh God, he was trying to work out where he knew me from.

'It . . . I'm . . . from the coffee shop.'

The question mark fell from his face. 'Ah yeah. Sorry! You OK?'

'Yes, thanks, you?'

'Grand . . .'

A girl appeared at his side and claimed one of the two pints. Her wrists were weighed down by grubby festival wristbands. Not Sanne, but she might as well have been. Pastel-pink hair, sure, but somehow more effortless than I will ever be. 'Mate, the queue in the ladies, seriously.' She was Australian. Well, of course she fucking was. Australians are cool. They have all the ease of a cold beer at a barbeque. She realised I was standing with him, not just near him. Not as near as she was, though. She was pressed to his hip. 'How's it going, darl?'

I hate her, but . . .

Dane sprang to life. 'Oh sorry. Taryn, this is . . . um . . .'

'Catherine,' I said.

⊰)|(⊱

MY EYE IS A BUTTON ON YOUR DRESS

HANAN AL-SHAYKH

translation from Arabic by Catherine Cobham

My beloved Amal,

Come and take my breath away.

Yusuf

I CLUTCHED AT MY heart for fear it would roll away, just like people in films and books. 'Come and take my breath away.' I became my own private earthquake: the ground was no longer in its normal place beneath my feet, my job didn't matter any more, my relationship with Simon had lost all meaning, in fact it seemed like a sheet of newspaper I'd fixed over a broken windowpane to keep out the draught. Freezing-cold London vanished in the warmth of his letter, and the Eye of Horus on the postage stamp looked kindly at me, pleading with me to return to the land of the sun where I was born and raised, and where I'd been madly in love with a man for ten years until he clipped my wings and I crashed to the ground.

I hurry to answer to Yusuf's email address, my fingers conveying my eagerness: 'I'm coming, I'm coming, I'm coming.' Then I rush to ask my boss if I can take a week off, clutching the letter and lying that I have to go to Cairo for a family emergency. I text Simon, telling him that my mother has to have an operation, reserve a seat on the plane for the next day, and return to my emails. I read Yusuf's reply: 'Your body will gather up the fragments of my body like Isis gathered Osiris and made him whole again.'

'I'm flying to you tomorrow.'

'Tomorrow? Not now? How can I wait till tomorrow?'

'You've lived without me for five years while I've suffered the torment of having you always here with me, on the sofa, in the bathroom, in the book I'm reading, in my bag, in the street, while I eat, wash my hair, dress and undress, sleep, yet despite all of that I never see you, touch you, hear from you.'

I don't write any of that, but ask if we can talk on Skype or FaceTime.

'Don't you think that would diminish the impact of our meeting, like someone fasting and breaking his fast on an onion?'

His refusal kindled my desire and made my passion grow.

He was a husband and a father. I never once asked him to divorce his wife, or to take me as a second wife. I was perfectly happy with our arrangement. I didn't try to make him jealous by telling him if men asked me out, or wanted to marry me, and I never tried to turn him against his wife. I remember when he used to tell me that she knew about our relationship and was threatening to leave, I just pretended to be busy moving the hands of my watch forwards or backwards.

But one day, five years, two months, and three days ago, he took my hands in his, telling me that we had to end our relationship for the time being.

We were in a nightclub called Aladdin, in Pyramid Street. I remember that everyone in the club was having a siesta, even the cats, as he had insisted on seeing me in the middle of the day. I was surprised when he asked to meet me there, and I suggested instead that we meet on the balcony of the Mina House Hotel, but he objected, and not as gently as usual.

'No, no.' And surrounded by the scary pictures of artistes, singers, and dancers, and the smell of cigarettes, he announced, the moment I sat down opposite him, that he loved me more than anyone else in the world, even more than he loved himself, and would love me for ever, for I had entered the pores of his skin and lived inside him, but that present circumstances were against us continuing our relationship.

'But why? I don't understand. Why?'

'Circumstances. The circumstances are very difficult.'

'Is there someone else?'

'You're totally crazy.'

'Your wife then?'

He shook his head uncertainly, then stood up and said, 'Yes, my wife.'

When he left without even a glance in my direction, I threw myself into my car, crying and screaming. I drove and joined the sit-in in Tahrir Square, pulling frantically at my hair, and people crowded around me telling me that I should calm down and that the people's will was strong and destiny would respond to them.* I suddenly felt embarrassed and got up to leave, claiming that I was needed at work at the radio station.

I pursued him like a dog following its master, to his workplace, to the flat where we used to meet. I turned the key in the lock as I always did before, trembling at the thought of what was going to happen between us shortly, but the keyhole rejected my key. So Yusuf had changed the lock even before ending our relationship. I went to the street where he lived, waiting for him opposite his house. I wrote letters to him because I thought they were safer than texts or emails, delivering them by hand to his secretary, and I hung around outside his barber's, his dentist's.

I also cut up the sheet stained with the blood of my virginity, which he'd kindly relieved me of, and sent it to his newspaper. I visited his sister, who'd always hated his wife, and clung to her, weeping, for her eyes were exactly like his, honey-coloured. She cried too, and told me that her brother was being followed by the security services, that

* A reference to the poem by Tunisian poet Abu'l Qasim al-Shabbi (1909–1934): 'If the people one day demand life, then destiny will surely respond'. This poem was used and repeated in various forms in the Arab uprisings beginning in 2010.

his life was in danger, and he was scared somebody might expose our relationship and use it against him in revenge for the way he'd reversed the politics of the newspaper he edited, so that now it was anti-regime. Then she begged me to think about my future. 'My future!' I shout. 'He's my future. I don't want to marry or have children.'

'No, you'll regret it. You're still young and beautiful, and you'll resent him, and life when you get older, especially if you don't have a child.'

'But I'm scared of pregnancy and childbirth. You can see how skinny I am!'

Cairo had risen up against its leader in protest against hunger, humiliation, injustice, and because people were treated like animals. The Arab Spring quickly gained momentum, and blazed like a firework display, bringing joy to all our hearts. The energy and excitement of the events going on around me and Yusuf began to have an effect on our relationship too. Despite the fact that I stayed in Tahrir Square all the time, and he never left his work except to go home in the early hours of the morning, we kept in touch on the phone and exchanged text messages: he asked me if I preferred chocolate to kissing, and I asked him if birds suffered from indigestion; he asked me if anyone had pinched my bottom in Tahrir Square, and I answered 'Yes, you.'

I pound away on the computer: 'You're quite right. It's better if we postpone our meeting till tomorrow when we're face to face,' and I'm thinking that the computer screen might show how crushed and depressed I look after our long separation.

'Tell me, are you married? Any kids?'

'No. I'm not married and I don't have children.'

'If you were waiting for me, now's the chance for us to be together, and I've arranged everything, that's of course if you want the same thing as I do.'

'Which is?'

'For you to be in my arms day and night. But you haven't told me why you went off to England?'

'Because I like fog!'

I'd decided to leave when I became like a sunflower, with a twisted neck from following him everywhere, and eyes stumbling unfocused and multiplying interminably as they searched for him and cried for him.

'We'll talk about everything. The important thing is that I'm waiting for you, waiting for your skinny body that must be dry as a stick, craving love and life!'

'I can hardly believe that you still remember your letters to me word for word. Do you remember what you wrote when I moved from my own radio programme to co-present with that idol of the masses, Hussam?'

The computer almost ignites when he answers me after a quarter of an hour. 'Sorry, I was making coffee. I remember I said, Watch out, my eye is a button on your dress, observing all your comings and goings!'

As I read this, all I can see is the balcony of the Mina House Hotel, and the pyramids reassuring me that everything will be fine between us, just as it used to be, and that I hadn't been in too much of a hurry to decide to travel the next day, even though when he kicked me out of his life, it was as if he'd cut off both my arms.

But what about his wife? Had they separated? Was she dead? I never hated her or felt jealous of her at any time in my relationship with him. Quite the contrary, I thought we shared something, our love for him, even though I did deliberately leave a pair of my tights in his house in Fayyoum when he'd asked me to put everything including the sugar jar and the packet of coffee back in its place, claiming his wife had begun to suspect that he took me to this holiday house of theirs. She'd even left home one day in protest at his relationship with me, and he'd finally come across her car parked in front of a hotel in the Cairo suburbs.

I write back to him, slyly trying to find out more about the situation with his wife. 'I want to hear your voice. Let me call you. Is your number the same as it was? I still remember it.'

'I'll call you, darling. Can you send me your number straight away?'

I send him my number and wait more than five minutes.

'Sorry, the electricity's been cut off and the lines are down. But maybe that happened for a reason, in case all the phone networks between Egypt and England burst into flames the moment we hear each other's voices.'

My phone rings again and I shout 'Hello! Hello!' but I only hear a crackling before the line is cut. Then I receive an email from someone whose name I don't recognise, telling

151

me that it's hard for our friend to contact me by phone, because it seems his phone is being tapped, but that there's no time to go into detail. I thank the writer of the email, only to receive a few seconds later a line from my beloved: 'Are you being unfaithful to me with my best friend? And I haven't asked you if you are happy in London, and in your work at the BBC?'

My heart thumps. Does he want to emigrate to London like millions of other Arabs, and that's why he's contacting me? I answer, 'I've got used to living in London and I like my work. Do you still like your work at the paper?'

'Should I understand from this that you're not coming back to Cairo for good any time soon? Be in no doubt that we're in dire need of you and all those like you who have emigrated and abandoned their homeland!'

I used to follow the news about Egypt, as it still affected me in London: how freedom had become a collar tightening around people's necks, the press was controlled by businessmen, poverty was almost at famine level, the streets had become car parks, the president wanted to amend the constitution to suit his own interests, friends rarely got together, and everyone complained of being hard up.

'We'll talk tomorrow, and I'll think about coming back to Cairo permanently.'

I get ready for the trip. I dye my hair its natural colour, honey brown, buy a new dress, shoes, handbag. I have to look as if I live a normal life in England. Since arriving in London I've neglected my appearance. I don't want it to seem that I take it more seriously than my job. What's more, the cold and rain, the public transport, and the long working hours don't encourage me to take the same interest in how I look as I did in Cairo. Back there, appearance, beauty, good looks are the first step to getting a job, and some kind of a smile from the world.

I arrived in Cairo, trembling inwardly as I queued at the passport office. Who knows, maybe my name was on a list, and I'd be interrogated because of my relationship with Yusuf, or I'd become an undesirable person since I'd criticised the regime and described the current leader as 'rubbish' in one of my radio interviews in London.

I took a taxi from the airport to Fayyoum where Yusuf was waiting for me. He had suggested we meet in the house where we had first made love. The grey jungles of Cairo were swallowed up in my longing to get to Fayyoum, still two hours away, and I felt no sorrow or guilt at the thought that I wasn't going to visit my mother till the end of my trip, even though I could picture her on her own in the sitting room listening to the news.

I texted him telling him I'd arrived and was on my way to Fayyoum.

'I can't believe it! Welcome, welcome! I can't believe I'm going to see you and hold you in my arms, dearest creature. I feel my spirit reviving after years of drought.'

My God, he remembers all the things he used to say to me before . . . no, he actually feels them. Our separation has fired up our emotions rather than subduing them.

I caught the driver glancing at me in his mirror from time to time, and I was suddenly afraid of him as we sat immersed in silence, for I felt myself opening up to the world, just as I did when Yusuf and I used to race to Fayyoum, because at last we were going to be together for two whole days, rather than a few stolen hours like our meetings in Cairo.

The moment we started driving through the town, my fear of the driver evaporated as I remembered wandering from shop to shop with Yusuf to buy tampons after my period had arrived unexpectedly; how, when he noticed the pain written all over my face, he'd insisted on taking me to the local pharmacy, unabashedly picking up the painkillers and the packet of tampons too, to the astonishment of the sales girl, who whispered to me, 'You're so lucky. He treats you like a princess.'

The lake appeared in the distance like a giant's blue eye, then his house, pink with blue window frames. The car sped towards the house, which appeared silent, with no visible signs of life. Its front door remained closed despite the scrunch of the wheels as we came to a halt. I slammed the door of the car firmly behind me, but the house remained shuttered and barred. I knocked gently and sighed in exasperation when nothing happened. Yusuf had always stuck to our arrangements in a way that used to fill me with awe.

I press the bell this time, take a deep breath, and press again.

Slow footsteps, moving quietly. An unhurried hand opens

the door. I prepare to throw myself at him, for years of absence to be erased as soon as our bodies touch.

I freeze. A middle-aged woman smiles at me, takes my bag, greeting me: 'Hello. Welcome. Glad you got here safely. Welcome. Come in. Tea or coffee, or lemonade?'

Had I gone to the wrong house? I see all the fossils hanging on the walls, petrified wood and other kinds, and a small whale's jawbone.

'Is Mr Yusuf in?'

'Yes. Do come in, please.'

I wonder if he's having a siesta. She puts my bag down and goes off down the corridor leading to the bedroom.

I didn't follow her. I was at a loss, utterly confused and angry, unable to believe he wasn't waiting for me at the front door. Was it the presence of this maid or cook that prevented him from coming to greet me? Maybe he was in the process of divorcing his wife and didn't want to look as if he had a relationship with another woman. When the maid – or cook – reached the bedroom door she turned back to me and said, 'Please madam, he's here.'

Before she could knock on the door, I stormed in past her and saw him sitting facing the window with his back to me. My heart leaped, and I rushed to embrace his head from behind, noticing the grey in his black hair. Was he asleep?

'Yusuf, Yusuf, I'm here.'

He turned round slowly, but not before I'd called his name again: 'Yusuf, Yusuf. I'm here, darling.'

When I saw his face, I gasped and the world spun around

me. It was him and not him, as if someone had blown him up with a pair of bellows; his eyes had glazed into two circles of broken glass, their honey colour turned waxen, his nose was still the same, but his lips had become a thin line etched hard into his face, yet trembling unaccountably.

He turned back to the window. I rushed to him, taking hold of his hands that were swollen, but still Yusuf's hands. I rubbed my face in them, kissing them and weeping. He looked right at me for a moment in complete bewilderment, then turned to face the window again. I gulped tearfully, mournfully. 'What's happened to you, my love? Yusuf, what happened?'

When his gaze remained fixed on the window, I brought my face close to his, in case my longing for him, my breath, my perfume, might rouse him, turn him back into Yusuf, but he moved his face away from mine and raised his hand to protect himself from me before focusing all of his attention on the lake once more.

'What can you see, Yusuf? Tell me, darling, what can you see?'

The horizon, violet, blue, with a line of green, and the lake itself, dusky with birds big and small, pink, white, black, brown, and the colour of the desert sand. I hear the moaning of the breeze, or is it the sound of my own breathing? I kneel down in front of him. He has put on weight. His feet are swollen. I look directly at him. Panic-stricken, he tries to move away from me, and when I don't let him he emits a terrified scream that makes my mouth go dry, but I take hold of his hand again, a hand that for sure didn't write that letter or exchange emails with me yesterday, or dial my number. He pulls his hand away, as if he's had an electric shock, covering it with his other hand and continuing to stare out of the window.

The woman hurries up to comfort him. 'What's the matter, Mr Yusuf? This lady is the new nurse. Don't be afraid of her.' Then she sighs in my direction and returns carrying a tray on which is a teapot, teacup, biscuits, and a glass of water. With a movement of my head I gesture towards him: 'How long?'

'Two years. God help him, and madam. Please help yourself. It's mint tea. Would you like something to eat?'

I thank her, shaking my head. 'Come, I'll take you to your room so you can rest for a while. The nurse before you has gone on holiday, and Madam Mervet left you this book.'

She went up to a table where there were a pile of books, a phone and a lamp, and brought a book over to me. The moment I saw it I pounced on it and opened it and saw my own handwriting: 'Happy Birthday to my love, today and always, my darling Yusuf.'

The book was *Wuthering Heights*, translated into Arabic, which I'd given Yusuf as a birthday present after we'd been together for two years. I stared at the inscription that had been so full of optimism and love at the time, with no thoughts of separation or illness or death.

I ask the book what has happened to my beloved, and take it to show Yusuf, whom now I know and don't know.

'Do you remember, do you remember this book, my love? Do you remember Heathcliff, Catherine?'

I turn the pages and notice a yellow sticker marking one of the pages and see the hearts that were red as roses when I drew them faded now, but still marking the following passage where I'd crossed out the name Heathcliff and substituted it with Yusuf: *'My love for ~~Heathcliff~~ Yusuf resembles the eternal rocks beneath: a source of little visible delight, but necessary. Nelly, I am ~~Heathcliff~~ Yusuf! He's always, always in my mind: not as a pleasure, any more than I am always a pleasure to myself, but as my own being. So don't talk of our separation again: it is impracticable . . .'*

Then the woman hands me a note that says: 'Welcome Ms Amal. It's a pleasure to welcome you to Fayyoum. Think of this as your home. Anyway, you're no stranger here, you know the house very well. Please don't forget to take your folder. You'll find it on the table.'

And sure enough I find a big folder with my name on it, and when I look inside it, I see my letters to him and his letters that I returned to him before I left for London. His wife has highlighted certain passages in blue so she could use them when she was talking to me yesterday as if she were Yusuf. I put them all back inside the folder and returned it to its place.

'Did the book tell you what sir likes to eat and drink?' asks the woman. 'Since madam left yesterday he hasn't let a morsel of food or a drop of water pass his lips.'

'When will madam return?'

'I've no idea. A week or ten days. God only knows!'

I find myself catching my breath, trying in vain to return it to my chest. Finally, I manage to sit down next to Yusuf, staring at the lake like him. But instead of wondering at the birds circling and alighting there, I'm like a cork twisting and turning around myself.

THE CORD

ALISON CASE

H E REACHED THE CRAG just as the clouds finished blotting out the moon, plunging him into perfect darkness. No rain, as yet, but a distant flash and crack of thunder told him it would come soon. Blinded, he dropped to his hands and knees, feeling for the edge of the stone and then the path that ran down along the far side of it. He crawled slowly down, backwards so that he faced up the hill, checking always that the stone was on his left, until he came to the bottom edge of the crag. Then he turned right. There was barely a path here; it was a matter of keeping level, moving neither up nor down the hillside, feeling for the slight gaps in the weeds, and checking what he felt against the map of his memory. It had been years since they were last here together, but before the old master died they had come often. Feeling in the darkness, he plunged his hand straight into a patch of nettles, and drew it back with a curse. But it reassured him – he remembered those nettles, or thought he did. It was hard to judge distance, crawling slowly where he was used to scrambling with confidence, but if he was right, he was halfway to his goal. The sting of the nettles was good, too. It kept him in the present, kept him sharp, and he needed that, because the thunder was getting closer and the first drops were falling. He could not let the storm find him on this open hillside. He moved a little faster, then stopped, suddenly confused. Had he gone too far? Did the path, if it was a path he was on, lead straight to the cave, or pass underneath it? He could not remember.

Another flash of lightning came to his rescue. It showed him the cave, directly uphill, further up than he had thought. Quickly, while the image remained burned on his eyes, he scrambled up towards it, until he felt the bare earth that floored it, and then knocked his head on the low overhang of rock above it. The heavens opened then. By the time he had worked himself into the back of the cave, away from the rain, he was wet, but not soaked through. Good enough, he thought. It would be a grim night, but that was nothing new. He curled himself into a tight ball and shivered. There was nothing to do but wait: for the rain to pass, for his body's warmth to dry his clothes, if it could, for daytime. One thing he could be sure of – there would be no sleep for him, not at this distance from Cathy, and certainly not with his blood still racing at her words.

He had drifted off into a light sleep in the warmth of the

kitchen, hidden from view behind the settle where Joseph was unlikely to spot him. He had woken to the sound of her voice, which never failed to rouse him from even the soundest slumber. His first impulse was to raise his head and claim her attention, turned from him during Edgar's long visit that afternoon, but then the words registered their meaning:

Today, Edgar Linton has asked me to marry him, and I've given him an answer.

His breath had stopped, his whole body frozen in place. She wouldn't tell Nelly her answer right away, wanting her advice, she said, and so for a while he had remained unbreathing, like a rabbit that hopes, if he just stays still enough, the fox will pass him by. She had said no, surely. But the teeth found him.

I accepted him, Nelly.

His blood ran cold. He had never known before how literal that was: ice water washed down his veins, to the ends of his fingers. He could not have moved or spoken if he tried. They were still talking. Nelly's voice was mere noise, but he could not escape Cathy's, each word a new twist wringing his heart tighter and tighter into a hard knot, like a sheet in the wash.

I love the ground under his feet, and the air over his head, and everything he touches, and every word he says. I love all his looks, and all his actions, and him entirely and altogether.

He had known that Edgar wanted her – who would not

want her? But for all his jealousy of the time stolen from him, he had never really thought that she – that *she*— Why was she still talking? Why keep grinding your thumb when the fly is already crushed beneath it? He pressed his hands over his ears and tried to shut out her words. She didn't know he was there. He had to get out before she discovered him, before she realised what he had heard and tried to make it right with him. Because she would succeed, he knew that. Once she turned on that – what was it? charm? glamour? – that *force* she had, all he would know was the Cathyness of her, and the impossibility of leaving. Quietly he rolled himself into a crouch, being careful to keep his head below the settle, but in so doing he took his hands off his ears again, and now he heard:

It would degrade me to marry Heathcliff now.

That was enough. He crept to the door. Nelly stirred the fire with the poker, and under cover of the noise he lifted the latch and slipped out. Once outside, he ran out of the yard, leaving the gate swinging behind him, and headed to the emptiest part of the moors, toward Penistone Crag. The twilight was fading fast, darkened by a pall of thunderclouds drawing itself over the sky, and in the dark he stumbled often, but it barely slowed him. The pain in his chest had to be lessened somehow, and wild exertion was the only relief. Another stumble, and he fell onto his knees with a curse. The terrain was rougher here, and the darkness had thickened. It was dangerous to run. A brief image came to him of himself broken, lying dead on the moors, and Cathy weeping over him, inconsolable. Perhaps that would be best: then she could marry Edgar, and he could haunt them both. Oh, how easily he could reduce that milk-pudding of a boy to a bundle of quivering nerves, starting at every shadow! And Cathy would see then what a poor excuse for a man she had chosen. Her love for Edgar would die, and she would grieve for Heathcliff, and long only to join him in death. A fitting end. But if he didn't die? He already had a lifetime of bitter experience in how much hunger, cold, and beatings he could endure and still live. What if he were discovered days from now, injured and ill, and dragged back to the Heights, weak and pitiable, to be nursed by her in mere charity, while Edgar came daily to offer her cheer and relief from the sad duty? That would be worst of all.

And so he slowed to a more careful walk, until the storm found him at the Crag, and now here he was, holed up like a badger in his sett, trying to think what Cathy's words meant for him, for them.

At this distance from her, the ache in his chest was intense. He had never before gone so far from her voluntarily. He had been in agony during the weeks she was at Thrushcross Grange. The invisible cord that bound him to her had been near its limit, stretched taut all day, twanging with pain while he was kept pent away from her at the Heights. Every night, as soon as everyone else was asleep, he would grab his blanket and sneak out toward the Grange, taking up a position on a hill that offered a view over the park wall to the house. He dared not scale the wall to get closer – the dogs were set loose to roam the park at night, and if they caught him without Cathy at his side this time, he had no doubt that the Lintons would let them tear him to shreds. But the hillside was near enough for the cord to slacken and give him some ease. The windows stayed lighted up in the Grange long after Wuthering Heights was asleep, illuminated with tier upon tier of expensive wax candles, and he could see the silhouettes of figures moving before them. Cathy's he always knew by the leap of his heart. She was so alive! The others' moved like pasteboard cut-outs, but hers flickered and danced like a flame. He would send his longing down the cord to her then, and often she would come to the window facing him and stare out into the darkness as if trying to see him, and he would be sure his longing had reached her and that it was her own for him that he felt flooding back. Then one of the Lintons would come and lead her away, and the lights would be extinguished but for a lone candle here and there lighting the inhabitants to their beds. When the last candle was put out, he would curl up in the blanket for a few hours' sleep.

He had been sure, then, that the cord was as deeply rooted in her heart as in his, that she could no more be at ease so far apart than he could. They had talked of it often, this bond between them, proud of its strangeness and its power, which seemed to set them apart from ordinary people. When they were touching, it seemed that they could enter each other's body at will, seeing and

hearing and feeling in the other's skin. Apart, even with
the whole of the yard between them, their emotions travelled down the cord from one to the other like raindrops
on a string, and they would reunite to exclaim over what
each had known the other was feeling when they were
apart. Over a mile apart, flashes of strong feeling still
came through.

Once only, he had tried to break it. It was after she
returned from Thrushcross Grange, when she was full of
the Lintons – their charms, their manners, and their
orderly, cleanly ways – and she reproached him for aban-
doning his studies, and for not bathing every day (how
could he study when he was kept at hard labour from dawn
to dusk, and what was the use of bathing when he had
only the one filthy set of clothes to put on after?). Then
he had stormed off. Driven by rage and resentment, he
had ignored the pain that began a little distance from
Wuthering Heights and grew the further he walked. But
at two miles he was gasping with it, and before he reached
three, the cord had dragged him to an agonised halt, quivering with nausea and pain. He could not do it. He had
turned back. When he returned, Cathy had stormed at him
and sobbed, saying that he was tearing her heart out and
making her ill, and he had heard in her words the echo of
his own experience. Whatever he suffered then, from the
hard labour without pay, Hindley's beatings, the loss of all
his schooling – yes, even from her, with her reproaches,
her new finicking ways, and all the time stolen from him

to entertain the Lintons while he hovered fuming in the yard – all of it had been worth enduring, because the alternative would be to rip out her heart along with his own, and that was unthinkable.

But if she really were bound as he was, she could never have thought of marrying Edgar, could not have said the things she said, that it would *degrade* her to marry him. Degrade? How could it degrade her to be with another part of herself? How could she think of promising to be one flesh with another, when they had so often rejoiced that *they* were united more closely than any marriage? *You are me and I am you*, she would say. But somehow *I am you* meant she was Cathy in him, seeing what he saw and feeling what he felt, but still fully herself, while *you are me* meant that he was swallowed up in the whole fullness of her person. He had told himself that they were equals, twin yolks in a single shell of consciousness, that she was as much his as he was hers. But had he ever been more than the dark supplement, the shadow cast by her brightness? *You complete me*, she liked to say. *We are one person.* Yes, he realised now, and that person was Cathy. He had accepted that because being hers, with her, of her, *being* her, was all that he had ever wanted. And who could wish to be him anyway – dark, despised, beaten as he was – even himself? Now he saw: for her it was only ever talk, a game she played at. Oh, the cord was real enough for him, he could not doubt that, with its tension even now feeling as if it would drag him from the cave back to her if he did not hold himself against it – but it was rooted in his heart alone: for her it was no more than a leash she held in her hand, something she could jerk to control him or drop at will to be free.

He would break it this time, he resolved. He would reach its limit and keep going until it snapped. It was only a question of bearing the pain, and he was used to that. He had failed before because he believed that his pain was also hers, and that he could not bear. But now he knew better. And if it ripped the heart from his chest and he died, so be it. Better that than to live as a mere pet to Edgar's wife, to be kicked or stroked, exiled or curled at her feet, according to her need or fancy.

He shifted in his dark hole to look out, and saw that the storm had passed. He crawled out from the cave and stood up. The clouds were gone, and there was moonlight enough to walk by. He made his way back to Penistone Crag and rested his hand on the stone. So many tales swirled round it – that it was sacred to the fairies, that it would grant wishes, for a price, that it could bind and unbind. Should he ask it for help in what lay ahead? He laughed bitterly and gave it a slap. 'I've been called a changeling, a demon, and the Devil's own child,' he said aloud. 'If I can't do this myself, I doubt you can help me.' He clambered back up to the footpath that ran along the ridge, set himself against the aching tug on his heart, and strode onward.

It was as it had been before, the pain intensifying with each step, until he had to stop, gasping, fighting the urgent demand of his whole being that he turn and run back to Wuthering Heights. He heard her voice in his head.

I am you and you are me.

'No,' he said. '*I* am Heathcliff. Not you.' He leaned into the tension, forcing himself on, panting as he fought the pull, and felt a few tiny fibres begin to snap and curl back on themselves, each sending a sharp *ping* to his chest.

You are more myself than I am.

'I am *Heathcliff*. I can,' – step – 'live,' – step – 'without you.' More fibres peeled away, but his heart was straining as if it would be pulled out of his chest. Grief and longing flooded him. Hers? No, it couldn't be. She felt nothing. She would be happier without him. She would marry Edgar. He gathered his strength and flung himself forward.

Snap.

The recoil knocked him to the ground and he screamed, curled tight around the excruciating pain in his chest. The ripping sensation had been so intense he expected to feel blood on his chest, but there was nothing there. For some time he could only lie there, moaning, sobbing as he had never sobbed even when Hindley beat him bloody. Hours passed, and then dawn began to lighten the eastern sky. He uncurled himself and climbed unsteadily to his feet. His whole body felt ravaged, and there was an ache in his breast he knew would never heal, but there was no drag on his heart. He stumbled a few paces in the direction away from the Heights. No change. He kept walking.

I am Heathcliff.

HEATHCLIFFS
I HAVE KNOWN

LOUISA YOUNG

FIRST ONE WAS THE bloke who hung about in the Woolworths car park opposite the gates of the Juniors. Yes, he had a heavy coat on and his collar up and his stupid willy hanging out, and he looked at me and said, broodingly, meaningfully, 'You're mine.'

I said, 'No I'm not, I'm my mum and dad's,' and walked on home, wondering if I'd got the possessives right. My mum's and dad's? My mum's and my dad's? Anyway I wasn't bloody his. I was theirs, and when I grew up I'd be my own.

I'm not going to get them in order.

Generally, I gave them short shrift and got off lightly. I never had a weakness for them, thank God. Not like some girls. But I'll only speak of what I know.

There was – Christ, I can't give him his real name, he's real, but by giving him a fake name I'm protecting him, to which I profoundly object. You can't win.

He was younger, we both rode motorbikes. He looked a bit cherubic, not my type, fat mouth and soft hair, big mean eyes, excitable. Once I was riding my Guzzi up the Wandsworth Road and I saw him coming towards me on the other side. I pulled towards the white line and so did he, and we were both in open-face helmets and that was the first time he kissed me, which I thought was well romantic. I went around to his a couple of times, and one time I stayed over because we'd had a bit to drink, but we didn't do anything. He wanted to, but he was being funny about it, starting and stopping, and I didn't really want to anyway. After a few weeks I wasn't very interested in him: he kept ringing up saying 'What are you doing tonight?' and I'd say 'I'm seeing my friends,' and he'd say, 'But what about me? What am *I* supposed to do?' and I wouldn't say, 'I have no idea; do what you bloody like,' but I would think – *twat alert.*

Then one night he drove his Honda 750 through the closed front door of the place I was living, right into the hallway, came into my room, called me a fat-titted witch, took my hair in his hands and banged my head on the wall, put his hands around my neck, and he was saying 'You're mine' – 'I'm fucking not', I couldn't say, because he was strangling me. 'I love you,' he said. 'I'm in love with you.' My flatmate came barrelling down the stairs, the creep ran up to get hold of him and threw him at the banisters, broke his rib, it turned out.

The police came around, said, 'Oh it's domestic,' and went

away. It was a long time ago. I rang them the next day and said, 'Oi.'

They picked him up in a dawn raid, and the DI said, 'Why didn't you tell me he was a coloured boy?' – because he wasn't, is why. He was half French or something, and a bit sallow.

Took it to court, he got off. The reason being, I felt bad for him, and didn't tell the truth. I was up as a witness – you weren't the victim then, you were a witness to what had been done to you. They said, 'You're his girlfriend.' I said 'No I'm not, I've only known him a few weeks and we've never had sex. That's not girlfriend to me.' I didn't say what he had told me: there was a thing in his family where the men's foreskins are too tight. His dad had it and his uncle; they got circumcised; it's fine. But he hadn't been circumcised. So every time he got a stiffy, he also got excruciating pain. So that had an effect on how he felt about women he fancied. So I became the reason for him getting severe sex-related dick-agony, and that's why he did what he did. But I was young and in court and didn't feel able to tell everyone in their wigs about his dick issues. I was sorry for him! Plus I thought my flatmate's broken rib and the busted-down door etc., etc., would tell the story without me having to go into details. More fool me. The lesson being, when you're up against the men, whatever kind of woman you are, use everything you've got.

His mum said to me in the public gallery, why did I get the police on him? I said, 'Because I was scared. And he might come back, or do it again.' She didn't say to me, 'He didn't do it.' She knew he'd done it. I could see in her eyes he'd done it before. Maybe to her. Then after it was over the DI asked me out on a date.

Hm, then what? Oh yeah, Greg. German-Sicilian physio-therapist. Bad combination. Same name problem. I'll call him Greg.

I'd gone to Los Angeles, as people do, if they can; saved some money and had some dreams and ended up on the furthest coast of the mad country, staying with an old school friend, male, Steven. He was American in London, English in LA. By blood, a Russian Jew. His mother was dead, and his nature made things as difficult as possible, always. I loved him. His face was tragedy like Groucho Marx and his body like a small and convenient Michelangelo that you could take around with you. We weren't lovers though. Not usually. One night there had been a very small earthquake. He'd woken me up because he knew I wouldn't want to miss it. The apartment (in a peach-coloured retro block set around a courtyard, south of Downtown, gas stations, crack houses, police helicopters overhead) was small, and we were sharing a bed. It didn't mean anything. We'd been teenagers together; we'd slept in piles like puppies throughout our teens.

I had a car. A 1978 Oldsmobile Delta Royale, eighteen feet long and six feet wide. I couldn't drive in those days. I'd bought it in Nashville, but the guy I'd come across the

States with wouldn't let me drive it. He was a driving snob – a driving dream, too. Had a way of steering with one hand, the other arm along the back of the long wide front seat, that made me want to curl up over on the other end and smile and think about cooking pancakes for his breakfast. So he drove, and I put my boots up on the dashboard. When we got to LA he stayed a few days, but he moved on because we really did hate each other by then. All the way across the US he'd refused to dance with me. In Memphis I'd wanted to find Al Green's church and go to Beale Street and daydream the Blues: he'd only wanted to do his laundry. We had one night there. In the launderette. Slept on the hard shoulder; a plant by the car, some southern vine, growing so fast it was over our wheel-arch by the time we woke up.

So he buggered off; and I was happy to be with my old school friend, who, if he didn't want to dance, would at least talk instead. After three months in the rural south-west an educated man was a joy.

The last weekend before I was to go home we decided to spend in Mexico. Tijuana! Road trip!

I loved the smell inside the car. Plasticky car seat, hot engine oil, something mosquitoey about it. Warm leatherette. Driving around LA, looking at palm trees. Actresses living in little white houses divided in two, in Hollywood. La Cienega. Silverlake. Melrose. Raymond Chandler. Nail bars. Desperate selfish young folk demanding the rewards they felt were due to their beauty and youth, and not getting them. All the same age: no children here, no old people. Twenty-one to thirty-two. Drug-taking.

Greg, a friend of Steven's, was going to come too. I didn't mind because he was going to buy my car for a thousand bucks. Five hundred more than I paid for it, four thousand miles later. I was happy to take his money because he was happy to give it. So he could come on our trip; that was all right.

We'd drive out to the Valley to pick him up. Wrong direction from Martin Luther King where Steven lived. Never mind – it was a trip! Fun like fishing! Get your stuff, pick up your friends, the sun is shining on a Southern California day.

Greg was a big bloke. Six foot four, and unaware of the effect of it. The kind of man who was always being asked to move his legs, and it never occurs to him just to keep them out of the way. Steven and I were both five foot five. We liked holding hands – Steven was used to holding hands with women, used to it being nice because he was the same height. For a woman, his height was a special treat. No inequality, no arm-stretching, no having to compensate. Greg went in the back of the Olds and I went in the mom seat, and Steven drove. The small Europeans were mum and dad, and US Greg was the big kid in the back seat. Off we went to Mexico.

We left the car at the border and then you walk across and you're there. First we went to a bar and drank some. Then we went up and down a tourist street. I bought little plaster skeletons: one with a desk and typewriter, one on a motorbike, one playing the trumpet. Mysterious roughly made little faces, gazing out and away. Teeth like piano keys. I could have chosen seventeen. Peered and peered at all the things they had the little skeletons doing: dancing and eating and driving and reading the paper. Like the dog in Old Mother Hubbard: She went to the cobbler to buy him some shoes, and when she came back he was reading the news. Bought a couple of dangly ones, their limbs held together with string, like puppets; and a couple of skulls, painted white, the jaws that could go up and down because of a piece of string knotted underneath. Mexican stuff! Greg had been to Mexico before and wasn't so excited about it.

Then there was a street stall selling oysters in their shells, so we ate them, with a ferocious thin hot red sauce, and squeezed lime. Greg wouldn't eat them. I thought I might get ill, but I didn't care, I could be ill on the plane and the stewardesses would look after me and I'd get home sick and thin and purged and jet-lagged and laden with skeletons and Greg's thousand dollars.

So we went and drank some more. We were drinking tequila. Of course we became extremely funny. There are photos Steven took: black-and-white eight-by-tens of the three of us on time lapse. Steven with his fading-out-of-reality face, his eyes and his voice blurring, his limited ability to bear the world wrapped up and protected by alcohol, retreating visibly. Greg big and smiley like a salesman at a convention. Me happy happy-happy. We're in Mexico, being funny. Not telling jokes but inventing them and running with them, building a gang thing, his bow tie is really a camera kind of funny. Only-we-would-get-it, You-had-to-be-there funny. I loved being in a Mexican bar with two handsome men and tequila and an Oldsmobile and a bagful of skeletons. Steven loved not thinking about his mother. Greg loved these funny European guys, this cute girl, the cute weird way they talk and are.

We got *so* drunk.

There was a bar on a roof terrace, with ads all around, and their grimy backs visible, all insects and fire-risk wiring and wooden frames. There was a greenness in the west, a sunset. A smell of carbon monoxide, hot traffic. A bar in a basement, with a mariachi band. There were some busy roads, and some pedestrianised roads. A street with trees and fairy lights, and tables outside the bars. Dark, purple and jasmine dark. There were waiters who found us amusing and waiters who didn't. Steven spoke Spanish. There was dancing; Greg was too big on the dance floor. There were people not as drunk as us and there were people drunker. Nothing closed. We were so funny. We were all arms around each other. The bags of skeletons got left behind and recovered. And left behind. And recovered because a waiter chased down the street to bring them back to us. The moon sailed on by.

Was it dark or light when we crossed the border back? That day or the next? It was overhead lighting and insects cracking on lilac light-tubes and sober people and it was terribly, terribly funny. God, we must have been young for being so drunk to be so funny for so long. There was a woman with a small child trying to cross over; border guards saying no. Young guys with guns and uniforms. Something had gone wrong for the woman; clearly she had believed she would be allowed to cross. She sat with her child in the corridor, on the floor. I gave her my passport. One of the uniform guys brought it back to me: 'Hey! Lady!'

Greg told me off and did a big sensible bloke/silly little woman/crazy English people number with the border guy. My mouth pulled together. Of course it was a stupid thing to do. That really wasn't the point. I didn't like Greg after that. Not to recognise a ludicrous poetic gesture for what it was . . . It shrank the glorious folly of our enterprise.

One of us drove, God help us. Then there was something wrong with the car, it was farting and jumping and any moment a police car would come and get us and we weren't in Mexico now. We drove very slowly – too slowly. Outside San Diego the car packed up and we drifted onto the hard shoulder. Was it dark? Was it dawn? What day was it? As far as I know the car is still there.

Across the flat brownish suburban nothing-land a yellow motel sign rattled against some kind of blue sky. We got there. We booked in. Three of us in a first-floor room you reach by a balcony along the front, with a Coke machine at the end by the stairs. Two double beds and a bathroom. Kind of disgusting. Shades of brown and pink.

Steven went in one bed and passed out. I went in the other and observed my head spinning and spinning and spinning. Greg came out of the bathroom and got in bed with me, wrapping himself around me with a great sigh of relief and desire.

'What are you doing?' I said, from the depths. 'Get off.'

He seemed to have passed out too. Great heavy huge lump. I was disgusted, tired beyond belief. He was all over me. Ugh. Pushed him off, shaking my head, wiping at my face, shaking myself, getting out of the bed. Pissed off. Got into the other bed. Steven out like a light. Pulled the cover up and sank into oblivion.

His arms were there again. On me. Steven? No: Steven's arms were small and strong and aware. This was that great breathing octopus, coming at me again – 'Greg! Fuck off!'

He was murmuring stuff. Possibly along the 'Come on baby' line. 'You're mine, baby,' he says. He's beside the bed, climbing in and blocking me. Steven is passed out on the other side. I push Greg and push back the cover and climb out and move away – he comes and puts his arms to go around me. 'Get off, Greg!' He's murmuring: 'You know you want me baby,' and so on.

'Shut up Greg,' I say. 'Go to sleep. You're being an idiot.' He's lurching after me, and I am out of bed and dodging him. Dodging him! A man I know, in a motel room, with my old buddy dead to the world in a bed right there. Greg has become completely stupid. He doesn't see, he doesn't hear.

He's a lumbering, huge, stupid lump of sexual hunger. He's really disgusting.

I went into the bathroom and closed the door and locked it. Greg knocked, and knocked, and begged, and kicked, and shouted. I sat on the bog and shivered in my T-shirt until he was quiet, then I put a towel in the bottom of the grubby bath and lay there and shivered. I was really angry. Stiff with anger and discomfort and a sense of the ridiculousness of it in the bottom of the bath.

When it had been quiet outside the door for a while, I got up and gently pushed it open. Quiet. Moonlight on the cheap carpet. Two beds, each with a lump, each quietly rising and falling. I sneaked across and slipped into Steven's, his friendly if comatose body between me and Greg's bed, and my mind reached down again for sleep.

Weight beside me. Hands on my body, up my T-shirt, trying to turn me over. A nasty little erection pressing against my thigh. 'Darling, darling . . .'

I shouted and pushed and I was back in the bathroom, door locked, my back against the door like someone in a film. Panting. Tired beyond belief. Pissed off. Scared? No. Angry.

'Sweetheart!' he was saying behind the door. 'Sweetheart what's the matter?'

Is there no end to this man's stupidity? What kind of no would mean no to him?

'Sweetheart, I'm sorry,' he's saying. 'Come on out. I'm sorry, I know, you're tired, let's speak in the morning. I'll go in with Steven. Come on, honey—'

183

The bathtub is cold. The floor is filthy. The towel is outside because I had had it around me when I came out last time. I sit. I sit cross-legged. I piss. I look at the bath. My head falls back against the cistern. I wake suddenly with a jerking nod, slipping sideways off the lid of the loo. I am swaying and shivering, teeth chattering with exhaustion.

Outside it's quiet.

Hardly upright, I slip out the door. The near bed is empty, and I fall into it and sleep.

A while later I am disturbed. He's on top of me, my T-shirt up, my knickers down, and he's burrowing his way up me. Six-foot four, fifteen stone, German-Sicilian Greg, the physiotherapist from the Valley. 'Get off me Greg, Greg, stop it, get off me Greg,' I'm saying, as best I can, smothered, under, squashed, small, his chest in my face, his big arms holding me and his big body weighing me down – I'm immobilised. I shout – do I shout? I want to tell him to fuck off, to make my rejection as clear as it can be made, but I can't say fuck – the word has become ambiguous. My face is all screwed up in disgust and my hands are pushing at him, but I don't want to touch him, his horrible hairy chest all over me, on my breasts – MY breasts – and I'm shaking and shaking and angry. I would bite him, but I don't want to touch him, don't want any of him anywhere near me and yet he's fucking me and saying oh baby oh baby. I'm so tense you'd think his body would just bounce off me, but it's so big and stupid it doesn't notice. A quick, sharp, clear thought appeared in the midst of my fury: he thinks I'm having sex with him. He thinks this is me joining in.

And I went limp. Just – died. Lay like a fish, dead and limp and nasty. I looked him in the face – his face swaying in some selfish ecstasy against the ceiling. Sarcasm caught me and made me hard and bright. 'OK,' I chirped. 'If that's what you want. Go on then. Don't mind me.' My cheeks stiff with fury, my belly quivering, my voice unspeakable, every word outlined in black sarcasm and hatred. 'Go on,' I said. 'Go on. Since it means so much to you. You just carry on, why don't you.'

And he fell on me, gentle, sweet, stroking and urging, kissing my neck, oh baby, oh *baby*, you know I love you, rolling my limp body around in his arms and heading in to kiss my mouth, as I turned my face away, my head sideways on the pillow. I began to weep, silently, coldly, about the time he started his blind, stupid, delirious, flailing orgasm.

And the next morning, he thought I was his girlfriend.

OK, who else?

That guy in Mumbai who grabbed my tit in the crowd, crying out 'Mrs I want you!'

The far-right Tory who decided because I was blonde and zaftig I'd make him a great Nazi wife, who sent me greetings cards with pictures of Valkyries on and the message written in that zigzag SS-style old German font.

∞

The guy on the boat on Dal Lake who thought because I was on a boat with him he could tear my shirt off. 'But I lent you my jacket,' he said. 'You wore it.'

Every man who shacked up with a woman and swore he loved her and was unfaithful and lied about it.

Every arse who ever said, 'But I want you', in that puzzled way, as if his wanting was the only thing in the world. His wanting delineated the world. He wants me? Then I must be his.

Every controlling bullying man who any woman ever thought she loved.

Every husband who comes on to a woman who is not his wife, assuming – knowing! – that because she's a decent person, she's not going to tell his wife about his proposition. Getting the woman to carry his misbehaviour – so whatever she does, she's somehow in the wrong. Though she didn't do anything. He did.

The dark and brooding man who felt I should have sex with him because his father died young. I said, 'No.' He said, 'Why?' I said, 'Because your wife is pregnant.' He said, 'Oh God don't tell me you're one of the *sisterhood*.' I said, 'If that means I care more about your wife than you do, well yeah, OK.'

∞

When I read *Wuthering Heights*, I wished afterwards I had taken notes and just added up his crimes. I wanted to draw up his charge sheet. Assault, assault, assault. Hanging a dog – because he's in *love*. Interfering with a corpse – two corpses! – because he's in *love*. Assault, assault. Trying to destroy her marriage, he loves her so much. Destroying her chances, he loves her so much. Being a violent controlling drunk, a bully, a narcissist, psychotic, but it's OK because he's in *love*.

I wish I was in his anger management group. I'd give him fucking borderline personality disorder. Not that borderline, is it? I couldn't read it again though, to make notes, for the Recording Angel and the Charge Officer. Too revolting.

And I'd like to be in Emily's creative writing class. Read your sister Anne's book, I'd say. Read a bit of honest truth about nasty men, and women who try to get away. Don't leave us this image and call it love. Sure, Cathy, he loves you. That's why he torments your daughter and kills your sister-in-law's pet and digs up your grave to look at your poor dead face and wants to get his dead body put in between yours and your husband's. That's quite the romantic over-ture, isn't it? What girl could resist? Yes, he was practically the only boy you'd ever met, yes you were only nineteen when you died, but you were a mother—

I'd like to be in your CBT session when they talk about co-dependency. 'I am Heathcliff,' you say. No you're not, love. You're really not.

Listen, when you come tapping on that window whining your Kate Bush lyrics, you'd better be coming for him. Coming to torment him for how he treated your daughter. Because, you know, *she* is yours. Made of the same stuff. *She* is you.

AMULET AND FEATHERS

LEILA ABOULELA

Today I set out to avenge my father's death. I took his dagger, the one with the two points, and I filled a pouch with poison leaves. I put on my brother's clothes and his turban so I would not be recognised. I hid the shells, feathers, and cowries deep in my pocket – I would only need them when I arrived in Gobir. I looped my amulet on a cord and tied it around my neck. I did not feel afraid.

My mother was alone in her room. She would mourn my father for months, not scenting her body or wearing gold. From outside, I heard her praying. She wanted to dream of him, to see how he was in his new life. But he had not yet visited any of us in a dream. I did not go into her room to say goodbye. She would stop me. She would say a young girl had no business travelling beyond the outskirts of town.

In our courtyard, I looked at everything – at one of our goats heavy with kid, our water pots with their reddish-brown colour, and the coop where the pigeons fluttered and cooed. I looked at the ashy remains of yesterday's cooking fire. I picked up my little cat. She knew who I was, she was not fooled. I kissed her and said, 'I will not play with you today or give you milk. Even tomorrow I will still be away.'

In the marketplace, I pulled down the sash that was wrapped around my turban and covered my mouth. I walked fast so that no one would recognise me. I bumped into my friend Aysha, her hair in corn rows. I almost cried out, 'Aysha, you have plaited your hair at last!' But she brushed past me and did not notice who I was.

Bello was buying guava from a seller, but he happened to glance my way. Unlike Aysha, he stopped and looked again. He started to follow me, and I pretended not to hear him. 'Maryam,' he said, 'it's you, isn't it, Maryam?' He looked like the village idiot, gaping and shadowing me.

At last I said, 'Bello, go away and don't tell my family that you have seen me.'

He started to ask one question after the other. 'Where are you going? Why are you dressed like that?'

Bello and I had left the marketplace by now and were at the outskirts of the town. There was hardly anyone around. I stopped under a tree and we sat down. I moved the wrapper from my mouth and said, 'I am going to Gobir to avenge my father's death.'

'But he has already been avenged. The man who killed him was stabbed immediately by your father's men.'

'I know all this,' I said, and started to remember when my heart hurt so much that I couldn't breathe, that bad bad day when my father's body was carried back from the mosque, his robes wet with blood.

I said to Bello, 'Do you know the name of the man who killed my father?'

'Yes, Ibra. He killed your father because in a land dispute your father ruled against him.'

'No,' I said, 'Ibra was sent by someone else.'

'Maryam, you can't know this. You have never set eyes on Ibra or spoken to him.'

'I saw him after he was killed. I went specially to see him.'

'Why?' Bello's eyes were wide.

I did not answer his question because he would not understand. Only my father would have understood because he was the Shehu, and a Shehu could see inside people, he was blessed. People came from far away to consult him because he could answer any question put to him. Sometimes my father made decisions that others didn't understand, but, because they had faith in him, they accepted his judgement. When he betrothed me to Bello, my mother wasn't happy – she complained to her friends, 'He teaches his daughter how to read and write. He takes her with him to the mosque. He says she is the best girl among the Fulani, and then he gives her to Bello!' There was nothing special about Bello. His family were neither skilled, nor high in position. I too was surprised at my father's choice because I had thought my future bridegroom would be a grown man and that I would be in awe of him. Instead Bello was a boy my age.

Now I brushed away his question. 'It does not matter why I wanted to see Ibra's face. What matters is that he told me he was sent by someone else.'

'Oh,' said Bello. 'He woke up from the dead and spoke to you! Maryam, you are not making sense. No one gave Ibra a chance to speak.'

'Don't mock me. Ibra came to me in a dream. He said Hind from the tribe of Gobir sent him to kill the Shehu.'

'Why would she do that?'

'I don't know, but tomorrow I will reach her and find out. And tomorrow I will avenge my father's death.'

It was not easy to get rid of Bello. He wanted to come with me, but at the end I threatened him that I would break off our engagement. He didn't argue with me. He knew it was my right. This was the dowry my father had decided upon – that Bello would give me freedom to do whatever I wanted. 'He is giving you away for nothing,' my mother grumbled. But my father was patient and explained. He said, 'Ambitious, proud men mould women and shape them as they wish. But no man could mould my daughter, he would break her if he tried. She needs someone modest and solid, someone who would encircle her but not come too close.' I understood my father's words, but my mother didn't.

At night I camped near a stream. The moon was yellow and bright. The wind was gentle, and nothing was still, not the grass, not the djinns, nor the tigers and hyenas who breathed and listened. I was not afraid because my amulet with the sacred verses protected me. But I could smell the animals' hunger. The djinns twisted and bounced around me, their breath warm against my face. Because they were so many I felt lonely and small. I missed my father. He was my mentor, and I shall never have that again. An ant bit my foot, and I guessed it was a viper that the amulet had reduced into an ant. 'We can never be fully protected,' my father used to say, 'we belong to this earth and we live by its rules. But prayers and amulets can make a calamity small and soften the blows that fall on us.' So instead of a deadly viper's bite, I had an ant's bite to scratch. Instead of hyenas and vultures, I only heard frogs and bats. All because of my amulet.

When I entered Gobir, I was no longer dressed like a boy. My braids were long on my shoulder, and I displayed my shells, cowries, and feathers. I walked about the market-place, calling out that I had fortunes for sale. People looked at me because I was a stranger, and they smiled their welcome. I found a tent where two hairstylists were plaiting women's hair. While their hair was being pulled and twisted, I tossed shells and read their fortunes in the sand. Soon a lot of women gathered around, pleased with what I was saying. I pretended to study the position of the shells when they fell, how they clustered or separated and which side they lay on – but I was really using my thinking. I could guess at a woman's personality by looking into her eyes. I could feel her anxieties and wishes by the way she sat and the payment she promised. I tossed my shells on the ground, and all the time my ears were ready to hear the name Hind. I was in Gobir, so she could not be far now. I had already spat on the poison herbs, kneaded a paste and smeared it onto the blade of my father's dagger.

Noon came and went, but no one mentioned Hind. I could not accept the Gobirs' hospitality. I could not swallow their food, and their water tasted sour. My mind hurt from making up lies and from the effort of guessing. I sat cross-legged on the ground, encircled by three young girls my age. They giggled as I told their fortune one after the other. They were only interested in who they were going to marry. I touched the shells on the ground and said, 'You will marry one of three brothers – see how these shells are close together – one, two, three.' I made up stories about their future. The silent, beautiful one would travel with her husband across the sea. The strong, fat one would prosper in the marketplace. The one who had a rough voice and was as restless as a boy would one day give birth to many sons. Now she said, grinning, 'There's Hind! Hind, come and have your fortune told.'

I looked up and saw the white light of the sun and the flutter of a large fan made of ostrich feathers. Hind was the most beautiful girl I had ever seen. Out loud I praised the Almighty for creating her and she smiled her thanks, her voice low and pleasant. She looked like she was older than me, her skin was clear, her hair plaited with gold beads. It was when her friends made room for her and she moved to sit down, that I noticed her slanting wary eyes, her nervous manner. Her movements were not smooth. Her head dipped forward as though she was an awkward bird, as if she were ill. I had expected her to be strong and smooth, and that was how she first looked, but now I saw that deep inside her was a kind of weakness that couldn't tell right from wrong. She sat hiding her mouth behind her fan, it made her eyes look bigger. Her turn now to have her fortune told. I shook the shells in my hands and tossed them onto the ground. They didn't cluster together, they broke apart.

'You have blood on your hands,' I said and my voice didn't break. 'You sent a man named Ibra, south to Soketo, to kill the Shehu.'

There was a hush in the gathering. None of the girls contradicted me. They were in awe of what they imagined to be my magical powers. Hind didn't stop fanning herself. I looked at the sway of the black-and-white ostrich feathers, smooth and pretty. In her eyes there was nothing, no guilt or sadness, just nothing.

My head throbbed and I felt sweaty. I blinked, but everything seemed blurred. I caught a vision of that day, when I lost the one I loved most. I saw how it had all happened. There was my father in the mosque just as he was about to lead the prayer. He turned first like he always did, tall and smiling, saying, 'Straighten your lines and stand close. Don't leave gaps for Satan to come between you.' Then Ibra, who was standing in the very front row, stepped forward and stabbed him in the neck.

I heard my voice, careful and soft, 'Tell me, Hind, why you wanted to kill the Shehu.'

She stopped fanning herself and instead held the fan in her lap, stroking each feather. Her voice was almost flirty, and her eyes shone with mischief and pleasure. 'Ibra was courting me. He asked me to set a sum for my bride-price. He was ready to give me everything.' She laughed, and her friends looked at her with admiration. I could imagine Ibra under her spell, wanting her at any cost. She went on, 'But I already had wealth, I told him, give me something more precious than wealth, give me life, not any life, but a mighty life, a life of a chief or a saint or a warrior. Ibra was meant to escape, I didn't want him captured or hurt, but he was stupid. He asked me, "Who should I kill?" I could think of five big men, but I couldn't choose which one. So I gave each a colour . . .' She giggled and shrugged. She was like a little girl describing a game.

'I dyed three of my feathers. I dyed one green and one red and one blue. I left one naturally black and one white. So I had five altogether, five men, five feathers. I put them all in a sack and closed my eyes. I put my hand in the sack and took out one feather. It was the green one – green for the Shehu.'

I stood up and said, 'I am Maryam and I am here to avenge my father's death.' Her mouth fell open but she didn't scream like the others. I reached into my pocket. Hind raised her fan and arms as if to protect herself. The dagger was too light, something was wrong. I raised it, and because it was too light my hand jerked forward. Hind lowered her arms and sighed. I looked at my hand, but instead of a dagger, I was holding a feather. It was as if sunset had come because I couldn't see very well and the cry that came from me didn't sound like my voice. I dropped the feather and ran.

I ran from Gobir, leaving my bag, my shells, even my brother's turban. I cried and kept running. Around me the light was purple and sleepy. I kept running until I reached a forest. I leaned against a tree and vomited, which made my head throb more. Why did my dagger turn into a feather? How could it, when Hind was the one to blame? I heard someone calling my name. It sounded like Bello, but I wasn't sure. I started running again and now it was completely dark. Now the bats came out and the owls. My feet caught on something and I tripped. I fell face forward. There was a pain in my foot, but it was good to lie on the ground. I was ashamed that I had got so close to Hind, heard her confess, and then, just like a weak girl, done nothing. I pressed my face into the dark sand.

I saw my father in his room at home, and knew I was dreaming. But still I felt relieved that he was standing up, tall, smiling, looking only at me. This was what my mother had prayed for – that my father would visit one of us in a dream. And he had chosen me. I wanted to tell him how sad I'd been, but I was so happy to see him. Here he was young in his new world. He was comfortable and laughing. I could hug him and we could sit on the rug in his room and, like in old times, I would ask him one question after another. 'Why did the dagger turn into a feather?'

'Because of your amulet,' he said.

'My amulet protected Hind?'

'No,' he laughed, 'it protected you from the consequences of hurting her. Besides it was my dagger, and a Shehu's dagger mustn't be used for revenge.'

I sat very quiet, knowing this was a dream and I shouldn't wake up. I must make it last as long as I could. He said, 'Why did you go to look at Ibra after he died?'

'Because I wanted to see the face of someone who was going to Hell. But he looked ordinary, just like anyone else.'

'And when you went looking for Hind,' he asked, 'what did you want to see?'

'Evil,' I said, 'I wanted to see the face of evil, and I saw a beautiful girl.'

He paused and then said, 'You will always want to know and learn. This is a good thing. But it is an eye for an eye and a life for a life and my death has already been matched by another's.'

'This is what Bello said. But it is not fair. Hind – how could she! She must be punished.'

'She would have been, if my friends had questioned Ibra instead of silencing him for ever.'

'They were angry,' I said, defending them. No one had ever criticised them, and now he, of all people, was!

'Well,' he went on, 'is anger a good thing?'

'No, because it does not let us see clearly.'

He smiled, and his voice became gentle again. 'I don't want you to be angry Maryam. When we are born, our day of death is already decided and nothing can change it. Every day we live, we are walking towards it. Listen good!'

My foot hurt, but I made myself listen good. He went on, 'If it wasn't Hind and Ibra, it would have been someone or something else. I am well and happy and I want you to be happy for me.'

I woke up in my room. My mother was looking over me. She smiled and kissed me. My foot was wrapped in a bandage. It hurt when I tried to move it. 'You broke your toe,' my mother said, 'don't worry, it will heal. Bello found you near the stream and carried you all the way here. He had been following you all along to keep an eye on you.'

She would start to like him after this. She would agree that he was the best husband for me, the only one who would embrace me without crushing me, who would encircle me without stopping me. Now she wanted me to drink warm milk with honey. Now she wanted me to speak. I told her how I went to Gobir and how I saw Hind. I told her how I did not, after all, avenge my father's death, and how I dreamed of him. How well he looked in my dream, and all the things that he said.

⊰║⊱

HOW THINGS
DISAPPEAR

ANNA JAMES

S HE WAS NINETEEN WHEN she started to disappear, although there had been signs when she was a child.

When she was six her parents took her to hospital, sure that her fingers had not formed properly, only to find they were entirely as expected by the time they reached the waiting room. When she was eight one of her teachers thought, just for a moment, that they had seen her freckles flicker on and off. She herself once thought she caught a glimpse of the colour in her irises fading away, but these things were only in the corner of someone's eye or just as she turned away from the mirror.

When she was fifteen she was convinced, temporarily, that her ribs were vanishing. She was sitting in an exam hall full of copy-and-paste rows of wooden desks and chairs, and copy-and-paste rows of students who were scared or confident or distracted or brave-faced. Just as the invigilator told them to turn over their papers she absent-mindedly scratched her side to discover a gap where her eleventh rib should have been. She dug her fingers deep between her tenth and twelfth without them meeting bone. She tried straightening her back, then curving it over, but however she sat, her eleventh rib proved elusive. *Explore the way Bertha Rochester is presented to the reader in* Jane Eyre *by Charlotte Brontë.* By the time the answer was written, the rib was back, and she assumed she had been mistaken that it ever went away.

'How did it go?' her parents asked her over dinner. 'Was it a question you'd practised before?'

'Near enough,' she said distractedly, thinking about how she didn't really know what ribs were for when it came down to it. She had a vague feeling that maybe they were for protection, but she couldn't remember if they were keeping something in or out, stopping something collapsing or holding something together. 'It was about Bertha.'

Her mother winced.

'Tricky,' her father said. 'She's so open to interpretation. What was the exact question?'

'What are ribcages for?' she asked.

Her parents paused, confused.

'I mean generally, not in *Jane Eyre.*'

'Oh, suddenly she's interested in biology, when she's already decided not to take any sciences next year,' her mother said, and, as usual, it wasn't clear whether she was joking. 'Do you know though, if you get the right results in the summer, maybe the school would let you pick up a science as an extra AS Level,' her mother mused, mainly to herself.

'Did you know,' her father said, 'that people used to think that men had one less rib than women because of the story of Adam and Eve?'

Maybe that's why men were so angry at women, she thought. Maybe that's why they invented corsets, to remind women to be grateful for the rib they had been permitted to keep. Later that night she counted the ribs that laddered down both sides of her chest and found all twenty-four. But for many months the eleventh rib on her left itched from the inside, like a reverse phantom limb, constantly reminding her that it had once thought about leaving.

During her first year of university the nerves inside her splintered, and she realised she should have been taking the disappearing more seriously. It was not until the world took so much of her without asking permission that she wondered if she ought to have protected herself better.

There had been a peg on the bathroom wall that she felt digging into the nape of her neck, and the blunt physical pain took her mind away from the far more complicated pain that was happening elsewhere. They had both been in fancy dress, and her brain had paused to wonder whether his sultan costume was maybe slightly racist. There was a fraction of a second where she nearly laughed that this thought had surfaced, considering the circumstances, but instead she vomited. It was a rich purple colour from the blackcurrant squash that had been mixed with the vodka they were drinking. It was only then that he registered any feeling of disgust, and years later it is still the stab of the peg in the back of her neck, and the repulsion on his face that lingers in her memory. That, and the blood; having to apologise to her housemate whose spare sheet she'd borrowed to fashion into a toga for the night, blaming an early period for the mess. After she'd been sick, the man looked as if he might vomit too, for a second, and as he left, he grabbed a towel and threw it at her. She felt the nerves inside her calcify and shatter where the towel hit her skin. She was given a reputation as a messy drunk, and laughed along any time someone brought that night up. And because the words had not been there when she first needed them, they became buried deep inside her, tangled up somewhere near her liver, which soaked them up before it too started to disappear.

For a long time her outer shell remained sturdy, and only the things inside shimmered into nothingness. She found she was able to register what was happening as if staring at a stranger, and she saw herself as though through a window of air distorted in the heat. There were times when she seized at things or people around her and tried to dig in a foundation, but the roots she set down found only dried mud that crumbled beneath her.

She found herself sitting at a top table in a white dress, a man next to her with a glass raised as people she thought she knew brayed and clinked their glasses in her direction. The light refracted through hundreds of champagne flutes, making her squint, and she flinched again and again as the glasses squeaked and smashed and the voices laughed and cheered and she looked at her hands and realised she could see the veins and the bones and the tendons as if she were looking through tissue paper. Another man stood up and talked about her, and another, and the loveliness of her and her bridesmaids were praised while she turned her hands over and over, fascinated by the blood and the mess inside. The man next to her never commented on her translucent skin, and so she thought he must not mind, but she later realised that he had never noticed.

She found that most people did not like to be reminded that they were made of the same tangle of blue and red that she was displaying. She felt like a patient smoking outside a hospital, attached to a drip, trying to ignore the resentful glances of the apparently healthy walking past. It was men in particular who recoiled from her. Children tended to react with curiosity, having not yet learned the appropriate response to such seemingly unapologetic messiness. With women it was often pity, feeling bad for her that she lacked the required discipline to keep the right things covered, although occasionally there were women who mentioned, so casually, that they thought her veins were lovely things, and did she want to see theirs? Men, on the whole, did not like seeing a woman so obviously made out of the same stuff as them, especially a woman who seemed to insist on displaying it so spitefully. They could see right through her, they said, and knew exactly what she was doing. It occurred to her that the world did not want to know that she bled, but still it wanted her blood.

Her heart did not vanish all at once, and so she did not really notice it happening. When she realised how much of it was missing, and tried to gather up all the jagged shards, she found it had shattered so finely that she could not remember what it looked like whole. A friend offered her a needle, in exchange for borrowing some thread, but the stitches were messy and made as many holes as they healed.

When she was a little older there was a child who did not belong to her but whose small hand took hers in the tea-and-coffee aisle at the supermarket.

'I'm so sorry,' a woman said, running up to her and reclaiming the sticky fingers. 'You know what they're like.'

'Do I?' she said, not meaning to sound as accusatory as she did. She knew the assumption was friendly, but it stuck in her like a fine needle, the entry wound not even visible.

'None of your own?' the woman blustered, disconcerted. 'Oh, but look how young you are. You've got plenty of time yet.'

The child started to shriek, mummy, mummy, and for a second she thought she saw the other woman's collarbone flutter in and out of existence.

'What's your name?' she asked, and the bone reasserted itself hard and sharp in the woman's skin.

Then there was a man who could not stop touching her gossamer skin, and so she showed him all the other things that had disappeared. He offered to take care of the parts that were still clinging on, and she thought maybe giving them to someone else might help, and she let him root around inside her.

He wanted to talk about her skin a lot, and when she told him about her shattered nerves, he liked to talk about that even more. He liked to hear all the details of how each thing had disappeared, and to promise he'd protect her, although she wasn't sure that was what she was asking for. And then later, although she'd already said she didn't really want to, he pawed at her breasts and she watched as they melted beneath his hand that seemed giant and monstrous where it was once tender.

Quite abruptly she realised she should probably claim back the parts of her she had entrusted to him, but he said he couldn't remember being given them, and if she had, he couldn't remember where he had put them, and what could you expect if you gave someone else the responsibility for the things that hold you together.

She did sense other people who were disappearing, but more often than not they weren't real. So, she stitched together the words of other people, in different times and places and worlds, and she made for herself a net that was full of holes, but that held when she tentatively first tried to walk on it. She searched libraries and bookshops for stories of other people who had vanished, and made self-help guides out of novels and poems. Once she had tested her weight on other people's words, she cautiously began to run the threads of her own in between them, weaving them tightly in together. The result was still messy, but it finally started to catch things before they escaped entirely. And so, slowly, she began to try to find the things that had disappeared.

Then there was a man, and when he looked at her she felt the black-and-white etching of her heart flicker into neon, and the scars that joined the broken pieces together pulse and glint. She opened her chest and took out her heart, the bright and precious thing she had rebuilt with bloodied aching hands. She disconnected the veins and the arteries with a careless tug, and it sat in her palm, and she shrugged as if to say, Well what else is there to do? She put it in his hand, gestured towards his chest, at a spot where she thought maybe it could stay for a while. His hand was too tight for a second, and it was as if it was around her throat instead, but then his fingers brushed her skin, each touch like oil in a hot pan. She wondered if his fingers would press too hard on the fault lines and send her heart crumbling again to dust.

But then the light caught it in just the right way, and there was a moment that passed too quickly where she thought she could see stars within, ones that would never have been visible if no cracks had ever been made. Not gently, although not without care, he pushed her heart back inside her own chest. He linked back up the parts he did not know the names of, and clicked her ribcage back into place around it. He put his hand on her cheek and it left a bloody mark there that was almost in the shape of a star.

THE WILDFLOWERS

———

DOROTHY KOOMSON

Saturday, 9.05 a.m.

THE BRAYING AT MY front door is enough to upset everyone down this street, not just my block of flats. I wrap my dressing gown around myself and hurry towards the front door. There'd better be an emergency for someone to be making this much noise on such an idyllic Saturday morning – before it began, I'd been about to open all the windows in the flat to let in the sea air.

'You!' she snarls when she sees me. '*You!*'

Before I can say anything, she raises the object in her hand – a large kitchen knife.

'I told you to stay away from my son. Now look what you've done.'

I should slam the door in her face, run for the phone, and call the police. I can't though, I'm frozen; petrified at what is happening and who is doing this.

'*Get inside,*' she hisses at me.

The blade seems to glint, and I seem to have forgotten how to move. I half expect a neighbour to come out of their flat to see what all the fuss is, but now she's being quieter – speaking in hushed, vicious tones, and no longer hammering – no one is going to come.

'*Get. Inside,*' she repeats and waves the knife for good measure. This time my body remembers how to move and takes a step back and lets in the woman holding a very large knife.

Twelve years ago

I ducked into this small art gallery in the centre of London to escape the rain. It was tipping it down outside, tapping belligerently on the skylights, rapping persistently at the doors and windows.

But I was grateful to the rain, because I had found the most beautiful canvas of wildflowers. A riotous explosion of colours, shapes, lines, paint splatters; all vibrant, alive, so very real . . . And looking at it took me to a field of flowers that grew unfettered, untamed, free.

'Hey,' a male voice said as he came to stand beside me.

I glanced at him and then returned to the painting. 'Hello,' I replied.

'It's my mother's birthday and I was thinking of buying this for her.' He sounded posh, but he was at least ten years younger than me, probably around the twenty-five mark. 'You're a woman, do you think she'd like it?'

I glanced around the gallery and clocked at least three other women more likely to be near his mother's age who he could have asked, but instead he chose me. I turned to face him. 'There are better chat-up lines, you know,' I told him.

Saturday, 9.07 a.m.

After some faffing around, she has 'requested' that I drag a chair over from the dining table in the bay of the window and place it in the middle of the room. That way she can sit on the sofa and watch to see if I make any sudden movements or attempts to escape. She almost collapses onto the sofa, so I'm assuming she has driven all the way down from her lavish country pile up in Yorkshire to confront me.

'Mrs Shibden, what are you doing?' I ask her.

She sits with the knife beside her, her grey-blonde hair a wiry, unruly mess around her head, her eyes out on fierce stalks, her thin lips pressed together in barely contained rage. 'I am doing, Zillah, what I should have done years ago – ridding myself of you once and for all.'

Eleven years ago

I tore off the brown wrapping paper with all the excitement of a woman receiving a first anniversary present from the man she loves. The flowers, our wildflowers, were hidden behind the brown paper.

'Oh my—' I covered my mouth with my hand. I couldn't believe he had done this. Fabian came from an extremely wealthy family, there was no escaping that, but this was too much.

'I couldn't give it to my mother, not when I saw how much you loved it. I promised myself I'd buy it for you if we were still together in a year. It reminds me of the flowers near where my parents live.'

'It's absolutely beautiful,' I said.

'I've been dying to tell you this, Zillah: when I was telling my grandfather about the picture and how I was going to buy it for you for our anniversary, he kept asking about your name and saying how striking it is.'

'That's nice of him.'

'He's brought it up more than once.'

'Maybe he knew someone who had the same name or something?' I replied not making too big a deal of it. Clearly Fabian had no idea about my name (and he hadn't looked it up), but his grandfather did.

'Maybe,' Fabian said.

I hadn't taken my eyes off the picture. Beautiful seemed such an insignificant word for it. And . . . 'I can't accept the picture,' I said to Fabian. 'It cost thousands of pounds. I just can't accept it.'

'All right,' he said, slipping his arms around me, not

fazed by my discomfort. 'How about we keep it here, at your flat, but officially, it stays mine? Will you accept it then?'

'Yes, I will accept it then.' I stood on tiptoes and kissed him. 'I love you.'

His eyes lit up at hearing those words for the first time. 'I love you, too,' he replied.

'Let's hang it in the bedroom so we can sleep each night in a field of wildflowers.'

'And make love there, too.'

Saturday, 9.15 a.m.

Mrs Shibden is glaring at me as though there is not much stopping her from doing me serious harm. No one would believe it if they knew. Mrs Shibden is a 'good egg'. She is involved in her local community: she makes jam for local fairs, she ferries elderly people to and from hospital, she sits on the boards of several charities. She has been in the papers, on the radio, and many television shows, fighting for her largest charity. It empowers girls and women in developing and third-world countries – helping brown-skinned girls to understand that they matter; they can be whoever they want, they can learn whatever they choose, they can love whoever they wish. Unless, of course, one of them happens to be sleeping with her son.

Ten years, six months ago

Fabian's parents' house in the Yorkshire countryside had a long driveway that allowed you to drink in the full, stately magnificence of it during the approach. My car seemed very small as I drove up to the front door. After the sixth request from Mr and Mrs Shibden to visit them without Fabian, I'd finally arranged a business meeting in Leeds so I could drive over to the Shibdens' afterwards.

When they first met me, their faces had become frozen caricatures of the people I'd seen in the photographs around Fabian's flat – horror was painted over with a rictus smile; shock was secreted away behind air kisses. I'd met them twice in two years, so I had a suspicion about why they wanted to see me alone – I was the problem that was not going away.

In the drawing room, Fabian's father stood by the fireplace, his mother sat beside me on the most uncomfortable sofa in the world, and his grandfather sat in a large leather seat between the sofa and the fireplace.

'It is so good of you to come along to visit us,' Mrs Shibden said pleasantly. 'Tell me, how are you getting on with your new clients, Thrushcross Endeavours? I hope they are not being too difficult.'

A creeping sensation wended up my spine, then spiralled down again. I did not talk about my work to anyone outside of the company – I had not told Fabian about Thrushcross

Endeavours. The only way she could know was if they had been checking up on me. This was going to be worse than I thought.

'We both know George Gimmerton, the current CEO of Thrushcross, very well. We maintain a lot of social as well as business contact with him.'

I managed to form a smile and forced myself to nod.

'But we're not here to talk about that,' she said with a genuine, warm smile. 'We're here to talk about when you will remove yourself from our son's life.'

'I'm not planning on finishing with him. I love him,' I replied. Those last three words sounded flimsy, weak. 'I love him,' I repeated to emphasise that my feelings were anything but feeble.

'And what of Douglas Carr, did you love him too?' Mrs Shibden asked.

They *had* been checking up on me. They had been digging through every area of my life if they were bringing up Douglas.

'And what of Kaiden Fincher? You married that one, so I assume you "loved" him also?'

I had made mistakes with the men I'd been involved with, but I wasn't going to let her shame me. We *all* made mistakes. 'I loved them both at different times of my life. What does that have to do with anything?' I said.

'We know all about you, Miss Landry,' Mr Shibden stated. 'We always conduct thorough background checks on the outsiders with whom our children become entangled.'

'If you know all about me, then you know that if you try to intimidate me, I will defend myself.'

'Yes, of course we know that,' Mr Shibden replied.

'Your parents, however . . . Will they be similarly able to defend themselves when scandal after scandal lands on their doorstep?' Mrs Shibden asked. 'And, of course, Thrushcross Endeavours have a decency clause associated with anyone working with them. How will they respond when they discover that the person in charge of their prestigious account has an ex-lover in prison for committing grand larceny? And that she met, married, and divorced a man in less than eighteen months?'

'I guess we'll find out when you tell them,' I replied. I sounded strong and fearless, but it felt like all the air had been sucked out of the room, and that my heart would beat itself out in less than five minutes. I'd had nothing to do with Douglas's crime or conviction; my thing with Kaiden was crazy-fun while it lasted, but they were parts of my past that I could not undo and would not want to undo. None of that had anything to do with Fabian.

'We love our son,' Fabian's father said. 'But we will not stand by any longer as he continues with you. I am grateful to you, Zillah, believe me. You encouraged our son to undertake his Masters degree. No one has been able to do that, except you. But that does not mean we approve or could ever approve of having you in his life.'

'What are you saying?'

'We are saying . . .' Mrs Shibden's look around the room encompassed not only her husband, the serious-looking ancestors watching from picture frames on the wall, but also Fabian's grandfather, 'we are saying that should you continue to be involved with our son, we will have no choice but to cut all contact with him.

'His siblings will be warned that if they see him we will cut them off without any financial support, and we will not have him at any of our family gatherings. Until you are out of his life, he will no longer be a part of our lives.'

'You would do that? To your own son?'

'For his own good.'

'For his own good,' Mr Shibden echoed.

Fabian would be devastated by this. He could survive without his family, but it would break his heart to know what they were truly like. He saw the world through rose-tinted glasses, and knowing this about the people he loved would destroy him. And our relationship would never be the same – instead of fun and laughter and joy and sharing, we would be forever ignoring the reality of what our togetherness had done to the people around him. I didn't want him or us to suffer like that.

Fabian's grandfather suddenly shifted forwards in his chair, as though finally ready to impart a great secret. His lips parted and he said something.

'Pardon, Father?' Mrs Shibden said loudly. 'What was that?'

I had heard what he said, and it sounded like, 'I am Heathcliff.'

'He doesn't know what he's saying,' Mr Shibden stated dismissively.

Grandfather Fabian flopped back in his seat. 'I am Heathcliff,' he mumbled again before shutting his eyes and seeming to fall asleep straight away. He must have remembered my name and its connection to *Wuthering Heights*. Probably all he recalled about me from what his grandson had told him.

'Please cooperate,' Fabian's mother said, not unkindly.

'Allow our family to move on from this unpleasantness,' his father continued. 'End things after he has completed his final examinations.'

'You want me to string him along for three more months and *then* finish with him?' I replied.

'If you love him, you will want nothing to disrupt his studies,' his mother replied.

If I didn't love him, I wouldn't be here now, would I? I thought.

I left without saying another word to them.

Saturday, 9.35 a.m.

Mrs Shibden springs forward suddenly, brings the knife dangerously close to my throat. I draw back in my seat. Is this it? Is this the moment she will do it? 'Tell me. Tell me why he did it. Tell me!'

Ten years, three months ago

Fabian smoked the cigarette right down to the edge of the filter, dragging every last molecule of nicotine from its fibres before he stubbed it out on the stone step. 'Why?' he asked.

My gaze strayed to the ring of grey-black he had scorched into the stone of the steps leading up to my flat – something to remember him and this moment by.

'It's not working,' I said. I was disgusted with myself. I'd had three months to come up with a proper answer to this question, and that was the best I could do? Pitiful. 'I mean, if you're honest with yourself, it isn't working.'

He gave a small, almost soundless snort through his nose. 'Not working.' He reached inside his jacket pocket and when he withdrew his hand, it was clenched around a dark-blue suede cube. Excitement and nausea hit the back of my throat at exactly the same time. He turned his palm towards me, his hand uncurled. The other hand reached over and opened the hinged lid. 'Not working,' he repeated.

Inside the box was a platinum band with a line of diamonds interspersed with emeralds – emeralds, the birth-stone for May, my birth month.

'Things aren't working so much, I had this made. And I planned to propose to you at my granddad's eightieth birthday party tomorrow night. I've been carrying it with me for courage.' He looked at me then, his eyes hard, his face harder. 'But you think it's not working. Right?'

I had to glance away from his accusatory gaze and stare

at the houses opposite instead. 'What happened today, Fabian?' I asked after a few seconds.

'Apart from you telling me it was over?'

'Yes, apart from that.'

'I had my last exam for my course,' he replied.

'And instead of being out with your friends, celebrating one of the best days of your life, you're here, with me.' I pointed to my dressing gown, my pyjamas underneath. 'It's not even nine thirty, and I'm in my nightwear, ready for bed. Compared to your friends, I am old, and I am holding you back. You need to go out, enjoy yourself.'

'Why are you saying these things? The age difference doesn't matter, none of the differences between us matter. We love each other, that's all that counts.'

'Do you know how young and naïve you sound? The world doesn't work like that. On the surface most people are tolerant, but scratch a little of that top coating off and things get "complicated", people "yeah, but" your feelings and situations. I've had enough of living with differences.'

'What if I haven't?' he replied.

We rarely talked about this, but it was there. Always. It walked with us every step of the way, it sat with us when we were together, it watched us as we made love. His parents had been more blatant about it than most, but people in his circle often dropped unsubtle hints that they couldn't see what Fabian and I had in common; people in my circle often acted as though I was betraying myself by choosing someone like him. We lived in the modern world, and people were still hung up on differences, status, wealth, appearance. But for two years, that hadn't mattered. For nearly twenty-four months we had lived in a glorious bubble, and now it had to burst.

'Is there someone else?' he asked.

I stared at him and did not speak. I should say 'yes'. *Yes, there's someone else, he's exactly like you, but the world around us is a different place so we can be together without problems.* My silence seemed to be confirmation that there was someone else.

Fabian's hand curled around the ring box, his face crumpled. 'How long has it been going on for?'

'Does it matter?'

'Do you love him?'

'Again, does it matter, if we're over?'

'Zillah, I can't believe—'

He got to his feet, unceremoniously shoved the closed box into his left-hand pocket.

'I'm sorry,' I said. I couldn't stand how much I'd hurt him. 'I'm so sorry.' He was about to leave, and the shock of that winded me. But I had to say something to keep him with me a little longer. 'Do you want the "Wildflowers" back?' I asked.

He looked at me, the hurt gushing out of him, and shook his head. He walked stiffly down the stairs and turned towards the sea end of my road.

I sat on the steps for a long time after he had walked out of my life.

Saturday, 9.40 a.m.

'Has something happened to Fabian?' I ask Mrs Shibden. That could be the only reason why she would be behaving like this – she has lost something precious and it has broken her. My heart slows down at the thought of something happening to him.

'No!' she barks. 'Because of you, something has happened to me!'

Two weeks ago

My mobile bleeped with a text message from my best friend, Lawrence. He was in his sweats, eating pizza and drinking beer on *my* sofa, regularly updating me on the evening I could have had if I hadn't had to sit through the world's longest awards ceremony. Everyone at my table who'd suffered through the evening with me had gone either to dance or to get more drinks.

'Hey. I'm thinking of getting a picture for my mother's birthday . . .' a voice said to me.

Fabian? Fabian!

I was half out of my seat, ready to throw my arms around him and greet him like a long-lost friend when I noticed the woman standing beside him. His wife.

She had the biggest, fakest smile I had ever seen on a real-life human. Her eyes were like flint, and she had her fingers clamped through his fingers, staking her claim.

'Hello, Zillah, it's good to see you,' he said. He had aged well. The ten years had made him seem more solid, more comfortable in his body. He wore a beard, he'd grown his hair, he stood with the demeanour of a proper grown-up.

'You too. What are you doing here?'

'Alice was up for an award,' he said. 'She's a young entrepreneur.'

'Congratulations on the nomination,' I said to Alice. 'Sorry you didn't win.'

'Thanks,' she replied with a thin smile. I had seen photos of them on their wedding day in the society pages of a magazine. Fabian Effram Shibden III and his 'princess' married less than eighteen months after I broke up with him. Their wedding had been lavish enough to rival a royal affair – celebrities, politicians, top business people were in attendance. The ceremony and reception were held at the Shibden family home. The bride wore an ivory princess gown and a diamond tiara, both designed especially for her; the bridegroom grinned like he had never been happier; the ex-girlfriend sat in her flat in Brighton, knowing their day would have been small and discreet, a registry office, a few friends for drinks afterwards, and absolutely one of the best days of her life.

'I, um, I was just leaving,' I said and grabbed my clutch bag and phone. 'I hope you enjoy the rest of your evening.'

'We will,' Alice replied. She moved closer to her husband, slipped an arm around his waist, almost automatically he slipped an arm around her shoulders, kissed the top of her head. The gut-wrench of that one little move, their short-hand for saying 'I love you' in front of other people, was like being driven through with a pickaxe.

'Are you driving?' Fabian asked.

'Yes,' I replied. 'Too long a journey to get a taxi.'

'You still live in Brighton, then?'

I nod. 'S—'

'Drive safe,' Alice cut in, obviously wanting me gone.

'Thank you,' I replied.

I used my dignity to prop me up, to force one leg to move and then the other, to keep my head raised, my shoulders back, and my breathing deep and even. I walked out of the ballroom, my steps picking up pace as I moved across the polished marble floor of the reception area. My heels clacked against the floor; the sound a *rat-tat* of the past knocking for me, telling me it was time for us to face each other.

Outside the hotel, my footsteps moved faster. And faster.

Faster and faster, until I was almost running across the dark car park, weaving around other vehicles, heading for my car. I needed to get to safety, to shut myself away from the world before the tears caught up with me.

I didn't cry ten years ago – I held myself together, the pragmatism and resignation to the way the world *really* worked shored up my weaker parts, keeping tears and outward hurt in check. I was strong, I was capable, I'd simply ended a relationship like millions of people do all over the world. Nothing unusual, nothing special, I'd just had to get on with it.

I threw myself into the driver's seat as the first howl, from deep inside, ripped its way out of me and shattered the stillness inside safety. I curled forwards and gave in to another wail of grief. It hurt. It'd hurt for so many years, and I'd been ignoring the pain, carrying on through the anguish, not allowing myself to feel even a sliver of the agony. *I loved him, I loved him, I loved him.*

I clung to the steering wheel, an anchor, something solid to stop me completely breaking apart.

I love him, I love him, I love him.

Saturday, 9.45 a.m.

'I knew you were trouble the second I saw you.'

I say nothing because I do not understand any of this.

'You have taken everything from me. My son. My money. *My* money. Do you know how long I had to suffer that old fool? I ran around after him, bent myself to his every whim, and all for nothing. *Nothing.*'

'What are you talking about? *Who* are you talking about?' I ask.

'My father-in-law! Fabian senior. I even named my only son after him. I HATED that name. But I knew, if I didn't, he would cut us out of his will. We always had to do what he wanted because otherwise it would mean being cut out of his will. He controlled my whole life.'

'You used Fabian losing his family to get me to do what you wanted,' I remind her. 'Isn't that the same thing?'

'Of course it isn't!' she screeches.

'Why? Because when you do it, it's fine, when someone does it to you, it's wrong?'

'You did not fit in with our family.'

'But Alice does?'

'Of course she does! She is from the right background, the right stock. *Everything* you are not.'

'If you've got the perfect daughter-in-law, what is your problem? Why are you here acting like some kind of wannabe serial killer?'

'Don't pretend you don't know.'

'I'm not pretending – I don't know. *Why are you here?*'

'Fabian senior cut us out of his will. We do not get a single penny.' She speaks slowly, carefully, venomously, so I can understand her.

'Oh.'

'Everything. *EVERY. THING.* Has been taken away from us. We are not even allowed to live in or take things from the house now he's dead.'

'He's passed away?' I ask. 'Oh no. That's sad to hear. Fabian loved his grandfather.'

'Yes, he's dead all right. And he has left his son and me destitute. We have fourteen days to vacate the property. The old bastard even had two psychiatrists certify that he was of sound mind before he changed his will, so it is water-tight. No grounds for appeal, apparently.'

Wow, he *really* screwed them over. 'I don't understand your problem. He obviously left it all to Fabian and your

other children. It shouldn't be too hard to convince them to
let you stay in the house. Your children love you, I'm sure
they'll share the money with you.'

'*What are you talking about?*' she screeches, brandishing
the knife. 'He left everything to you!'

Two weeks ago

I calmed down, pulled myself together, and changed my
shoes, ready for the long journey home. As I was driving
away, I saw Fabian standing at the hotel entrance, hands
in pockets as though waiting for me to drive by.

Saturday, 9.50 a.m.

I laugh in her face.

She has got to be joking! He wanted me out of Fabian's
life just as much as his parents, so why would he do something like that? 'Why on earth would he do that?' I ask.

'Because "he is Heathcliff". Whatever that means! That
was all it said in the letter. "I am Heathcliff."'

That was what he said that day they pushed me to leave
Fabian: I am Heathcliff. It'd crossed my mind over the
years, but I could never really work out why he'd said it at
that moment.

'Are you wanting me to sign all the money back to you?'
I query.

She waves the knife back and forth. 'Oh, no, no, no. In

the event of you being unable or unwilling to take on the responsibility of *my* money and *my* estate, the money will go straight to my main charity, and the estate will be sold, and all proceeds will support the local children's homes in the area.'

'Well that's something,' I say diplomatically. I'm pretty impressed by how comprehensively Fabian senior has stitched up his son and his wife.

'Is it?' she snarls. 'Is it really?'

I suppose to her, facing destitution after a lifetime of luxury, it isn't 'something' at all.

She comes closer to me, the knife millimetres from my nose. 'You seem to be enjoying this just a little too much—'

I knock the knife out of her hand, then follow it up with an uppercut punch to make sure she doesn't go for the knife again. I'm not at all violent – unless I need to defend myself.

Unsurprisingly, Mrs Shibden has a glass jaw. She goes down like a lead balloon, and lies sprawled on the living-room floor, out cold. I know I should rush to the door, fling it open, and scream for help, but I need a minute or two. I lower myself into my seat again and try to gather myself together.

Saturday, 12.35 p.m.

My dear.

I sat at that meeting and remembered exactly how I felt when I was first brought to this house. A small boy

230

who was never to fit in amongst all the pomp and finery.
I stuck out, I was different, I was meant for something
lesser but Fate had intervened. I swore never to feel less
than; never to allow a person to feel less than. You see,
my dear, I am Heathcliff. I am the young, orphaned child
brought to wealth, educated, feted, reared in luxury –
and yet reminded every day how lowly I was thought to
be. I am the young child who knew no matter what, I
would never be accepted into the higher echelons of
society. Money would not allow me to become one of
them. I would never truly belong. I have managed to
create a pleasing façade, over the years. The memories of
those who you come up with fade, the newer generation
is dazzled by wealth and not so much by status.

I am Heathcliff. I fought for a position in this higher
society, but in all of it, forgot who I truly am. In all of
this, the slow transition to acceptance, I had forgotten my
vow: to not allow another person to feel less than. I failed.

I have kept my eye on you, all these years.
I have watched you continue your rise up the ranks, I
have seen how you never seem to treat others as less
than anyone else. My son, his wife, they have always felt
inferior, but have always felt entitled to the very best. I
intend to change this. Upon my death, I am bequeathing
to you all of my wealth, accumulated and inherited. I
know you will do great things with it. I am sorry I did
not stand up for you when I should have. I am sorry for
all the hurt you felt.

I hope you will, one day, find it in your heart to forgive me.

Fabian Effram Shibden, Snr

Fabian sits beside me on the steps outside my building while I read and re-read the letter from his grandfather. Fabian had been on his way here to deliver it, when he was confronted with his conscious and incensed mother being carted away in a police car.

He'd gone to the police station to be with her – until he heard a list of her crimes. Then he'd come straight back to check I was OK.

'Wow,' I say to him for about the twentieth time. 'I'm, like, a gazillionaire.'

'Yes, Zillah, you are,' he says as patiently as he has said it the first nineteen times. 'What are you going to do with it all?'

'Give it to charity and the children's homes like he wanted.'

'Are you sure?'

'Yes. He was right, money doesn't change who you fundamentally are. You can be the richest person in the world and still feel inferior.'

'True.'

'Although I will give some of it to my family, they could do with a bit of respite.'

We fall into silence for a few minutes. We haven't been

able to talk properly since he arrived back – too much to say, too much emotion to know where to begin. Eventually, Fabian breaks our awkwardness with: 'In his letter explaining everything to me, Grandpa told me what they did – my parents, him. The choice you were forced to make. He said you stood up to them in a way he'd never seen anyone fight back before. He also told me to grow a spine and marry you.'

'Shame you can't remind him that you're already married.'

'I'm not. Alice and I were divorced last year. Marry in public, divorce in private.'

'So what was all that stuff about at the awards? She was on the verge of fighting me.'

'We're still the best of friends. She knows all about how you broke my heart. She's very protective.'

'I don't believe you,' I say to him. He wouldn't be the first married man to tell tall tales.

'I hoped you might say that,' he replies, and reaches for his inside pocket. 'Exhibit one, divorce papers.'

'You brought your divorce papers?'

'How else could I make you believe me?' He removes his mobile from another pocket, plays around with it until he produces a wedding picture of two women in bridal gowns. 'Exhibit two, Alice on her second wedding day with her wife.'

'Wow,' I say.

'And exhibit three . . .' Fabian kisses me.

Our lips linger on the kiss, the sound of the sea gently playing in the air around us; very soon, I know, we'll be making love under our field of wildflowers.

HEATHCLIFF
IS NOT MY NAME

———

MICHAEL STEWART

YOU ARE WALKING THROUGH Butcher's Bog, along the path at Birch Brink. You traipse across Stanbury Moor, to the Crow Stones. A morass of tussock grass, peat wilderness and rock. There are no stars to guide you, just the moaning of the wind. Stunted firs and gaunt thorns, your only companions.

Perhaps you will die out here, unloved and unhomed. There was the tale of Old Tom. Last winter, went out looking for a lost lamb. Found a week on, icicles on his eyelids, half-eaten by foxes. Or was it the last wolf? Said to roam these moors. The ravens will eat out your eyes and the crows will pick at your bones. The worms will turn you into loam. You've forgotten your name and your language. Mr Earnshaw called you 'it' when first he came across you. Mrs Earnshaw called you 'brat' when first she took you by the chuck. Mr Earnshaw telt to call him father and Mrs Earnshaw, mother, but they were not your real parents.

Starving when they took you in. They named you after their dead son. The man you called your father, carried you over moor and fell, in rain and in snow. When finally you got to the gates of the farm it was dark and the man could hardly stand. He took you into the main room and plonked himself in a rocker. By the fire you stood, a ghost in their home. Next to you a living girl and living boy, who spat and kicked. This was their welcome to your new hovel. Over ten years ago now. You'd spent weeks on the streets, eating scraps from bin and midden. Kipped by the docks and ligged in doorways. You'd trusted no one, loved no one, believed in nothing.

It was tough in the new place but you'd had it worse. You'd almost died many times. You'd been beaten inside an inch of your life. Gone five days without food. Slept with rats and maggots. Nothing this new place had in store could harm you more than you'd been harmed before. Or so you thought. The girl was called Cathy, the boy Hindley, and you hated them apiece.

Over ten years ago. But you can still feel her hot spit on your face, and his boot in your groin. None of it ever hurt you as much as her words. Words that cut to the bone. Words that stab you in the back.

You stand on top of the Crow Stones on the brink of the wilderness. It is said that the stones were used for ritual sacrifice. The slit throat of a slaughtered goat. The gushing blood of a lamb seeping into the craggy carpet beneath your feet. The wind tries to blow you off your perch. Blow harder.

You are the goat, the lamb, you care not for sacrifice. Let them take you. Let them bleed you. Fuck the lot of them.

For two years your adopted father tried to protect you from Hindley. From his maniac beatings, with fist and boot and club. Sometimes it worked. Until your adopted mother died and your father retreated into himself. The jutting stones of your adopted home were fitting symbols. The grotesque carvings and crumbling griffins were your companions. But not now. Walking without direction. It doesn't matter where you go as long as you go away from that place of torture, that palace of hate.

They called you dark-skinned gypsy, dirty Lascar, vagabond, devil. You'll give them dark, dirt, devil. Cathy wanted a whip. Hindley a fiddle. You'll give her whip, him fiddle. You took a seat at the end of the hearthstone. Petted a liver-coloured bitch. There was some warmth in the room and it came from an open fire. Flames that licked, peat that steamed, coals that glowed, and wood that hissed.

Hindley called you dog and beat you with an iron bar. Mr Earnshaw tried once more to stop him. He sent Hindley to college, just to get the maniac away. And things picked up for a while. Then you watched your father die, watched the life drain from his eyes, his last breath leave his lips. You knelt at his feet and wept. You held on to his lifeless hand, the skin as brittle as a wren's shell. Cathy wiped the tears from your eyes. Hindley came back from the funeral with a wife. She was soft in the head and as thin as a whippet. Always coughing her guts up. Things got bad again.

Banished from the house, set to work outside, in the pissing wind and whirling rain. You were flogged, locked out, spent your evenings shivering in a corner while that cunt stuffed his face, supping ale and brandy. Eating and drinking, singing and laughing with his slut.

The wind has lulled now and you listen to its hush. You hear a fox scream and an owl cry. The night gathers in pleats of black and blue. The cold rain falls. You teeter on the brink. It would be so easy to tumble and smash your skull on the rocks. Let the life bleed out of the cracks and let the slimy things take you. No one would miss you. Not even you. The only thing that is real is the hardness of the rock and the pestilent air that festers. You could dive head-first onto the granite. Dead in an instant. Released from the teeth of experience.

You think about the Lintons that day, when they came to visit. Supping mulled ale from silver mugs. You were a stain on their polished tray. You were the muck on their well-scrubbed floor. Leave them to it. You had turned your back on them and gone inside to feed the beasts. Fuck 'em. Fuck the rotten lot. Spoke to no one except the dogs. And when they had all gone to church, you went onto the moor. Fasted and thought. Had to turn things round. Had to get Cathy back.

You came in through the kitchen door, went to Nelly and said, 'Make me decent.' You were younger than Edgar but taller and twice as broad. Could knock him down in a twinkle.

You wanted light hair and fair skin. Nelly washed and combed your curls. Then she washed you again. But she couldn't wash the black off your face. Then you saw them, descending from a fancy carriage, smothered in furs. Faces white as wealth. You thought you'd show them that you were just as good as them and you opened the door to where they were sitting. But Hindley pushed you back and said, 'Keep him in the garret. He'll only steal the fruit.' How ashamed you'd felt that day. How cold and lonely you'd been in that garret with just the buzzing of the flies for company.

That cunt Edgar had started, saying your hair was like the hair of a horse. You'd grabbed a bowl of hot sauce and flung it in the cunt's face. Edgar had screamed like a girl and covered his face with his hands. Hindley grabbing hold of you, dragging you outside. Punched you in the gut. When you didn't react, he went for the iron weight and smashed it over your back. Go down. Kicking you in the ribs. In the face. Stomping on your head. Then he got the horse whip and flogged you till you passed out.

Cold stone slabs. When you had woken the next day from Hindley's flogging, you discovered that he'd locked you in the shed. Aching all over, bruises everywhere, caked in dried blood. It wasn't the first time he'd beaten you sense- less, nor was it the first time he'd shoved you in the shed. You could cope with the beatings, and the cold stone flags for a cushion, but the humiliation still stung like a fresh wound. A razor's edge had a kinder bite. You could hear them in the house. There was a band playing, trumpets and horns, clatter and bang. You could hear them chatting and laughing as you lay in the dark, bruised and battered. Your whole body a dull ache and a sharp pain. You swallowed and tasted the metal of your own blood. How to get the cunt? You didn't care how long it took. Didn't care how long you had to wait. As long as he didn't die before you did. And if you burned in hell for all eternity it would be worth it. At least the flames would keep you warm and the screams would keep you company. Kicking the cunt was not enough. He must suffer in every bone of his body and in his mind too. His every thought must be a separate torture. He must have no peace, waking or asleep. His whole life, every minute of every hour of every day must be torture. Nothing less would do.

You think back to the day his slut gave birth to a son. She was ill, crying out in pain, and it was such joy to watch Hindley suffer. That week, as she lay dying, the cunt was in agony. How you laughed behind Hindley's back. Thank you God, you said under your breath, or thank you Devil. You'd prayed to both, not knowing which would hear you first. All your prayers were answered. You knew what Hindley loved the most and it was his slut. You knew what would hurt the cunt the most – the slow painful death of his slut.

The doctor's medicine was useless. Your spell was stronger. Your anti-medicine had worked. You watched her cough and splutter. Watched her chuck up blood. Watched the life drain from her face. Watched the wretched slut die in front of the cunt. You went to the funeral so you could observe his agony some more. How you'd wanted to laugh when they'd lowered the coffin into the ground and tears had rolled down his cheeks. Each tear was a sugared treat. And afterwards in the church hall, he was inconsolable. The curate had patted him on the back, said he was sorry for his loss, and offered him some brandy. But Hindley was unreachable in his grief. Only you knew how to reach him. Later that night you'd put your ear to his chamber door and listened to him sob. Sweet music.

Hareton was the bairn. The fruit of Hindley and the slut's union. Cathy was fifteen, all curves and skin. You taunted Hindley so that he beat you. Called his bairn a witless mooncalf. And you laughed when he fired and lost his temper. So that his beating brought no satisfaction. Fuck the lot of them: Isabella, Edgar, Hareton, Hindley. You'll make them pay. Make them all suffer. They called you vulgar, called you brute. But they had no inkling of the depths of your brutality.

You remember another night as black as this. Your love had lost her shoes in the bog beneath Whitestone Clough. You crept through a broken hedge, groping your way up the path in the dark, planting yourselves on a flowerpot, under the drawing-room window. They hadn't put the shutters up and the light poured out. You clung to the ledge and peered in. It was carpeted in crimson and there were crimson-covered chairs. A shining white ceiling fretted with gold. A shower of glass drops hanging on silver chains, shimmering. It was Edgar and his sister Isabella. She was screaming, shrieking as if witches were ramming red-hot needles in her eyes. Edgar was stood on the hearth weeping. In the middle of a table sat a little dog, shaking its paw and yelping. They were crying over that dog, the silly cunts. Both had wanted to hold it and neither had let the other do so. You laughed, you and Cathy. They were like toy dogs themselves, all prim and prettified. Milksopped and mollycoddled.

They stopped yelping. They must have heard you laugh. Then Edgar saw you at the window and started shouting. You ran for it, but they'd let the bulldog loose, a big bastard with a big bastard head and it had got Cathy by the ankle. It sunk its bastard teeth in and wouldn't let go. You got a stone and thrust it between its bastard jaws, crammed it down its bastard throat, throttled that bastard dog with your bare hands. Its huge purple tongue was hanging half a foot out of its mouth, and blood and slaver dripped from its lips.

Then there was a servant running towards you. A big bear of a man. He grabbed Cathy and dragged her in. You followed him. Mr Linton was running down the hallway shouting, 'What is it?' The man grabbed you inside too and pulled you under the chandelier. Mr Linton was looking over his spectacles. Isabella said, 'Put him in the cellar.' 'That's Mr Earnshaw's daughter,' said another. 'Her foot is bleeding.' You cursed the servant, swore like a trooper. He dragged you into the garden, threw you on the grass, then went back to the house and locked the door behind him.

You went to the window again. Thought about smashing it in. She was sitting on the sofa. A servant brought a bowl of water. They took off her shoes and stockings. They washed her feet. They fed her cake. Edgar stood and gawped. They dried her wild hair and combed it sober. They wheeled her to the fire. The Lintons stood there staring.

You should shelter. Soaked to the bone and shivering, teeth chatter in your skull. You think about a nook beneath Nab Hill where the earth is soft and the rocks block the wind. It was the first place you and Cathy fucked. She took hold and put you inside her. Her white thighs astride your black hips. Your teacher, your lover, your sister, your mother. She was all you needed in the world. The rest could go to hell.

She stayed at Thrushcross Grange for five weeks. Till Christmas. Hardly knew her when she returned. Turned up on a black pony, hair all done up, wearing a fancy hat with a feather in the ribbon. Even her speech was altered. She was dressed in a silk frock. You felt ashamed of your appearance, felt dirty. Your hair was coarse and uncombed. She said you looked grim and laughed in your face. You couldn't stand to listen to that laugh, couldn't stand to be so black next to one so white. You ran out of the room, burning with shame. Your flesh was a fire of disgust. The next day the Lintons were invited to the house. You were banished to the outbuildings. They called you dog, called you devil. You'll give them dog, give them devil.

Your thoughts are jumbled. They whir like the storm

around you. They make a flaysome din in your skull. Shelter. There's a cave under Penistone Crags. A roof over your head. A hole to lig in. Get out of the storm. Where are you? Somehow you are lost. The moor so familiar, but you don't recognise the landscape. You make out black shapes, skeletal outlines of withered hawthorns. Whinstone and mud. The ground keels. You are somewhere. You are nowhere. You are here. The night is as black as your shame, as black as your face. You are wandering like a blind man. You don't know anything any more. Not what's up. Not what's down. You don't know who you are, where you came from. You don't even know your own name.

ONLY JOSEPH

SOPHIE HANNAH

'So you're actually going to do it,' says Rich. 'You're taking Kitty for a taster day at a school where a female pupil was murdered.' He's using the same tone he used the other day to say, 'I can't clean the outside bin, it's too disgusting. There are maggots in it. I haven't got the right equipment. It needs a professional.' While he complained at length, I whipped out my phone and found a local wheelie-bin cleaner and everything was sorted that same day.

This latest complaint is harder to deal with. I doubt I'd find anything online about how to handle taster days at schools with unsolved murders in their recent history, or husbands who don't like the idea of them.

'Why do you say "a female pupil", as if Kitty's at greater risk because of her sex? There's no reason to think that's true.'

'How do you know? A girl got pushed out of a window, Sonia. To her death. A talented, clever, attractive girl –

like Kitty. She was fourteen when she died. That's how old Kitty'll be in September. Two years on and still no-one's got a clue who murdered Lucy Ross. What if the killer's got a thing for pushing teenage girls out of windows and he's just waiting for the next suitable victim to come along?'

I want to tell Rich he's being ridiculous but I can't, which makes his words more irritating. What he fears is within the bounds of possibility. Just about.

'If you want me to cancel the taster day, just say so,' I tell him. 'Don't put all the responsibility on me. Say, "On no account will I allow my daughter to go to that school."'

'I can't do that, can I? It's not only up to me. You say The Morrow's amazing for performing arts, and their anti-bullying—'

'God, this is what I can't stand! Make up your mind: either you're worried Kitty might get murdered or you aren't. If you are, you shouldn't care about the brand new state-of-the-art theatre they've just built. Keeping Kitty safe is paramount, right? Dead girls can't star in musical theatre extravaganzas.' *Careful. Don't give him the perfect form of expression for a sentiment you don't want him to express.* 'Look, Rich, I'm not saying it's ideal. Obviously I'd rather no one had been murdered at The Morrow, but we've got to be rational, not hysterical. I mean, we live in London! Think how many people have been murdered here over the years. Probably more than in any other part of the UK, but we don't go round thinking it's going to happen to us.'

'Until we decide to send Kitty to a school where there's a killer prowling the corridors. And then we do.'

'What's the alternative, if we don't send her to The Morrow?' I prepare, for at least the twentieth time, to lay out the facts. 'I've contacted every half-decent school within commuting distance. The Morrow's the only one with a place—'

'Hey, if they didn't have a place available for Kitty, they could always create one by pushing another student out of a third floor window,' Rich quips.

'They get brilliant results, their music and drama departments are world class and that's no exaggeration – and music and drama are the only subjects Kitty gives a shit about. And they've offered us a bursary, they're so keen to have her. Rich, Lucy Ross's murder – and it wasn't even definitely a murder, remember? It could have been an accident—'

'No, it couldn't.'

'It was two years ago. No one's—' I stop, but it's too late.

'No one's been murdered at The Morrow since then? Is that what you were going to say? Well . . . brilliant! What's "We only murder a pupil once every three years" in Latin? That could be the official school motto.'

I exhale slowly. Then I say, 'A taster day is only a visit. I partly agree with you. I *mainly* agree with you, much as I don't want to. We probably won't send Kitty there – though God knows where she'll end up instead. But, Rich, she can't stay at Vinery Road. We have to get her away from Philip Oxley. The nightmare's lasted too long. None of us can take much more.'

I feel as if I've used an illegitimate tactic, though Rich and I have never formally agreed that we won't mention the boy we both wish didn't exist. We usually refer to 'the problem' or 'the issue'.

Now it feels as if Philip Oxley is in the room with us, making it darker and heavier.

'I know', Rich says with a shudder. He hates hearing the name as much as I hate saying it. Even thinking about its owner makes me feel as if I might throw up. Rich turns away, and I wonder if his cartoon-like fears of a murderer on the prowl at The Morrow are a comforting distraction for him. His true terror might be the same as mine: that we will never be able to get Kitty away from Vinery Road; that she will be trapped in a classroom with Philip Oxley for another four years.

The Morrow is an independent day school in Hampshire with extensive grounds and beautiful gothic buildings of pale-grey stone. From the look of it, there might be as many mullioned arch-topped windows as there are students. The head teacher, Dr Nina Adebayo, is a stocky, muscular woman in her mid-forties with short, no-nonsense hair. She's wearing a red trouser-suit with a white blouse and red high-heeled shoes. She takes me to her office for a chat, once we've dropped Kitty off with her possible future form teacher and classmates.

'I'm sorry you've had such a terrible experience at Kitty's present school,' she says, handing me a mug of tea. 'I'll be frank with you: we get a lot of children coming here whose original schools couldn't quite cut the mustard on the pastoral-care front. It's one of The Morrow's great strengths.'

I imagine what Rich would say to that if he were here.

'Vinery Road's a great school,' I say, though it's an effort to produce the words. I don't really believe them any more. No school that can't adequately protect its pupils from extreme distress should ever be called great. 'I'm not sure it's their fault that they couldn't do anything,' I tell Dr Adebayo. 'The boy in question . . . none of his behaviour falls into the categories listed as bullying in their anti-bullying policy. According to him, he simply likes Kitty and feels a special affinity with her – one based on nothing. They've barely spoken. He claims all he wants is to be friends with her and make sure she's okay. And that leads to him staring at her all day long, hovering near her, sending her messages saying she's all that matters to him. Sitting there silently weeping at his desk when she speaks to other people – and not only boys. Even girls, even if all she's saying is, "Chloe, pass me that ruler,"' I add bitterly. 'It's got so bad that Kitty's having panic attacks every day, not sleeping much more than three hours a night. She's paralysed with terror that something she might do could make him try to kill himself.'

I hear Rich's voice again in my mind: *Stop, Sonia. If you go too far, you'll lose sympathy.* The truth is that I would love nothing more than for Philip Oxley to commit suicide, as long as Kitty didn't blame herself for it. I don't care if that makes me a terrible person. My most urgent wish is for that boy to not exist.

'He's never unkind, and he falls into the category of vulnerable, protected student, so the school won't expel him. All they can do, all they've done and will ever do, is have long, sensitive talks with him where they explain that he needs to give Kitty space. When he denies that he spends all day staring at her – that he picks up her hairs when they fall on the floor and adds them to his collection of Kitty memorabilia – they ask Kitty if she might be imagining things!'

'Mrs Woolford, you don't need to tell me. I know, believe me. Why do you think we drafted our anti-bullying policy in the precise way that we did? What this boy's doing to poor Kitty is stalking. He's menacing her, and putting her mental health at risk.'

'Yes,' I whisper, fighting back tears. 'Thank you.' I'm Dr Woolford, not Mrs Woolford, but I don't bother to correct her. Her take on Philip Oxley is the right one – that's what matters.

Dr Adebayo pulls her chair in closer to her desk. 'I can promise you this: a child at The Morrow who behaved in that way would be given two warnings and then, if the problem didn't stop, they would be asked to leave the school. All parents sign a contract when their children start here. In doing so, they agree that if their child's behaviour creates an intolerable environment for another pupil, they will accept the school's decision that the child must be removed. It's non-negotiable. We get to decide who's creating hostile environments and who isn't – me and the board. I can personally promise you that I won't let anyone make this school an unpleasant place for Kitty to spend her days.'

In which case, I don't care if, as my husband quipped, somebody pushes a child out of a top floor window every three years. As long as it's not my child, or anyone she likes. Or the child of any parents I grow to like. Oh, all right, I obviously would care...but not as much as I need never to see or think about Philip Oxley again.

'I'll give you the tour of the school in a moment, but first: do you have any questions?'

I open my mouth, then freeze, thinking that Dr Adebayo might react to the name 'Lucy Ross' in the way Rich and I react to hearing That Boy's name.

'Shall I answer the question you're not asking me?' She smiles. 'I can't believe you don't want to know about the death of Lucy Ross.'

I nod. There's no point denying it.

'That's fine. I wanted to know too, when I came to The Morrow. Oh, I've only been head here for a year. Most of the staff and pupils are relatively new. When a tragedy like

Lucy Ross happens, there's a mass exodus, as you can imagine. All I can say is that this is the same school she died in in name only. Yes, it's the same building, the same physical grounds. But it's not the same people, which means that effectively it's a completely different school. You'll see when I show you round: the atmosphere is lovely and positive. Nurturing. Creative.'

'But there are some people still here from two years ago?' I ask. If only there were none – nobody at all left at The Morrow from when Lucy Ross died – I could feel happy about sending Kitty here.

'Yes, a handful,' says Nina Adebayo. 'But really no more than five or six people. Garry Phelps, a physics teacher. Our office manager, Jenny Pethers, her son Max, Ariella Huxley and her brother Rocky.' She raises an eyebrow, and I wonder if she's tacitly acknowledging that the Huxley siblings' names tell us something about their parents. 'And Nelly,' she adds in a different tone altogether, with a worried expression on her face.

'Who's Nelly?'

Her frown quickly converts to a grin, but it's not convincing. 'Nelly Dean. From *Wuthering Heights.*'

'What do you mean?'

'You've probably heard that Lucy Ross died just as we were due to stage a big show at the school – *I Am Heathcliff!*, the musical?'

'I'd forgotten what the show was but . . . yes.'

'The pupils wrote the songs themselves. I've listened to

some of the rehearsal recordings – it would have been amazing, I'm sure. Obviously after Lucy died, it was cancelled. The girl who had the part of Nelly Dean in the show, she's still here. Her name's Florence Liddon – Florrie – but I can't help thinking of her as Nelly. She's not recovered well from Lucy's death, I don't think. She was only twelve when it happened – the youngest member of the cast. She's stunningly talented. Personally, I think her parents should have moved her whether she wanted to leave or not. Still, they didn't, and Florrie's obsession with Lucy, her death, the show that never happened . . . it seems to grow and grow. I've found her once or twice just sitting by the window. You know . . . '

'Yes,' I say quickly, so that she doesn't have to explain.

'Lately she's been to see me twice, crying, begging me to let the school do the musical now, with a new cast. She says it would provide closure, but . . . ' Dr Adebayo breaks off. 'As I've told her, I can't allow it. I think it's a terrible idea.' She sighs and shakes her head. 'I shouldn't be telling you all this, but . . . well, I wanted to be absolutely upfront with you: here at The Morrow, the past is the past – apart from in the mind of one traumatised pupil.'

'God,' I murmur, glad of her honesty. Rich was right. We can't send Kitty here. Maybe there's no killer roaming the corridors, but now I know that The Morrow contains at least one unhappy ghost from the past who sits staring out of the Window of Death – no doubt at the spot on the ground below where her friend's body landed.

'Oh, I should stress that Nelly's the kindest girl I've ever met,' says Dr Adebayo. 'Yes, she has her problems, but she's very responsible in the way she handles them. She never says a word to the other girls about Lucy's death. "I wouldn't want to inflict my emotional baggage on anyone else, Dr A", she told me once. If you're worried that she might have a negative effect on Kitty, I promise you she wouldn't.'

I'm worried that you, the head teacher, openly refer to your haunted, troubled pupil as Nelly, and don't think that might freak me out. That you see her primarily as Nelly Dean from a musical version of Wuthering Heights *that was never staged, and not as Florence Liddon, which is her real name. That you don't realise that I don't want my daughter anywhere near a girl everyone sees as lovely and good-hearted but damaged and vulnerable. That's what people at Vinery Road think about Philip Oxley.*

'What happened?' I blurt out. 'I mean, I know no one knows, but . . . I've heard conflicting stories – that it could have been an accident, that it definitely couldn't have been an accident . . . '

'Well . . . the inquest didn't deliver a verdict of accidental death,' Dr Adebayo says in a no-nonsense voice. 'The police believed it was deliberate.'

'You mean . . . '

'Suicide was never suspected by anybody, I don't think. Since nothing was ever established for certain, most people at The Morrow like to tell themselves it was an accident – kids messing about and it went horribly wrong, that kind of thing. Personally, I'd rather face facts. It's an unsolved murder.'

The phone on the desk starts to ring and Dr Adebayo picks it up. 'Hello? *What?*' She sighs. 'All right, I'll come now.' To me she says, 'I'm so sorry, I'm going to have to leave you here for a few minutes. Apparently there's an angry villager at the gates demanding to see me and only me, and threatening to vandalise one of our vehicles. Most of the local folk are lovely and don't mind us one bit, but there's one or two of the more elderly ladies who regard our school buses as the enemy of their green and pleasant village, which they believe we've ruined forever. I'll be back as soon as I've calmed the old dear down – sit tight.'

She marches out of the room on her red heels, closing the door behind her.

I'm not going to sit tight. I'm going to do the opposite – find Kitty and leave without wasting any more time here. Traumatised servant characters from a cancelled *Wuthering Heights* musical and vicious revenge-seeking old ladies beating down the doors? No thanks. There has to be another school for Kitty. We can move house if we need to; I can relocate to the Boston office. Kitty can go to an American school.

I open the door to leave Dr Adebayo's room and find an obstacle in my way: an unusually tall, bony girl with dark-brown shoulder-length hair and a heavy fringe that falls to just above her eyes, which are large and a pale, clear blue. She looks like a peculiar grown-up in school uniform and is holding a navy rucksack with the school's name and crest on it in white.

'You're Dr Sonia Woolford,' she says. I don't know who she is or how she knows. I nod. Fleetingly, I worry that she's about to tell me Dr Adebayo has been slaughtered by the furious pensioner.

'My name's Florrie. Florence Liddon.'

Nelly.

The next words she comes out with nearly stop my heart. 'I need to talk to you. We haven't got much time.'

'Is Kitty okay?'

Florrie looks puzzled. 'Your daughter? Yes, she's fine. Oh! I'm so sorry if I worried you. No, this isn't anything to do with your daughter.'

I exhale slowly.

Florence Liddon starts to talk. Fast. 'I knew you were coming – that Kitty was coming. Always very exciting when a prospective new girl comes for a taster day!' She attempts a light-hearted grin, but it soon falls off her excessively serious face. 'You know how gossip spreads in a place like this. I heard that the new girl's mum was a famous scientist, and I Googled you, and you are.'

'I'm not sure I'd call myself—'

'Yes, you are – you've been interviewed on TV. You work for a company that's about to launch a new way of testing for early cancer, a test that needs only a few strands of a person's hair. That's right, isn't it? Your company's going to be the next multi-billion-pound company in the UK?'

'Well, I wouldn't like to—'

'You're a brilliant scientist,' Florence insists. 'That means you're clever.'

Not clever enough to get myself out of this situation as fast I'd like to. 'Florence, I can't really—'

'Yes, you can.' Her wide blue eyes drill into me. 'You have to talk to me. There was no angry old woman!'

'What?'

'It was me that rang Dr A and said that, pretending to be one of the gate staff. I do good accents.' After a pause, she adds with an undertone of pride, 'I'm an actor.'

I know, Nelly.

Her meaning takes a second or two to sink in. She's telling me that she deliberately lied to get Nina Adebayo out of the way. So that she could talk to me.

'I know you know about Lucy. Everyone knows – everyone who comes here finds out. She was murdered. It was never solved. She was my friend. The thing is, I've been going over and over everything, since it happened. I've got stacks of notes. Then a few weeks ago, I spotted something I hadn't noticed before, and now I think I know who did it – I'm sure I do – but I can't think how to prove it. And then we were told about Kitty coming today and that her mother was this great scientist and I thought, "She must be one of the cleverest people in the country. She'll know what to do." I tried talking to Dr A about my suspicions but she told me I was being ridiculous. She said that if I carried on like that, I'd have to leave The Morrow.'

These last words are whispered, as if to leave would be a dreadful fate.

'I refuse to leave until I've solved Lucy's murder.' Florence straightens her back defiantly. 'No one cares about it except me!'

'Florence, I'm sorry, but I'm in no position to—'

'Ssh!' she hisses, cutting me off. 'Did you hear that? She's coming.' Florence opens her rucksack, pulls out a large envelope and a book: *Wuthering Heights*. 'Read Charlotte's introduction and read all my notes. Lucy's family was from Yorkshire too – she'd lived there most of her life, and only started at The Morrow six months or so before the auditions for the show. That's one reason why she was such a brilliant Cathy – her Yorkshire accent. And the man missed—'

Florence breaks off as she hears what I hear: high heels clacking on stone steps. They sound near.

'What man?' I ask.

Florence shakes her head, gestures at my bag and whispers, 'Hide them.'

And I do. I can't think why I don't refuse. I could so easily say, 'I'm afraid I can't get involved in this, Florence. I'm very sorry.'

By the time Nina Adebayo appears on the landing beside us, Florrie-the-actor is composed and ready to perform. 'Hello, Dr A. I was just entertaining Dr Woolford, in case she got lonely without you, haha.'

'That's very kind of you, Florrie.'

As soon as we're alone together inside her office, Dr

Adebayo asks, 'She didn't . . . say anything about Lucy Ross, did she? I'd hate to think she'd been pestering you.'

'No,' I lie. 'She hardly said anything at all. She just asked me if I needed anything.'

All the way home, while Kitty chats excitedly beside me in the car about the lovely day she's had, I think about the sentence Florence Liddon didn't finish. *And the man missed.* What had she wanted to tell me? Was the man Lucy Ross's murderer? Had he missed some crucial piece of evidence that he'd left behind, something Florence had recently found. Was that how Florence knew who had killed Lucy? Or was the man a policeman – the investigating detective, maybe – who'd neglected to notice something essential.

Florence's Liddon's extensive notes give me a lot more information than I got from Nina Adebayo. I've had to wait until today, Saturday, to read them. I persuaded Rich to give Kitty the lift I was supposed to be giving her, to a sleepover at her friend Isobel's house. 'Remember to remind Isobel's mum to look out for *any* sign of That Boy hanging around outside her house, and to ring us immediately if anything happens.' Rich nodded wearily. We'd both told Kitty not to tell too many people about her social plans, just in case, but it was important to be vigilant all the same.

Once she and Rich had left the house, I opened the envelope Florence had given me. It's taken me a while, but I've got to grips with all the information now, I think.

Wow. Who'd have guessed that a teenage production of a *Wuthering-Heights*-based musical could cause so much misery? There's a vast amount of detail here, but nothing I've noticed so far gives any indication of who might have pushed Lucy Ross out of a window.

I realise I'm assuming Florence Liddon is a reliable source. Why? For all I know, she might be entirely detached from reality. I think about her sitting morosely beside the Death Window, maybe hoping to notice some detail even now that would offer a clue: a jagged piece of red material attached to a splinter in the window frame or something like that.

In my mind, I hear her say, *She was murdered. It was never solved. She was my friend. No one cares about it except me.*

I know how it feels to be the only one who cares. The staff at Vinery Road, the students, the other parents . . . they don't really care that the behaviour of Philip Oxley is ruining my daughter's life, turning her into someone who's scared of other human beings, scared to leave the house. When they're not busy pointing out that Kitty's tormentor is in foster care and suffering from post-traumatic stress himself, they make sympathetic noises in our direction, but not a single one of them loses sleep, or can't eat properly any more, or ever rushes to the bathroom to vomit, or makes a silent pact with God that she'll immediately donate ten thousand pounds to charity if only He would make That Boy drop dead.

I torment myself, often, by considering what will happen at Vinery Road once we take Kitty out. Will the teachers be relieved that the Philip Oxley problem has been solved? Maybe without Kitty around, he'll behave more normally and it'll be as if the whole thing never happened. There will be no Florence Liddon, that's for sure – no one unable to forget that beautiful, talented, kind Kitty Woolford was driven away by the obsessive lunacy of Philip Oxley; no one determined to address that injustice by, for example, pushing Philip out of a high window.

I wipe my eyes and turn my attention back to Florence's notes. There were two Heathcliffs in The Morrow's musical rendition of *Wuthering Heights*, or, rather, there would have been had the show gone ahead: Giorgio Frasco and Cameron Lee. This, according to Florence, was because Cameron was by far the better actor and singer – definitely leading-man material – but Giorgio was dark and 'slightly savage', whatever that means, and more suitable for Heathcliff. Cameron was a brilliant student who could learn any number of lines within days, whereas Giorgio had already been suspended once for violence against another boy, and there was talk of him maybe being expelled. The two teachers in charge of the production were the music and drama teachers: Tracey Maxwell and Susannah Gate.

Maxwell was adamant, according to Florence, that, since he'd auditioned, Giorgio should be given the chance to play Heathcliff, that he'd be brilliant, that this great opportunity would be the very thing to turn his behaviour around. Gate was vehemently against this plan and had been overheard by pupils referring to Giorgio as 'a nasty little shit'. She wanted her star drama student, Cameron Lee, to play the part, and argued that it didn't matter one jot that Cameron was tall and skinny with pale skin and ash blond hair. Lucy Ross, who was playing Cathy, very much wanted Cameron Lee as Heathcliff too, but Giorgio Frasco's mother, Maria, was able to make a convincing case to the then headteacher that her son was being slandered in a most unprofessional way by the drama teacher. She lobbied for Susannah Gate to be fired. In the end, the only solution that seemed to calm the situation and keep everyone happy was for Giorgio and Cameron to share the part of Heathcliff, appearing in two each of the four performances.

However, according to Florence, the peace brought about by this compromise was an uneasy one. A girl called Ariella Braelin-Louise Huxley, whose name turned out to be even more ridiculous than Nina Adebayo had led me to believe, refused to accept that she hadn't got the part of Heathcliff. She knew she wasn't as good a singer as Lucy Ross, so the role of Cathy was beyond her reasonable reach, but she was easily as good a singer as both Giorgio Frasco and Cameron Lee. Both she and her mother believed she was the best actor in school, and that to assume that Heathcliff must go to a boy was pure sexism. Ariella produced many documents expounding the virtues of 'colourblind casting', which was common practice in professional theatre, apparently, and meant that one didn't necessarily cast white characters in white roles – and indeed, the notion of 'white roles' was thought to be racist.

There were several other problems too. Max Pethers, who was due to play Joseph, Heathcliff's servant, fled from the drama studio in tears one day after his costume shrank in the wash, Giorgio Frasco teased him about it, and Ariella Huxley said, 'What does it matter, really? He's only Joseph.' Max's mother, school office manager Jenny Pethers, went to the head and demanded a letter of apology, with specific reference to the words 'only Joseph'. Next to this information, Florence has written in brackets: 'This wasn't a we're-all-a-team-and-we-all-matter-equally thing. Jenny P has a massive chip on her shoulder because her husband is one of the school's gardeners, and he used to be a driver for a barrister called Simon Appleton-Drake, and she sees her family as being the servant classes. Most Morrow families are wealthy. The Petherses aren't at all.'

Beneath this note Florence has added, with a different pen and in new brackets: 'But Jenny Pethers PRETENDED it was about valuing all cast members equally. But that's a lie. If e.g. Max had been playing middle-class Mr Linton, Edgar's dad, and Ariella had said, "He's only Mr Linton", Max would still have got upset, but Jenny wouldn't have. No proof of this but I KNOW. It wasn't a minor character thing for Jenny, it was a servant character thing. You can totally tell she loathes the Morrow kids she sees as rich and privileged, like me, though she tries to hide it.'

It's clear from Florence's notes that something horrendous happened at almost every rehearsal. Ariella Huxley's mother burst into one and announced that, after the insult of her daughter being cast as Isabella Linton, she had handed in notice for both her children to leave The Morrow the following term. Florence has inserted an asterisk here, with a linked note at the bottom of the page: 'After Lucy's death, the Huxley family changed their minds and decided to keep Ariella and Rocky at The Morrow. It's pretty obvious they wanted to be on hand to enjoy every minute of the school's misery. Also, with no more Lucy Ross at the school, Ariella H was definitely the best female singer, so Lucy's death must have felt like a promotion for Ariella.'

The boy playing Hindley Earnshaw came down with glandular fever; Lucy Ross had a fight with Cameron Lee and snogged Giorgio Frasco purely to annoy him; music teacher Tracey Maxwell argued bitterly with drama teacher Susannah Gate about whether one of Heathcliff's songs could and should contain the word 'cunt'.

Lucy Ross's mother, a child psychologist who uses puppet-work and role-play to resolve disputes between children and teenagers, volunteered to come into school to do a conflict-resolution workshop, and her offer was eagerly accepted. She talked to the whole cast of *I Am Heathcliff!* about the benefits of Emotional Freedom Therapy,

Meditation and something called the Bob Snape Technique. Florence has added here in brackets: 'Emotional Freedom Therapy means tapping pressure points on your body while reciting positive statements e.g. "Even though a terrible thing has happened, I deeply and completely love myself." The Bob Snape Technique is something Lucy's mum invented herself and is very proud of. It's a technique for dealing with people we can't stand in a way that minimises conflict and drama. Bob Snape is a painter/decorator/repair man who used to do work for Lucy's family. He is a really decent man but the most boring person Lucy's mum has ever met. She wanted to minimise contact with him but definitely didn't want to hurt his feelings or cause trouble, so she was very polite and friendly to him, at the same time as making sure she didn't have to spend more time with him than necessary.

'So, e.g., the Bob Snape Technique means saying, "Thank you for inviting me for afternoon tea, Bob. I'd have loved to come, but I'm busy that night." The Bob Snape technique for The Morrow students would have meant Giorgio being polite and friendly to Cameron at all times, and Mrs Maxwell being polite and friendly to Mrs Gate at all times, and if they didn't want to hang out together and didn't actually like each other, instead of saying "I hate you, leave me alone", they should have smiled and said, "Oh, I'd have loved to do X with you but I'm afraid I'm busy." The key is to treat people at all times as if you don't want to hurt them or distress them, though you do want to make sure you're not with them any more than you need to be. It's protecting yourself at the same time as protecting other people. Lucy's mum has found that if you don't express hostility, your anger and dislike of the person actually decreases, and soon the basic polite friendliness is easier to achieve. She thought that too many people at The Morrow, both staff and students, mistakenly believed that honestly airing every feeling and grievance was a route to peace. Lucy's mum saw it as a route to more war. She was about to make us all do an embarrassing Bob-Snape-Technique role-play exercise, but luckily Max Pethers said he was feeling sick, and he looked a bit pale, so Mrs Gate said maybe we should end the session early and all get some fresh air.'

I'm shaking my head as I read this. Spare me these shrinks and their well-meaning advice, I think. The Bob Snape Technique wouldn't work with Philip Oxley. Nothing works with him: not polite and friendly firmness and not a screamed 'Fucking leave my daughter alone, you pasty-faced stalker freak!'

On and on the notes go, with disasters piling up at every turn: the parents of Linton Heathcliff announced they were getting divorced and the poor boy wept through every rehearsal thereafter; it transpired that Hareton Earnshaw had a theatrical agent and had secretly auditioned for a part in the chorus of a West End show. He got the part, had to drop out of *I Am Heathcliff!*, and, by the sound of it, was loathed and ostracised for his betrayal by teachers and pupils alike.

Florence has made an effort to ensure that her notes are as chronological as they can be, so I come across Lucy Ross's death only on the third-to-last page.

There was a room on the third floor of The Morrow where pupils were allowed to go if they had free periods, or during breaks and lunchtimes – a sort of students' common room. The window from which Lucy Ross was pushed was in that room. A group of her fellow pupils had gathered on the grass beneath. There were five of them. One was Cameron Lee, the ash-blond Heathcliff. Lucy hit the ground a few centimetres from where they were standing.

Florence's notes tell me that all five were in unanimous agreement about what they'd seen and heard. First, they'd heard a girl's voice coming from above, shouting, 'Heathcliff!' They'd looked up and seen Lucy leaning out of the window, waving. She'd seemed fine, they said, and not unhappy. She and Cameron had by this point resolved their differences, and all snogging of unhappy, abandoned Giorgio Frasco had ceased.

The five reported that Lucy had then turned back into the room and said first, 'I'm sorry,' and then 'What are you doing?', followed by – in a tone that was a mix of bewilderment and indignation – '*Who?*' And then she'd fallen.

The obvious suspects are listed by Florence: Giorgio Frasco and Ariella Huxley. No one else, as far as anyone could see, had a motive for wanting Lucy Ross dead. Her death occurred at a time when most of the pupils and teachers were in lessons. Both Giorgio and Ariella had been in a Spanish lesson together and couldn't have pushed Lucy.

Florence obviously imagined that whoever would read her notes might suspect Mrs Maxwell and Mrs Gate, the music and drama teachers, because she's underlined the note that they were both teaching classes when Lucy died.

The only people with free periods at the relevant time were the dyslexic pupils who were excused from some of the language classes, Florence has written. She's listed them, and the only two names I recognise are Lucy Ross and Max Pethers. Max could have been in the room with Lucy when she died, according to Florence, but he and Lucy were quite close friends and she'd stuck up for him when Ariella Huxley had made her 'only Joseph' remark. Florence believes there's no way that Max would have harmed Lucy, or indeed anybody. Max has apparently developed a range of nervous tics since Lucy died and his body now makes uncontrollable twitching movements. He is often not at school because of his psychological issues.

I frown. Dr Adebayo didn't mention this when she was telling me that, for everyone but Florence Liddon, the past was the past. Not for twitching Max Pethers, if Florence's account can be relied upon.

My eyes widen when I read the next paragraph: 'Max has never said where he was when Lucy died. He says he wasn't in the room with her, or anywhere near it, but he refuses to say where he was at the time. I've tried to talk to him about this, but it's hard, and once I got a day's detention for forcing a conversation and upsetting him. I don't understand why he won't just say where he was!! Max is the kind of boy who would no way have been doing anything wrong or forbidden. He's just not that sort of person. My theory, which I can't prove, is that maybe he was on his way to the room at the start of his free period, and he saw someone push Lucy out of the window. If the person didn't see him, then of course he wouldn't want to admit he was anywhere near there, in case the killer worked out that he might have seen something, and killed him too.'

I put down the notes and think. If Florence believes that Max Pethers would never harm Lucy, might that mean that he liked her rather a lot – enough to seethe with envy as the two Heathcliffs, blond and dark, competed for her attention, while he – only Joseph, after all - didn't get a look-in?

Of all the Morrow pupils I've read about in Florence's notes, Max Pethers sounds the closest in type to Philip Oxley: a weird boy with lots of problems, behaving strangely. I know I shouldn't allow this to influence me.

I pick up the copy of *Wuthering Heights* that Florence gave me and start to read Charlotte Brontë's introduction to the novel, as instructed. Florence mentioned Yorkshire as if it was significant. Lucy was from Yorkshire too, she said – but why did that matter? The girl playing Cathy in a school show came from the same place as the author of the original book. So what?

Charlotte's introduction starts with a defence of her sister's novel. I read the opening.

I have just read over 'Wuthering Heights,' and, for the first time, have obtained a clear glimpse of what are termed (and, perhaps, really are) its faults; have gained a definite notion of how it appears to other people – to strangers who knew nothing of the author; who are unacquainted with the locality where the scenes of the story are laid; to whom the inhabitants, the customs, the natural characteristics of the outlying hills and hamlets in the West Riding of Yorkshire are things alien and unfamiliar.

To all such 'Wuthering Heights' must appear a rude and strange production. The wild moors of the North of England can for them have no interest: the language, the manners, the very dwellings and household customs of the scattered inhabitants of those districts must be to such readers in a great measure unintelligible, and – where intelligible – repulsive. Men and women who, perhaps, naturally very calm, and with feelings moderate in degree, and little marked in kind, have been trained from their cradle to observe the utmost evenness of manner and guardedness of language, will hardly know what to make of the rough, strong utterance, the harshly manifested passions, the unbridled aversions, and headlong partialities of unlettered moorland hinds and rugged moorland squires, who have grown up untaught and unchecked, except by Mentors as harsh as themselves.

I can't help smiling. Charlotte seems to be saying, 'You try living where I live and then come and tell me people are much nicer and better behaved than Hindley Earnshaw and Heathcliff.' Why, though, would Florence Liddon stress that Lucy Ross was from Yorkshire too? Was she trying to hint that Lucy was savage in some way – as feral as a character from Emily Brontë's novel? Did Lucy play off Cameron Lee and Giorgio Frasco against one another, like Cathy Earnshaw messed with the heads of Edgar Linton and Heathcliff?

I can't think of any intention Florence might have had apart from to convey the message that people from Yorkshire are bad. Dangerous. And I can't see why she'd do that if it was a purely random opinion of hers, unrelated to the notes and book she was pressing into my hands as she spoke. She surely had to be implying that someone from Yorkshire had murdered Lucy Ross.

Wait . . .

Let's be logical about this. Emily Brontë, Charlotte Brontë and all the inhabitants of Yorkshire they might have been acquainted with . . . none of those people could have murdered Lucy Ross. They're all long dead.

Heathcliff, Hindley, Cathy, Only- Joseph . . . none of those fictional characters could have killed Lucy either; they don't exist apart from on paper.

Lucy Ross was the victim, and therefore not the culprit. If what Florence was trying to tell me was that Yorkshire people are harsh and potentially lethal, how could the 'too' be significant? *Lucy was from Yorkshire too*. Was the implication that she'd somehow brought about her own murder with some character flaw resulting from her Yorkshire origins?

Someone else must have a Yorkshire connection, I conclude. That's the only thing that makes sense. 'Lucy was from Yorkshire too' cannot have meant 'as well as Emily and Charlotte Brontë'. It must have meant 'as well as her murderer.'

And the man missed—

I run through a theory in my head: Lucy Ross used to live in Yorkshire. So did The Man, a man, whoever he was. When she left, he missed her. So he followed her to Hampshire and to The Morrow and . . . No, that's ridiculous. Utterly ludicrous.

I pick up my phone again. Time to do a bit more internet searching.

Three days later, I'm back in Nina Adebayo's office. 'I think I might know who killed Lucy Ross,' I tell her.

She smiles sadly. 'I knew it. I knew Nelly had got to you.'

'Florence Liddon told me nothing,' I lie. I don't want to get her expelled. 'But I've done some independent research and—'

'Nelly's worried I'll punish her, but she needn't be,' Dr Adebayo talks over me. 'I won't. I never would. I only said that for her sake, hoping it would shake her out of her obsession. I should have known it wouldn't work. The thing is, Mrs Woolford, if there's no proof then there's only slander. Do you see what I'm saying?'

'You know, don't you?' I say coldly. 'You've done the same legwork I've done, and you know the truth as well as I do. As well as Florence does.'

'I happen to believe there's no such thing as knowledge without proof.'

'You could think up any number of reasons to fire Jenny Pethers,' I tell her. 'Instead, you allow a murderer to continue to work at your school. Why?'

'Mrs Woolford, I'm not going to engage in slanderous speculation with you. I will only say that unless and until someone has been found guilty of a crime, it's quite wrong to penalise them as if they had committed said crime. If I were to terminate Jenny Pethers' employment here, do you really think word wouldn't spread about my secret and officially unjustifiable reason for doing so? Jenny's an excellent administrator. I can't fault her professional behaviour.'

'Lucy Ross's family should know the truth. Lucy deserves justice.'

Dr Adebayo's patient smile remains in place. 'Mrs Woolford, as a scientist, you must know as well as I do that you can arrange an assortment of random facts in a particular order and create a false pattern – something that looks as if it must be the truth, but that nevertheless is not. If you think about what you believe you now know – *really* think about it, I mean – you'll realise that in spite of the pattern you think you've recognised, it's equally likely that, for example, Garry Phelps pushed Lucy Ross to her death.'

'Who's Garry Phelps?'

'A perfectly delightful physics teacher here. Think of everything you've found out, and tell me which item on your list makes it impossible for Lucy Ross's killer to be Garry Phelps.'

'Did he have a reason to want Lucy dead?'

'Not as far as I know, but he might have. How should I know? And the trouble is that when one accuses a person of murder with zero evidence, that person often says, "No, it wasn't me. I'm innocent." Then, perhaps, the parents of the murder victim pursue some sort of vigilante justice outcome . . . and we have more violence. More tragedy.'

I shake my head in disbelief.

'What would you do in my position?' Dr Adebayo asks. 'Do you think Lucy Ross's mother would feel better or worse if she found out what you and Florence Liddon believe was the catalyst for her daughter's murder, if there's no way to ensure the guilty party is punished?'

'But what did she mean by that?' asks Rich, rubbing his eyes. I've worn him out. 'You're telling the story the wrong way round.'

'Because I want to prove to you that it's obvious that Nina Adebayo – the head teacher of the school – knows what I know, *knows* that Jenny Pethers killed Lucy Ross. Everything she said to me in her office makes it clear that she thinks exactly what I think. So when I tell you why I think it – or rather, how I know it – please bear in mind that it isn't just me that's dreamed this up. There are at least three of us with the same opinion.'

'All right. Go on. I still can't see any reason why Jenny Pethers should want to murder the girl playing Cathy in the show. It's not as if her Max would get the part once Lucy's out of the way.'

'Lucy's murder had nothing to do with Heathcliff, Cathy, the musical, casting – it was nothing like that. Although it did have something to do with Only-Joseph, even if only thematically.'

'Thematically?' Rich winces. 'What are you talking about?' He's read Florence's notes, so he doesn't need to ask about Only-Joseph.

'When Ariella Huxley said that Max Pethers' costume didn't matter because he was only Joseph, she was revealing something we all know: that status matters. It *really* matters. Joseph's a minor character, and therefore low status. Heathcliff and Cathy: main characters, high status. Jenny Pethers had a class-and-status-themed chip on her shoulder. She resented the rich, privileged kids, and it showed. She was highly sensitive to any hint that servants mattered less, because her husband was the school's gardener, because he used to be a driver for a posh barrister with a double-barrelled surname—'

'I know all this from the notes, but so what? Are you saying Jenny Pethers killed Lucy Ross because she had a high-status part and Max only had a servant's part?'

'No. If you just listen, I'll explain. When I realised that Florrie Liddon had hinted to me that Lucy Ross's murderer came from Yorkshire, I investigated my favourite suspect first: Max Pethers. It took me about three seconds to find out that the Pethers family had lived in Yorkshire for many years. That's when I realised what Florence had meant by "And the man missed".'

'What? What the hell does that mean?'

'Never mind. That's not important. What's important is that the *man mist-er* Pethers, Max's dad and Jenny's husband, used to be a driver for – the barrister, Simon Appleton-Drake – has practised law in Yorkshire for more than twenty years. Therefore . . . the Pethers family lived in Yorkshire for all the years Mr Pethers was Appleton-Drake's driver. I did a bit of digging around and happened to stumble across Jenny Pethers's maiden name. I found a photograph of her and her husband at a do with Appleton-Drake – this was before they were married. Underneath the photo was a caption with their names: Simon Appleton-Drake, Nigel Pethers and Jenny Snape. Her maiden name is Snape, Rich.'

'So?' He sighs. 'Who cares what her maiden name was?'

'The surname Snape doesn't ring any bells for you?'

'No.'

'How about the Bob Snape Technique, from Florence's notes?'

'What—' Rich falls silent. Blinks a few times.

'Bob Snape: the extremely boring workman who did work

for Lucy Ross's family. The one Lucy's mum based a theory around, about how to deal kindly with awful people one wanted to avoid.'

'Are you saying . . . ?'

'He's Jenny Pethers' dad. Yeah.'

'Fuck!'

'Yep. Max Pethers had to sit in that conflict-resolution session at school with all his fellow pupils and hear a smug, privileged psychologist cheerfully telling everyone that his no doubt beloved grandfather was the dullest man in the world – so unpalatable as company that a special technique had to be devised to limit contact with him. Max must have gone home very upset that night. Florence says in her notes that the session had to be cut short because Max felt sick. Imagine how Jenny Pethers felt when she heard the story. I know exactly what she'll have thought.'

Rich nods. 'That Lucy Ross's mother valued Bob Snape so little that she'd happily sit and slag him off as "lovely but unbearable" in front of dozens of people without for a second considering that he was, in fact, a real person. With feelings that might be hurt if news ever reached him that the Bob Snape Technique was now a thing in therapy circles. With relatives whose feelings might be hurt.'

'Precisely. And Jenny Pethers, with her social-class chip on both shoulders, will have known in her heart of hearts that the reason Lucy Ross's mother didn't think of Bob Snape in this way – as a fellow human being with feelings – was because Bob was just some guy who did work for her,

277

just a member of the servant class. Just like Only-Joseph, Jenny's son, whose costume didn't matter.'

'So . . . Jenny Pethers pushed Lucy Ross out of the window—'

'To punish Lucy's mother, yes. Nothing to do with Lucy herself. Jenny wanted Lucy's mother to suffer. "You don't give a shit about my closest and dearest family? Then guess what: I don't give a shit about yours."'

'Sonia, this is – Fuck!'

'What Dr Adebayo was trying to say to me was: do you really think Lucy Ross's mother will benefit from finding this out – that something she said while she was trying to resolve conflict at The Morrow caused someone to murder her daughter? She'd blame and torment herself for ever. The fact is, what she did was and is terrible. It should have occurred to her that to broadcast her theory as if Bob Snape didn't matter was quite unfair. And fucking ironic too, given that the whole point of the technique, originally, was not to hurt Bob Snape.'

'She would,' Rich agrees. 'She'd blame herself. I sure as hell would if I were her. But at the same time, Lucy Ross was murdered. And Jenny Pethers, thus far, has got away with it.'

'I suppose it might have been Max Pethers who did it,' I say. 'I don't think so, though. I think it was Jenny. Florence's description of her inability to conceal her resentment towards anyone privileged . . . And I think Max might have seen his mother do it.'

'So what are you going to do?' asks Rich. 'What do we do now?'

'We do the unthinkable.'

'You mean . . . *nothing?*'

'What? Oh, no, I've already laid all this out for the police in great detail. I did that straight away: contacted the detective who investigated Lucy's death at the time. I even told him my theory about why Lucy's first words, when she turned back into the room just before she fell, were "I'm sorry." I think she saw a member of staff coming angrily towards her – Jenny Pethers – and assumed she was going to get a bollocking for leaning out of the window.'

'You did the right thing. Telling the police is the only thing to do. So what's the unthinkable?'

I swallow hard and, with a shudder, force myself to utter the word: 'Home-schooling.' Rich recoils.

It's horrible, but it's the only path I'm willing to consider now. I can't send Kitty to a school. I don't trust schools. I'm school-phobic, school-averse. I'm a school-denier. Schools ruin lives and they kill. What was the name of the school where the oldest two Brontë sisters died of cholera or scurvy or whatever it was?

We can join a home-schooling collective so that Kitty meets other kids her age. I'll stage productions of *Showboat* and *Oklahoma!* in my lounge if I have to. I'm never setting foot in one of those toxic, evil places ever again, and neither is Kitty.

⊰⧚⊱

NOTES ON THE CONTRIBUTORS

Louise Doughty is the author of eight novels, one work of non-fiction, and five plays for radio. Her latest book, *Black Water*, is out now from Faber & Faber UK and Farrar Straus & Giroux in the US, where it was nominated as one of the *New York Times Book Review* Notable Books of 2016. Her seventh novel was the number-one bestseller *Apple Tree Yard*. Shortlisted for the CWA Steel Dagger Award and the National Book Award Thriller of the Year, it has sold half a million copies in the UK alone to date and been translated into thirty languages worldwide. A four-part TV adaptation with Emily Watson in the lead role was broadcast on Sunday nights on BBC1. Doughty's sixth novel, *Whatever You Love*, was shortlisted for the Costa Novel Award and longlisted for the Orange Prize for Fiction. She has also won awards for radio drama and short stories, along with publishing one work of non-fiction, *A Novel in a Year*, based on her popular newspaper column. She is a critic and cultural commentator for UK and international newspapers, and broadcasts regularly for the BBC, and has been the judge for many prizes and awards including the Man Booker Prize and the Costa Novel Award. She lives in London.

Nikesh Shukla is a columnist for the *Observer* and the author of three novels for adults, *Coconut Unlimited* (shortlisted for the Costa First Novel Award 2010), *Meatspace*, *The One Who Wrote Destiny* and one YA novel, *Run, Riot*. Nikesh has written for the *Guardian*, *Esquire*, *BuzzFeed*, *VICE*, *Noisey*, Channel 4, BBC2, *Lit Hub*, *Guernica*, and BBC Radio 4. Nikesh is the editor of the bestselling essay collection, *The Good Immigrant*, which won the readers' choice at the Books Are My Bag Awards. Nikesh was one of *Foreign Policy* magazine's 100 Global Thinkers, the co-founders of the Jhalak Prize for British Writers of Colour and the *Bookseller*'s 100 most influential people in publishing in 2016 and 2017.

Hanan al-Shaykh is one of the most acclaimed writers in the contemporary Arab world. She is the author of seven novels, including *The Story of Zahra*, *Women of Sand & Myrrh*, *Beirut Blues*, *Only in London*, as well as a collection of stories, *I Sweep the Sun off Rooftops*, and her much praised memoir of her mother's life: *The Locust and the Bird*. She has written two plays, *Dark Afternoon Tea* and *Paper Husband*, and published *One Thousand and One Nights*, an adaptation of some of the stories from the legendary *Alf Layla Wa Layla – the Arabian Nights*. Her latest novel, *The Occasional Virgin*, was published by Bloomsbury in 2018. Her work has been translated into twenty-eight languages. She lives in London.

Louisa Young was born in London, and read history at Trinity College, Cambridge. She lives in London with her daughter, with whom she co-wrote the best-selling *Lionboy* trilogy. Her work is published in 36 languages and she is the author of fourteen previous books, including her first novel, *Babylove* (longlisted for the Orange Prize) and the bestselling *My Dear I Wanted to Tell You* (shortlisted for the Costa Novel Award and a Richard and Judy Book Club choice). Her latest work, a memoir, *You Left Early: A True Story of Love and Alcohol*, is out now. Her first novel, *Baby Love* was longlisted for the Orange Prize. Her work is published in 36 languages.

Leila Aboulela is the author of five novels, *Bird Summons*, *The Translator*, a *New York Times* 100 Notable Books of the Year, *The Kindness of Enemies*, *Minaret* and *Lyrics Alley*, Fiction Winner of the Scottish Book Awards. She was the first winner of the Caine Prize for African Writing and her latest story collection, *Elsewhere, Home* was shortlisted for the Saltire Fiction Book of the Year. Leila's work has been translated into fifteen languages and she was longlisted three times for the Women's Prize for Fiction. Leila grew up in Sudan and moved, in her mid-twenties, to Scotland.

Anna James is a freelance journalist and writer who lives in north London. *Tilly and the Bookwanderers* is Anna's debut novel, and the first in the *Pages & Co* series. It was published by HarperCollins Children's Books in September 2018. You can find her on Twitter: @ACaseForBooks.

Michael Stewart is a multi-award-winning writer, born and brought up in Salford, who moved to Yorkshire in 1995 and is now based in Bradford. He has written several full-length stage plays, one of which, *Karry Owky*, was joint winner of the King's Cross Award for New Writing. His debut novel, *King Crow*, was published in January 2011. It is the winner of the *Guardian*'s Not-the-Booker Award, and has been selected as a recommended read for World Book Night. Michael works as a senior lecturer in Creative Writing at the University of Huddersfield, where he is the publisher of Grist Books. His latest novel, *Ill Will*, was published by HQ in November 2018.

Juno Dawson is the author of seven novels for young adults as well as the non-fiction titles *This Book is Gay*, and *The Gender Games*. She is also a regular contributor to *Stylist*, *Glamour*, *The Pool*, and *Attitude Magazine*.

Grace McCleen's first novel, *The Land of Decoration*, was published in 2012 and was awarded the Desmond Elliott Prize for the best first novel of the year. It was also chosen for Richard & Judy's Book Club and won her the Betty

Trask Prize in 2013. Her second novel, *The Professor of Poetry*, was shortlisted for the Encore Award and her latest, *The Offering*, was published by Sceptre in 2015. She read English at the University of Oxford and has an MA from York, and currently lives in London.

Erin Kelly is the author of six novels including *The Poison Tree*, *He Said/She Said* and *Broadchurch: The Novel*, inspired by the mega-hit TV series. In 2013, *The Poison Tree* became a major ITV drama and was a Richard & Judy Summer Read in 2011. Born in London in 1976, Erin lives in north London with her husband and daughters.

Joanna Cannon graduated from Leicester Medical School and worked as a hospital doctor, before specialising in psychiatry. Her most recent novel *Three Things About Elsie* was published in 2018 and was a top-ten hardback bestseller and her first novel *The Trouble with Goats and Sheep* was a top-ten bestseller in both hardback and paperback and was a Richard and Judy pick. She lives in the Peak District with her family and her dog.

Laurie Penny is a writer and journalist. She writes for *Vice*, the *Guardian* and many other publications, and is a columnist and Contributing Editor at the *New Statesman* magazine. She was the youngest person to be shortlisted for the Orwell Prize for political writing on her blog 'Penny Red'. She has reported on radical politics, protest, digital culture and feminism from around the world, working with activists from the Occupy movement and the European youth uprisings. She has 160,000 followers on Twitter and in 2012 won the British Media Awards' 'Twitter Public Personality of the Year' prize. Laurie is a nerd, a nomad and an activist. She is thirty years old and lives in London.

Lisa McInerney's work has featured in *Winter Papers*, *Stinging Fly*, *Granta* and on BBC Radio 4, and in the anthologies *Beyond the Centre*, *The Long Gaze Back* and *Town and Country*. Her debut novel, *The Glorious Heresies*, won the Baileys Women's Prize for Fiction 2016 and the Desmond Elliott Prize. Her second novel, *The Blood Miracles*, was published by John Murray in April 2017.

Alison Case received her BA from Oberlin College and her PhD in English Literature from Cornell University. A Professor of English at Williams College in Williamstown, Massachusetts, she has published two books and many articles on nineteenth-century British fiction and poetry. Her debut novel *Nelly Dean* was published in 2015 by The Borough Press.

Dorothy Koomson has been making up stories since she was thirteen and hasn't stopped since. She is the award-winning author of fourteen novels including *The Brighton Mermaid*, *The Friend*, *When I Was Invisible*, *The Chocolate Run*, *My Best Friend's Girl* and *The Woman He Loved Before*.

Dorothy's books have been translated into more than 30 languages and have regularly topped the charts across the globe. In 2013 a TV series based on Dorothy's *The Ice Cream Girls* was shown on ITV1 and her Quick Read book, *The Beach Wedding* was one of the 2018 World Book Night giveaway titles.

Sophie Hannah is an internationally bestselling crime fiction writer. Her crime novels have been translated into 34 languages and published in 51 countries. Her psychological thriller *The Carrier* won the Specsavers National Book Award for Crime Thriller of the Year in 2013. In 2014 and 2016, Sophie published *The Monogram Murders* and *Closed Casket*, the first new Hercule Poirot mysteries since Agatha Christie's death, both of which were national and international bestsellers. Sophie is an Honorary Fellow of Lucy Cavendish College, Cambridge.

A NOTE ON EMILY BRONTË

EMILY JANE BRONTË, AUTHOR of *Wuthering Heights*, was born on 30 July 1818, the fifth of six children of the reverend Patrick Brontë and his wife Maria. She was born at Thornton, near Bradford, in West Yorkshire. In 1820 Patrick Brontë was appointed perpetual curate of Haworth church, five miles away. The bleak parsonage at Haworth, and the windswept moorland surrounding it, became central to Emily's creative life, and had a profound influence on her writing.

Emily and her sisters were taught the essential female skills of needlework and household management by their Aunt Branwell, who made her home with the family following the death of Mrs Brontë in 1821, when Emily was just three years of age. The children studied the Bible, as well as history and geography, with their father. In 1824 Emily joined her elder sisters at the Clergy Daughters' School at Cowan Bridge, near Kirkby Lonsdale. Conditions at the school were harsh, and later provided Charlotte with a model for the infamous Lowood School in her novel *Jane Eyre*. This first experience of leaving home ended tragically with the deaths of the two eldest girls, Maria and Elizabeth, who died within a few weeks of each other in 1825, aged just eleven and ten years. Charlotte and Emily were withdrawn from the school and spent the next few years at home, together with their youngest sister Anne, and brother Branwell, resuming lessons with their father and aunt. Patrick Brontë instilled a love of learning in all his children, and they read anything they could lay hands on, delighting in the novels of Sir Walter Scott and the poetry of Lord Byron.

Outside lesson time the children created a rich imaginary world sparked by their father's gift to Branwell of a set of toy soldiers. Each of the soldiers was given a name and a character by the children, and an increasingly complex sequence of stories and plays developed around them. Whilst Charlotte and Branwell joined forces to create the kingdom of Angria, Emily and Anne went on to form Gondal, an imaginary island in the North Pacific, with a cold climate and bleak moorland landscape reminiscent of Haworth. The central characters were as wild as any of the inhabitants of Wuthering Heights, and the Gondal saga continued to absorb Emily into adulthood.

In 1835 Emily was sent away for a second stint at boarding school, this time to Roe Head, near Mirfield, a much more genteel affair than Cowan Bridge, where her sister Charlotte was employed as a teacher. At seventeen, Emily was older than the other pupils; she did not make friends and failed to adapt to school life. Her health declined, and within three months Emily was back at Haworth. She had established her right to remain at home, and, with only two exceptions, never left it again.

In 1838, despite her lack of formal education, she obtained a teaching post at Miss Patchett's school at Law Hill, near Halifax. Emily survived the uncongenial employment for just six months before heading back to Haworth. Shortly after, the sisters' decision to set up a school of their own at the parsonage provided Charlotte with the impetus to improve her language skills by spending time studying at a school on the continent. It seems surprising that she suggested Emily should accompany her, and more surprising still that Emily agreed to go.

The sisters' stay at the Pensionnat Heger in Brussels, funded by their Aunt Branwell, was cut short after nine months by news of their aunt's illness and death. While Charlotte returned to Brussels for another year, Emily remained at the parsonage as housekeeper. She threw herself into the old routine of household tasks combined with writing, and wasn't overly disappointed when the school project came to nothing.

One day in 1845 Charlotte discovered a collection of Emily's poems and was awestruck by their quality. She hatched a plan to publish a selection of poems by all three sisters, and, although Emily was initially furious at the invasion of her privacy, she was eventually persuaded that the poems should be published. Branwell was not included in the project, despite the fact that several of his poems had already been published in local newspapers. After a series of disappointments and ill-fated career attempts, his early promise had been blighted by alcoholism. It's unclear whether he even knew about his sisters' publications, which all appeared under the androgynous-sounding pseudonyms, Currer, Ellis, and Acton Bell. The book of poems was published in 1846, but despite some favourable reviews, the small volume sold only two copies. 'Ill success failed to crush us,' Charlotte later wrote, adding that 'the mere effort to succeed had given a wonderful zest to existence: it must be pursued.' The sisters set to work again, and three prose tales by the Bells were soon winging their way to the first on a long list of publishing houses.

Emily's *Wuthering Heights* was published in December 1847. Branwell died the following year, and it is said that his funeral was the last occasion on which Emily left the parsonage. She died on 19 December 1848, at the age of thirty, from tuberculosis. It soon became clear that Anne was also ill; she died from tuberculosis in the following year, aged twenty-nine years. Charlotte lived on at the parsonage with her elderly father, and published a total of three novels in her lifetime (a fourth was published posthumously). In 1854 she married her father's curate, Arthur Bell Nicholls, but died nine months later in the early stages of pregnancy. For the remainder of the nineteenth century, Charlotte was regarded as the famous Brontë. Although the originality of *Wuthering Heights* was acknowledged, the novel repelled many of its early readers, and Emily Brontë never lived to see the huge impact her writing would have.

Ann Dinsdale
Principal Curator, Brontë Parsonage Museum